THE EAGLE
HAS FLOWN

Also available in Large Print
by Jack Higgins:

Memoirs of a Dance-Hall Romeo
A Season in Hell
Confessional
Touch the Devil
Luciano's Luck
Solo

THE EAGLE HAS FLOWN

A NOVEL

JACK HIGGINS

G.K. HALL & CO.
Boston, Massachusetts
1992

Published in Large Print by arrangement with
Simon & Schuster.

G.K. Hall Large Print Book Series.

Set in 18 pt. Plantin.

Library of Congress Cataloging-in-Publication Data

Higgins, Jack, 1929–
    The eagle has flown / Jack Higgins.—Large print ed.
      p.   cm—(G.K. Hall large print book series)
    ISBN 0-8161-5363-9.—ISBN 0-8161-5364-7 (pbk.)
    1. Large type books. I. Title.
[PR6058.I343E15 1992]
823′.914—dc20   91-38957

FOR MY MOTHER
HENRIETTA HIGGINS BELL

At one o'clock on the morning of Saturday, November 6, 1943, Heinrich Himmler, Reichsführer of the SS and Chief of State Police, received a simple message: The Eagle has landed. *A small force of German paratroopers under the command of Oberstleutnant Kurt Steiner, aided by IRA gunman Liam Devlin, were at that moment safely in England and poised to snatch the British Prime Minister, Winston Churchill, from the Norfolk country house where he was spending a quiet weekend near the sea. By the end of the day—thanks to a bloody confrontation in the village of Studley Constable between American Rangers and the Germans—the mission was a failure, Liam Devlin apparently the only survivor. As for Kurt Steiner . . .*

LONDON
BELFAST
1975

1

THERE WAS an Angel of Death on top of an ornate mausoleum in one corner, arms extended. I remember that well because someone was practicing the organ and light drifted across the churchyard in colored bands through stained-glass windows. The church wasn't particularly old, built on a high tide of Victorian prosperity like the tall houses surrounding it. St. Martin's Square. A good address once. Now just a shabby backwater in Belsize Park, but a nice, quiet area where a woman alone might walk down to the corner shop at midnight in safety and people minded their own business.

The flat at number thirteen was on the ground floor. My agent had borrowed it for me from a cousin who had gone to New York for six months. It was old-fashioned and comfortable and suited me fine. I was on the downhill slope of a new novel and needed to visit the reading room at the British Museum most days.

But that November evening, the evening it all started, it was raining heavily, and just after six I passed through the iron gates and followed the path through the forest of Gothic monuments and gravestones. In spite of my umbrella, the shoulders of my trench coat were soaked, not that it bothered me. I've always liked the rain, the city at night, wet streets stretching into winter darkness, a peculiar feeling of freedom that it contains. And things had gone well that day with the work; the end was very definitely in sight.

The Angel of Death was closer now, shadowed in the half-light from the church, the two marble attendants on guard at the mausoleum's bronze doors, everything as usual, except that tonight I could have sworn there was a third figure and that it moved out of the darkness toward me.

For a moment I knew genuine fear, and then, as it came into the light, I saw a young woman, quite small and wearing a black beret and soaked raincoat. She had a briefcase in one hand. The face was pale, the eyes dark and somehow anxious.

"Mr. Higgins? You are Jack Higgins, aren't you?"

She was American, that much was obvious. I took a deep breath to steady my nerves. "That's right. What can I do for you?"

"I must talk to you, Mr. Higgins. Is there somewhere we could go?"

I hesitated, reluctant for all sorts of obvious reasons to take this any further, and yet there was something quite out of the ordinary about her. Something not to be resisted.

I said, "My flat's just over the square there."

"I know," she said. I still hesitated, and she added, "You won't regret it, believe me. I've information of vital importance to you."

"About what?" I asked.

"What really happened afterward at Studley Constable. Oh, lots of things you don't know."

Which was enough. I took her arm and said, "Right, let's get in out of this damn rain before you catch your death, and you can tell me what the hell this is all about."

The house interior had changed very little, certainly not in my flat, where the tenant had stayed with a late Victorian decor, lots of mahogany furniture, red velvet curtains at the bow window and a sort of Chinese wallpaper in gold and green, heavily patterned with birds. Except for the central heating radiators, the only other concession to modern living was the kind of gas fire which made it seem as if logs burned brightly in a stainless steel basket.

"That's nice," she said and turned to face me, even smaller than I had thought. She held out her right hand awkwardly, still clutching the briefcase in the other. "Cohen," she said. "Ruth Cohen."

I said, "Let's have that coat. I'll put it in front of one of the radiators."

"Thank you." She fumbled at her belt awkwardly with one hand, and I laughed and took the briefcase from her.

"Here, let me." As I put it down on the table, I saw that her initials were etched on the flap in black. The only difference was that it said Ph.D. at the end of it.

"Ph.D.?" I said.

She smiled slightly as she struggled out of the coat. "Harvard, modern history."

"That's interesting," I said. "I'll make some tea, or would you prefer coffee?"

She smiled again. "Six months post doc at London University, Mr. Higgins. I'd very definitely prefer your tea."

I went through to the kitchen and put on the kettle and made a tray ready. I lit a ciga-

6

rette as I waited and turned to find her leaning on the doorway, arms folded.

"Your thesis," I said. "For your doctorate. What was the subject?"

"Certain aspects of the Third Reich in the Second World War."

"Interesting. Cohen—are you Jewish?" I turned to make the tea.

"My father was a German Jew. He survived Auschwitz and made it to the U.S., but died the year after I was born."

I could think of no more than the usual inadequate response. "I'm sorry."

She stared at me blankly for a moment, then turned and went back to the sitting room. I followed with the tray, placed it on a small coffee table by the fire, and we sat opposite each other in wingback chairs.

"Which explains your interest in the Third Reich," I said as I poured the tea.

She frowned and took the cup of tea I handed her. "I'm just a historian. No ax to grind. My particular obsession is with the Abwehr, German Military Intelligence. Why they were so good and why they were so bad at the same time."

"Admiral Wilhelm Canaris and his merry men?" I shrugged. "I'd say his heart was never in it, but as the SS hanged him at

Flossenburg concentration camp in April forty-five, we'll never know."

"Which brings me to you," she said. "And your book *The Eagle Has Landed.*"

"A novel, Dr. Cohen," I said, "Pure speculation."

"At least fifty percent of which is documented historical fact; you claim that yourself at the beginning of the book."

She leaned forward, hands clenched on her knees, a kind of fierceness there. I said softly, "All right, so what exactly are you getting at?"

"Remember how you found out about the affair in the first place?" she said. "The thing that started you off?"

"Of course," I said. "The tombstone to Steiner and his men that the villagers of Studley Constable had hidden under another tombstone in the churchyard."

"Remember what it said?"

"Hier ruhen Oberstleutnant Kurt Steiner und thirteen Deutsche Fallschirmjäjer gefallen am six November nineteen forty-three."

"Exactly," she said. " 'Here lies Lieutenant Colonel Kurt Steiner and thirteen German paratroopers killed in action on six November nineteen forty-three.' "

"So what's your point?"

"Thirteen plus one makes fourteen, only there aren't fourteen bodies in that grave. There are only thirteen."

I stared at her incredulously. "How in the hell do you make that out?"

"Because Kurt Steiner didn't die that night on the terrace at Meltham House, Mr. Higgins." She reached for the briefcase, had it open in a second and produced a brown manila folder. "And I have the proof right here."

Which very definitely called for Bushmills whiskey. I poured one and said, "All right, do I get to see it?"

"Of course, that's why I'm here, but first let me explain. Any study of Abwehr intelligence affairs during the Second World War constantly refers to the work of SOE, the Special Operations Executive set up by British intelligence in 1940 on Churchill's instructions to coordinate resistance and the underground movement in Europe."

"Set Europe ablaze, that's what the old man ordered," I said.

"I was fascinated to discover that a number of Americans worked for SOE before America came into the war. I thought there might be a book in it. I arranged to come over here to do the research, and a name that came up again

9

and again was Munro—Brigadier Dougal Munro. Before the war he was an archeologist at Oxford. At SOE he was head of Section D. What was commonly known as the dirty-tricks department."

"I had heard of him," I said.

"I did most of my research at the Public Records Office. As you know, few files dealing with intelligence matters are immediately available. Some are on a twenty-five-year hold, some fifty—"

"And exceptionally sensitive material, a hundred years," I said.

"That's what I have here." She held up the folder. "A hundred-year hold file concerning Dougal Munro, Kurt Steiner, Liam Devlin and others. Quite a story, believe me."

She passed it across, and I held it on my knees without opening it. "How on earth did you come by this?"

"I checked out some files concerning Munro yesterday. There was a young clerk on duty on his own. Got careless, I guess. I found the file sandwiched in between two others, sealed, of course. You have to do your research on the premises at the Records Office, but since it wasn't on the booking-out form, I slipped it into my briefcase."

"A criminal offense under the Defence of the Realm Act," I told her.

"I know. I opened the seals as carefully as I could and read the file. It's only a thirty-page resumé of certain events—certain astonishing events."

"And then?"

"I photocopied it."

"The wonders of modern technology allow them to tell when that's been done."

"I know. Anyway, I resealed the file and took it back this morning."

"And how did you manage to return it?" I asked.

"Checked out the same file yesterday. Took the Munro file back to the desk and told the duty clerk there'd been an error."

"Did he believe you?"

"I suppose so. I mean, why wouldn't he?"

"The same clerk?"

"No—an older man."

I sat there thinking about it, feeling decidedly uneasy. Finally I said, "Why don't you make us some fresh tea while I have a go at this?"

"All right."

She took the tray and went out. I hesitated, then opened the file and started to read.

I wasn't even aware that she was there, so gripped was I by the events recorded in that file. When I was finished, I closed it and looked up. She was back in the other chair watching me, a curiously intent look on her face.

I said, "I can understand the hundred-year hold. The powers that be wouldn't want this to come out, not even now."

"That's what I thought."

"Can I hang on to it for a while?"

She hesitated, then nodded. "Till tomorrow if you like. I'm going back to the States on the evening flight. Pan Am."

"A sudden decision?"

She went and got her raincoat. "That's right. I've decided I'd rather be back in my own country."

"Worried?" I asked.

"I'm probably being hypersensitive, but sure. I'll pick the file up tomorrow afternoon. Say three o'clock on my way to Heathrow?"

"Fine." I put the file down on top of my coffee table.

The clock on the mantelpiece chimed the half-hour, seven-thirty, as I walked her to the door. I opened it and we stood for a moment, rain driving down hard.

"Of course there is someone who could confirm the truth of that file," she said. "Liam Devlin. You said in your book he was still around, operating with the Provisional IRA in Ireland."

"Last I heard," I said. "Sixty-seven he'll be now, but lively with it."

"Well, then." She smiled again. "I'll see you tomorrow afternoon."

She went down the steps and walked away through the rain, vanishing in the early evening mist at the end of the street.

I sat by the fire and read the file twice, then I went back into the kitchen, made myself some more tea and a chicken sandwich and sat at the table eating the sandwich and thinking about things.

Extraordinary how events coming right out of the blue can change everything. It had happened to me once before, the discovery of that hidden memorial to Steiner and his men in the churchyard at Studley Constable. I'd been researching an article for a historical magazine. Instead, I'd found something unlooked-for that had changed the course of my entire life. Produced a book which had gone around the world from New York to

Moscow, made me rich. Now this—Ruth Cohen and her stolen file, and I was filled with the same strange, tingling excitement.

I needed to come down. Get things in perspective. So I went to have a shower, took my time over it, shaved and dressed again. It was only eight-thirty, and it didn't seem likely that I'd go to bed early, if I went at all.

I didn't have any more whiskey. I needed to think, so I made even more tea and settled on the chair by the fire, lit a cigarette and started to work my way through the file again.

The doorbell rang, shaking me from my reverie. I glanced at the clock. It was just before nine. The bell rang again insistently, and I replaced the file in the folder, put it on the coffee table and went out into the hall. It occurred to me that it might be Ruth Cohen again, but I couldn't have been more wrong, for when I opened the door I found a young police constable standing there, his navy-blue mac wet with rain.

"Mr. Higgins?" He looked at a piece of paper in his left hand. "Mr. Jack Higgins?"

Strange the certainty of bad news so that we don't even need to be told. "Yes," I said.

He stepped into the hall. "Sorry to trouble

14

you, sir, but I'm making an inquiry relevant to a Miss Ruth Cohen. Would you be a friend of hers, sir?"

"Not exactly," I said. "Is there a problem?"

"I'm afraid the young lady's dead, sir. Hit-and-run accident at the back of the British Museum an hour ago."

"My God!" I whispered.

"The thing is, sir, we found your name and address on a card in her handbag."

It was so difficult to take in. She'd stood there at the door where he was, such a short time before. He was no more than twenty-one or -two. Still young enough to feel concern and he put a hand on my arm.

"Are you all right, sir?"

I said, "Rather shocked, that's all." I took a deep breath. "What is it you want of me?"

"It seems the young lady was at London University. We've checked the student accommodation she was using. No one there, with it being the weekend. It's a question of official identification. For the coroner's office."

"And you'd like me to do it?"

"If you wouldn't mind, sir. It's not far. She's at Kensington Mortuary."

I took another deep breath to steady myself. "All right. Just let me get my raincoat."

The mortuary was a depressing-looking building in a side street, more like a warehouse than anything else. When we went into the foyer, there was a uniformed porter on duty at the desk and a small dark man in his early fifties standing at the window looking out at the rain, a cigarette dangling from the corner of his mouth. He wore a trilby hat and trench coat.

He turned to meet me, hands in pockets. "Mr. Higgins, is it?"

"Yes," I said.

He didn't take his hands out of his pockets and coughed, ash falling from the tip of his cigarette onto his coat. "Detective Chief Superintendent Fox. An unfortunate business, sir."

"Yes," I said.

"This young lady, Ruth Cohen, was she a friend of yours?"

"No," I said. "I only met her for the first time earlier this evening."

"Your name and address were in her handbag." Before I could reply, he carried on. "Anyway, best to get it over with. If you'd come this way."

16

The room they took me into was walled with white tiles and bright fluorescent lighting. There was a line of operating tables. The body was on the end one covered with a white rubber sheet. Ruth Cohen looked very calm, eyes closed, but her head was enclosed in a plastic hood and blood seeped through.

"Would you formally identify the deceased as Ruth Cohen, sir?" the constable asked.

I nodded. "Yes, that's her." And he replaced the sheet.

When I turned, Fox was sitting on the end of the table in the corner lighting another cigarette. "As I said, we found your name in her handbag."

It was then, as if something had gone click in my head, that I came back to reality. Hit and run—a serious offense, but when had it merited the attention of a detective chief superintendent, and wasn't there something about Fox with his saturnine face and dark watchful eyes? This was no ordinary policeman. I smelled Special Branch.

It always pays to stick as closely to the truth as possible, I found that out a long time ago. I said, "She told me she was over from

17

Boston, working at London University, researching a book."

"About what, sir?"

Which confirmed my suspicions instantly. "Something to do with the Second World War, Superintendent, which happens to be an area I've written about myself."

"I see. She was looking for help, advice, that sort of thing?"

Which was when I lied totally. "Not at all. Hardly needed it. A Ph.D., I believe. The fact is, Superintendent, I wrote a rather successful book set during the Second World War. She simply wanted to meet me. As I understood it, she was flying back to the States tomorrow."

The contents of her handbag and briefcase were on the table beside him, the Pan Am ticket conspicuous. He picked it up. "So it would appear."

"Can I go now?"

"Of course. The constable will run you home."

We went out into the foyer and paused at the door. He coughed as he lit another cigarette. "Damn rain. I suppose the driver of that car skidded. An accident really, but then he shouldn't have driven away. We can't have that, can we?"

"Goodnight, Superintendent," I told him and went down the steps to the police car.

I'd left the light on in the hall. When I went in, I went into the kitchen without taking my coat off, put the kettle on and then went into the living room. I poured a Bushmills and turned toward the fire. It was then that I saw that the folder I'd left on the coffee table was gone. For a wild moment I thought I'd made a mistake, had put it elsewhere, but that was nonsense of course.

I put the glass of whiskey down and lit a cigarette, thinking about it. The mysterious Fox—I was more certain than ever that he was Special Branch now—that wretched young woman lying there in the mortuary, and I remembered my unease when she'd told me how she had returned that file at the Records Office. I thought of her walking along the pavement and crossing that street in the rain at the back of the British Museum, and then the car. A wet night and a skidding car, as Fox had said. It could have been an accident, but I knew that was hardly likely, not with the file missing. Which raised the problem of my own continued existence.

Time to move on for a while, but where?

And then I remembered what she had said. There was one person still left who could confirm the story in that file. I packed an overnight bag and went and checked the street through a chink in the curtain. Cars parked everywhere, so it was impossible to see if I was being watched.

I left by the kitchen door at the rear of the house, walked cautiously up the back alley and quickly worked my way through a maze of quiet back streets thinking about it. It had to be a security matter, of course. Some anonymous little department at D15 that took care of people who got out of line, but would that necessarily mean they'd have a go at me? After all, the girl was dead, the file back in the Records Office, the only copy recovered. What could I say that could be proved or in any way be believed? On the other hand, I had to prove it to my own satisfaction, and I hailed a cab on the next corner.

The Green Man, in Kilburn, an area of London popular with the Irish, featured an impressive painting of an Irish tinker over the door which indicated the kind of custom the place enjoyed. The bar was full. I could see that through the saloon window, and I went around to the yard at the rear. The curtains were drawn, and Sean Riley sat at a crowded desk doing his accounts. He was a small man with cropped white hair, active for his age, which I knew was seventy-two. He owned The Green Man, but more importantly was an organizer for Sinn Fein, the political wing of the IRA, in London. I knocked at the window, he got up and moved to peer out. He turned and moved away. A moment later the door opened.

"Mr. Higgins. What brings you here?"

"I won't come in, Sean. I'm on my way to Heathrow."

"Is that a fact. A holiday in the sun, is it?"

"Not exactly. Belfast. I'll probably miss the last shuttle, but I'll be on the breakfast plane. Get word to Liam Devlin. Tell him I'll be staying at the Europa Hotel and I must see him."

"Jesus, Mr. Higgins, and how would I be knowing such a desperate fella as that?"

Through the door I could hear the music from the bar. They were singing "Guns of the IRA." "Don't argue, Sean, just do it," I said. "It's important."

I knew he would, of course, and turned away without another word. A couple of minutes later I hailed a cab and was on my way to Heathrow.

The Europa Hotel in Belfast was legendary among newspaper men from all over the world. It had survived numerous bombing attacks by the IRA and stood in Great Victoria Street next to the railway station. I stayed in my room on the eighth floor for most of the day, just waiting. Things seemed quiet enough, but it was an uneasy calm, and in the late afternoon there was a crump of a bomb; and when I looked out of the window, I saw a black pall of smoke in the distance.

Just after six, with darkness falling, I decided to go down to the bar for a drink, was pulling on my jacket when the phone rang. A voice said, "Mr. Higgins? Reception here, sir. Your taxi's waiting."

It was a black cab, the London variety, and the driver was a middle-aged woman, a pleasant-faced lady who looked like your favorite aunt. I pulled back the glass panel between us and gave her the ritual Belfast greeting: "Goodnight to you."

"And you."

"Not often I see a lady cab driver, not in London anyway."

"A terrible place that. What would you

expect? You sit quiet now like a good gentleman and enjoy the trip."

She closed the panel with one hand. The journey took no more than ten minutes. We passed along the Falls Road, a Catholic area I remembered well from boyhood, and turned into a warren of mean side streets, finally stopping outside a church. She opened the glass panel.

"The first confessional box on the right as you go in."

"If you say so."

I got out and she drove away instantly. The board said *Church of the Holy Name*, and it was in surprisingly good condition, the times of Mass and Confession listed in gold paint. I opened the door at the top of the steps and went in. It was not too large and dimly lit, candles flickering down at the altar, the Virgin in a chapel to one side. Instinctively, I dipped my fingers in the holy water and crossed myself, remembering the Catholic aunt in South Armagh who'd raised me for a while as a child and had anguished over my black little Protestant soul.

The confessional boxes stood to one side. No one waited, which was hardly surprising, for according to the board outside I was an hour early. I went in the first on the right and closed the door. I sat there in the darkness for a moment and then the grille slid open.

"Yes?" a voice asked softly.

I answered automatically. "Bless me, Father, for I have sinned."

"You certainly have, my old son." The light was switched on in the other box, and Liam Devlin smiled through at me.

He looked remarkably well. In fact, rather better than he'd seemed the last time I'd seen him. Sixty-seven, but as I'd said to Ruth Cohen, lively with it. A small man with enormous vitality, hair as black as ever, and vivid blue eyes. There was the scar of an old bullet wound on the left side of his forehead, and a slight ironic smile was permanently in place. He wore a priest's cassock and clerical collar and seemed perfectly at home in the sacristy at the back of the church to which he'd taken me.

"You're looking well, son. All that success and money." He grinned. "We'll drink to it. There's a bottle here surely."

He opened a cupboard and found a bottle of Bushmills and two glasses. "And what would the usual occupant think of all this?" I asked.

"Father Murphy?" He splashed whiskey into the glasses. "Heart of corn, that one. Out doing good, as usual."

"He looks the other way, then?"

"Something like that." He raised his glass. "To you, my old son."

"And you, Liam." I toasted him back. "You never cease to amaze me. On the British army's most wanted list for the last five years and you still have the nerve to sit here in the middle of Belfast."

"Ah, well, a man has to have some fun." He took a cigarette from a silver case and offered me one. "Anyway, to what do I owe the pleasure of this visit?"

"Does the name Dougal Munro mean anything to you?"

His eyes widened in astonishment. "What in the hell have you come up with now? I haven't heard that old bastard's name mentioned in years."

"Or Schellenberg?"

"Walter Schellenberg? There was a man for you. General at thirty. Schellenberg— Munro? What is this?"

"And Kurt Steiner," I said, "who, according to everyone, including you, died trying to shoot the fake Churchill on the terrace at Meltham House."

Devlin swallowed some of his whiskey and smiled amiably. "I was always the terrible liar. Now, tell me what this is all about."

So I told him about Ruth Cohen, the file and its contents, everything, and he listened intently without interrupting.

When I was finished, he said, "Convenient, the girl's death, you were right about that."

"Which doesn't look very good for me."

There was an explosion not too far away and, as he went to open the door to the rear yard, the rattle of small-arms fire.

"It sounds like a lively night," I said.

"Oh, it will be. Safer off the streets at the moment."

He closed the door and turned to face me. I said, "The facts in that file. Were they true?"

"A good story."

"In outline."

"Which means you'd like to hear the rest?"

"I need to hear it."

"Why not." He smiled, sat down at a table in the corner and reached for the Bushmills. "Sure and it'll keep me out of mischief for a while. Now, where would you like me to begin?"

BERLIN
LISBON
LONDON
1943

2

BRIGADIER DOUGAL Munro's flat in Haston Place was only ten minutes' walk from the London headquarters of SOE in Baker Street. As head of Section D, he needed to be on call twenty-four hours a day, and besides the normal phone he had a secure line routed directly to his office. It was this particular phone he answered on that late November evening as he sat by the fire working on some files.

"Carter here, Brigadier. Just back from Norfolk."

"Good," Munro told him. "Call in on your way home and tell me about it."

He put the phone down and went and got himself a malt whisky, a squat, powerful-looking man with white hair who wore steel-rimmed spectacles. Strictly a nonprofessional, his rank of brigadier was simply for purposes of authority in certain quarters; and at sixty-five, an age when most men faced retirement, even at Oxford, the war had been the saving of him, that was the blunt truth. He was thinking about that when the doorbell rang and he admitted Captain Jack Carter.

"You look frozen, Jack. Help yourself to a drink."

Jack Carter leaned his walking stick against a chair and shrugged off his greatcoat. He was in the uniform of a captain in the Green Howards, the ribbon of the Military Cross on his battledress. His false leg was a legacy of Dunkirk, and he limped noticeably as he went to the drinks cupboard and poured a whisky.

"So, what's the situation at Studley Constable?" Munro asked.

"Back to normal, sir. All the German paratroopers buried in a common grave in the churchyard."

"No marker of course?"

"Not at the moment, but they're a funny lot those villagers. They actually seem to think quite highly of Steiner."

"Yes, well, one of his sergeants was killed saving the lives of two village children who fell into the millrace, remember. In fact, that single action was the one thing that blew their cover, caused the failure of the entire operation."

"And he did let the villagers go before the worst of the fighting started," Carter said.

"Exactly. Have you got the file on him?"

Carter got his briefcase and extracted a couple of sheets stapled together. Munro examined them. "Oberstleutnant Kurt Steiner, age twenty-seven. Remarkable record. Crete, North Africa, Stalingrad. Knight's Cross with Oak Leaves."

"I'm always intrigued by his mother, sir. Boston socialite. What they call 'Boston Brahmin.'"

"All very fine, Jack, but don't forget his father was a German general and a damn good one. Now, what about Steiner? How is he?"

"There seems no reason to doubt a complete recovery. There's an RAF hospital for bomber crews with burn problems just outside Norwich. Rather small. Used to be a nursing home. We have Steiner there under secure guard. The cover story is that he's a downed Luftwaffe pilot. Rather convenient that German paratroopers and Luftwaffe aircrews wear roughly the same uniform."

"And his wounds?"

"He was damn lucky there, sir. One round hit him in the right shoulder, at the rear. The second was a heart shot, but it turned on the breastbone. The surgeon doesn't think it will take long, especially as he's in remarkable physical shape."

Munro went and got another small whisky. "Let's go over what we know, Jack. The whole business, the plot to kidnap Churchill, the planning. Everything was done without Admiral Canaris's knowledge?"

"Apparently so, sir, all Himmler's doing. He pressured Max Radl at Abwehr headquarters to plan it all behind the admiral's back. At least that's what our sources in Berlin tell us."

"He knows all about it now, though?" Munro said. "The admiral, I mean."

"Apparently, sir, and not best pleased, not that there's anything he can do about it. Can't exactly go running to the Führer."

"And neither can Himmler," Munro said. "Not when the whole project was mounted without the Führer's knowledge."

"Of course Himmler did give Max Radl a letter of authorization signed by Hitler himself," Carter said.

"*Purporting* to be signed by Hitler, Jack. I bet that was the first thing to go into the fire. No, Himmler won't want to advertise this one."

"And we don't want it on the front of the *Daily Express*, sir. German paratroopers trying to grab the Prime Minister, battling it out with American Rangers in an English country village."

"Yes, it wouldn't exactly help the war effort." Munro looked at the file again. "This IRA chap, Devlin. Quite a character. You say that your information is that he was wounded?"

"That's right, sir. He was in hospital in Holland and simply took off one night. We understand he's in Lisbon."

"Probably hoping to make it to the States in some way. Are we keeping an eye on him? Who's SOE's man in Lisbon?"

"Major Arthur Frear, sir. Military attaché at the Embassy. He's been notified," Carter told him.

"Good." Munro nodded.

"So what do we do about Steiner, sir?"

Munro frowned, thinking about it. "The moment he's fit enough, bring him to London. Do we still house German prisoners of war in the Tower?"

"Only occasionally, sir, transients passing through the small hospital. Not like the early days of the war when most of the captured U-boat people were housed there."

"And Hess."

"A special case, sir."

"All right. We'll have Steiner at the Tower. He can stay in the hospital till we decide on a safe house. Anything else?"

"One development, sir. Steiner's father was involved, as you know, in a series of army plots aimed at assassinating Hitler. The punishment is statutory. Hanging by piano wire, and by the Führer's orders the whole thing is recorded on film."

"How unpleasant," Munro said.

"The thing is, sir, we've received a copy of the film of General Steiner's death. One of our Berlin sources got it out via Sweden. I don't know if you'll want to see it. It's not very nice."

Munro was angry, got up and paced the room. He paused suddenly, a slight smile on his mouth. "Tell me, Jack, is that little toad Vargas still at the Spanish Embassy?"

"José Vargas, sir, trade attaché. We haven't used him in a while."

"But German intelligence are convinced he's on their side?"

"The only side Vargas is on is the one with the biggest bankbook, sir. Works through his cousin at the Spanish Embassy in Berlin."

"Excellent." Munro was smiling now. "Tell him to pass the word to Berlin that we have Kurt Steiner. Tell him to say in the Tower of London. Sounds very dramatic. Most important, he makes sure that *both* Canaris and Himmler get the information. That should get them stirred up."

"What on earth are you playing at, sir?" Carter asked.

"War, Jack, war. Now have another drink, then get yourself off home to bed. You're going to have a full day tomorrow."

Near Paderborn in Westphalia in the small town of Wewelsburg was the castle of that name which Heinrich Himmler had taken over from the local council in 1934. His original intention had been to convert it into a school for Reich SS leaders, but by the time the architects and builders had finished and many millions of marks had been spent, he had created a Gothic monstrosity worthy of stage six at MGM, a vast film set of the kind Hollywood was fond of when historical pictures were the vogue. The castle had three wings, towers, a moat, and in the southern wing the Reichsführer had his own apartments and his special pride, the enormous dining hall where selected members of the

35

SS would meet in a kind of court of honor. The whole thing had been influenced by Himmler's obsession with King Arthur and the Knights of the Round Table, with a liberal dose of occultism thrown in.

Ten miles away on that December evening, Walter Schellenberg lit a cigarette in the back of the Mercedes which was speeding him toward the castle. He'd received the order to meet the Reichsführer in Berlin that afternoon. The reason had not been specified. He certainly didn't take it as any evidence of preferment.

He'd been to Wewelsburg on several occasions, had even inspected the castle's plans at SD headquarters, so he knew it well. He also knew that the only men to sit around that table with the Reichsführer were cranks like Himmler himself who believed all the dark-age twaddle about Saxon superiority, or timeservers who had their own chairs with names inscribed on a silver plate. The fact that King Arthur had been Romano-British engaged in a struggle against Saxon invaders made the whole thing even more nonsensical, but Schellenberg had long since ceased to be amused by the excesses of the Third Reich.

In deference to the demands of Wewelsburg, he wore the black dress uniform of the SS, the Iron Cross First Class pinned to the left side of his tunic.

"What a world we live in," he said softly as the car took the road up to the castle, snow falling gently. "I sometimes really do wonder who is running the lunatic asylum."

He smiled as he sat back, looking suddenly quite charming, although the dueling scar on one cheek hinted at a more ruthless side to his nature. It was a relic of student days at the University of Bonn. In spite of a gift for languages, he'd started in the Faculty of Medicine, had then switched to law. But times in Germany in 1933 were hard, even for well-qualified young men just out of university.

The SS were recruiting gifted young scholars for their upper echelons. Like many others, Schellenberg had seen it as employment, not as a political ideal, and his rise had been astonishing. Because of his language ability, Reinhard Heydrich himself had pulled him into the Sicherheitsdienst, the SS security service known as the SD. His main responsibility had always been intelligence work abroad, often a conflict with the Abwehr, although his personal relationship with Canaris was excellent. A series of brilliant intel-

37

ligence coups had pushed him up the ladder rapidly. By the age of thirty, he was an SS Brigadeführer and Major General of Police.

The really astonishing thing was that Walter Schellenberg didn't consider himself a Nazi, looked on the Third Reich as a sorry charade, its main protagonists actors of a very low order indeed. There were Jews who owed their survival to him, intended victims of the concentration camps rerouted to Sweden and safety. A dangerous game, a sop to his conscience, he told himself, and he had his enemies. He had survived for one reason only. Himmler needed his brains and his considerable talents, and that was enough.

There was only a powdering of snow in the moat, no water. As the Mercedes crossed the bridge to the gate, he leaned back and said softly, "Too late to get off the roundabout now, Walter, far too late."

Himmler received him in his private sitting room in the south wing. Schellenberg was escorted there by an SS sergeant in dress uniform and found Himmler's personal aide, a Sturmbannführer named Rossman, sitting at a table outside the door, also in dress uniform.

"Major." Schellenberg nodded.

Rossman dismissed the sergeant. "A pleasure to see you, General. He's waiting. The mood isn't good, by the way."

"I'll remember that."

Rossman opened the door and Schellenberg entered a large room with a vaulted ceiling and flagged floor. There were tapestries on the walls and lots of dark oak furniture. A log fire burned on a great stone hearth. The Reichsführer sat at an oak table working his way through a mound of papers. He was not in uniform, unusual for him, wore a tweed suit, white shirt and black tie. The silver pince-nez gave him the air of a rather unpleasant schoolmaster.

Unlike Heydrich, who had always addressed Schellenberg by his Christian name, Himmler was invariably formal. "General Schellenberg." He looked up. "You got here."

There was an implied rebuke, and Schellenberg said, "I left Berlin the moment I received your message, Reichsführer. In what way can I serve you?"

"Operation Eagle, the Churchill affair. I didn't employ you on that business because you had other duties. However, you by now will be familiar with most of the details."

"Of course, Reichsführer."

Himmler abruptly changed the subject.

"Schellenberg, I am increasingly concerned at the treasonable activities of many members of the High Command. As you know, some wretched young major was blown up in his car outside the entrance to the Führer's headquarters at Rastenburg last week. Obviously another attempt on our Führer's life."

"I'm afraid so, Reichsführer."

Himmler stood up and put a hand on Schellenberg's shoulder. "You and I, General, are bound by a common brotherhood, the SS. We are sworn to protect the Führer and yet are constantly threatened by this conspiracy of generals."

"There is no direct proof, Reichsführer," Schellenberg said, which was not strictly true.

Himmler said, "General von Stülpnagel, Von Falkenhausen, Stieff, Wagner and others, even your good friend Admiral Wilhelm Canaris, Schellenberg. Would that surprise you?"

Schellenberg tried to stay calm, envisaging the distinct possibility that *he* might be named next. "What can I say, Reichsführer?"

"And Rommel, General, the Desert Fox himself. The people's hero."

"My God!" Schellenberg gasped, mainly because it seemed the right thing to do.

"Proof." Himmler snorted. "I'll have my proof before I'm done. They have a date with the hangman, all of them. But to other things." He returned to the table and sat. "Have you ever had any dealings with an agent named Vargas?" He examined a paper in front of him. "José Vargas."

"I know of him. An Abwehr contact. A commercial attaché at the Spanish Embassy in London. As far as I know, he has only been used occasionally."

"He has a cousin who is also a commercial attaché at the Spanish Embassy here in Berlin. One Juan Rivera." Himmler glanced up. "Am I right?"

"So I understand, Reichsführer. Vargas would use the Spanish diplomatic bag from London. Most messages would reach his cousin here in Berlin within thirty-six hours. Highly illegal, of course."

"And thank God for it," Himmler said. "This Operation Eagle affair. You say you are familiar with the details?"

"I am, Reichsführer," Schellenberg said smoothly.

"There is a problem here, General. Although the idea was suggested by the Führer, it was, how shall I put it, more a flight of fancy than anything else? One couldn't rely on Canaris to do anything about it. I'm afraid that total victory for the Third Reich is low on his list of priorities. That is why I personally put the plan into operation aided by Colonel Radl of the Abwehr, who's had a heart attack, I understand, and is not expected to live."

Schellenberg said cautiously, "So the Führer knows nothing of the affair?"

"My dear Schellenberg, he carries the responsibility for the war, its every aspect, on his own shoulders. It is our duty to lighten that load as much as possible."

"Of course, Reichsführer."

"Operation Eagle, however brilliantly conceived, ended in failure, and who would wish to take failure into the Führer's office and place it on his desk?" Before Schellenberg could reply, he carried on. "Which brings me to this report which has reached me from Vargas in London via his cousin here in Berlin, the man Rivera."

He handed across a signal flimsy and Schellenberg glanced at it. "Incredible!" he said. "Kurt Steiner alive."

"And in the Tower of London." Himmler took the signal back.

"They won't keep him there for very long," Schellenberg said. "It may sound dramatic, but the Tower isn't really suitable to house high-security prisoners long-term. They'll move him to some safe house just as they did with Hess."

"Have you any other opinion in the matter?"

"Only that the British will keep quiet about the fact that he's in their hands."

"Why do you say that?"

"Operation Eagle almost succeeded."

"But Churchill wasn't Churchill," Himmler reminded him. "Our intelligence people discovered that."

"Of course, Reichsführer, but German paratroopers did land on English soil and fought a bloody battle. If the story was publicized, the effect on the British people at this stage of the war would be appalling. The very fact that it's SOE and their Brigadier Munro who are handling the matter is further proof."

"You know the man?"

"Know of him only, Reichsführer. A highly capable intelligence officer."

Himmler said, "My sources indicate that Rivera has also passed this news on to Canaris. How do you think he will react?"

"I've no idea, Reichsführer."

"You can see him when you get back to Berlin. Find out. My opinion is that he will do nothing. He certainly won't go running to the Führer." Himmler examined another sheet in front of him. "I'll never understand men like Steiner. A war hero. Knight's Cross with Oak Leaves, a brilliant soldier, and yet he ruined his career, failure, everything, for the sake of some little Jewish bitch he tried to help in Warsaw. It was only Operation Eagle that saved him and his men from the penal unit they were serving in." He put the sheet down. "The Irishman, of course, is a different matter."

"Devlin, Reichsführer?"

"Yes, a thoroughly obnoxious man. You know what the Irish are like, Schellenberg. Everything a joke."

"I must say that from all reports he seems to know his business."

"I agree, but then he was only in it for the money. Someone was singularly careless to allow him to walk out of that hospital in Holland."

"I agree, Reichsführer."

"My reports indicate that he's in Lisbon now," Himmler said. He pushed another sheet across. "You'll find the details there.

He's trying to get to America, but no money. According to that, he's been working as a barman."

Schellenberg examined the signal quickly, then said, "What would you like me to do on this matter, Reichsführer?"

"You'll return to Berlin tonight, fly to Lisbon tomorrow. Persuade this rogue Devlin to return with you. I shouldn't think that would prove too difficult. Radl gave him twenty thousand pounds for taking part in Operation Eagle. It was paid into a numbered account in Geneva." Himmler smiled thinly. "He'll do anything for money. He's that sort. Offer him the same—more if you have to. I'll authorize payments up to thirty thousand pounds."

"But for what, Reichsführer?"

"Why, to arrange Steiner's escape, of course. I should have thought that's obvious. The man is a hero of the Reich, a true hero. We can't leave him in British hands."

Remembering how General Steiner had met his end in the Gestapo cellars at Prinz Albrechtstrasse, it seemed likely to Schellenberg that Himmler might have other reasons. He said calmly, "I take your point, Reichsführer."

"You know the confidence I repose in

you, General," Himmler said. "And you've never let me down. I leave the whole matter in your capable hands." He passed an envelope across. "You'll find a letter of authorization in there that should take care of all contingencies."

Schellenberg didn't open it. Instead he said, "You said you wanted me to go to Lisbon tomorrow, Reichsführer. May I remind you it's Christmas Eve?"

"What on earth has that got to do with anything?" Himmler seemed genuinely surprised. "Speed is of the essence here, Schellenberg, and reminding you of your oath as a member of the SS, I will now tell you why. In approximately four weeks, the Führer will fly to Cherbourg in Normandy. January twenty-first. I shall accompany him. From there we proceed down the coast to a place called Château de Belle-Île. Such strange names the French employ."

"May I ask the purpose of the visit?"

"The Führer intends to meet with Field Marshal Rommel personally, to confirm his appointment as Commander of Army Group B. This will give him direct responsibility for the Atlantic Wall defenses. The meeting will be concerned with the strategy necessary if our enemies decide to invade next year.

The Führer has given to me the honor of organizing the conference and, of course, responsibility for his safety. It will be purely an SS matter. As I've said, Rommel will be there, probably Canaris. The Führer particularly asked for him."

He started to sort his papers into a neat pile, putting some of them into a briefcase. Schellenberg said, "But the urgency on the Steiner affair, Reichsführer, I don't understand."

"I intend to introduce him to the Führer at that meeting, General. A great coup for the SS, his escape and near victory. His presence, of course, will make things rather difficult for Canaris, which will be all to the good." He closed the briefcase and his eyes narrowed. "That is all you need to know."

Schellenberg, who felt that he was only hanging on to his sanity by his fingernails, said, "But, Reichsführer, what if Devlin doesn't wish to be persuaded?"

"Then you must take appropriate action. To that end, I have selected a Gestapo man I wish to accompany you to Lisbon as your bodyguard." He rang a bell on the desk and Rossman entered. "Ah, Rossman. I'll see Sturmbannführer Berger now."

Schellenberg waited, desperate for a cigarette, but aware also of how totally Himmler disapproved of smoking, and then the door opened and Rossman appeared with another man. Something of a surprise, this one. A young man, only twenty-five or -six, with blond hair that was almost white. Good-looking once, but one side of his face had been badly burned. Schellenberg could see where the skin graft stretched tightly.

He held out his hand. "General Schellenberg. Horst Berger. A pleasure to work with you."

He smiled, looking with that marred face like the devil himself and Schellenberg said, "Major." He turned to Himmler. "May I get started, Reichsführer?"

"Of course. Berger will join you in the courtyard. Send Rossman in." Schellenberg got the door open and Himmler added, "One more thing. Canaris is to know nothing. Not Devlin, not our intentions regarding Steiner and for the moment no mention of Château de Belle-Île. You understand the importance of this?"

"Of course, Reichsführer."

Schellenberg told Rossman to go in and walked along the corridor. On the next floor, he found a toilet, slipped in and lit a cigarette, then took the envelope Himmler had given him from his pocket and opened it.

FROM THE LEADER AND CHANCELLOR OF THE STATE
GENERAL SCHELLENBERG ACTS UPON MY DIRECT AND PERSONAL ORDERS IN A MATTER OF THE UTMOST IMPORTANCE TO THE REICH. HE IS ANSWERABLE ONLY TO ME. ALL PERSONNEL, MILITARY AND CIVIL, WITHOUT DISTINCTION OF RANK, WILL ASSIST HIM IN ANY WAY HE SEES FIT.

Adolf Hitler

Schellenberg shivered and put it back in the envelope. The signature certainly looked right, he'd seen it often enough, but then it would be easy for Himmler to get the Führer's signature on something, just one document among many. So, Himmler was giving him the same powers as he had given Max Radl for Operation Eagle. But why? Why was it so important to get Steiner back and in the time scale indicated?

There had to be more to the whole business than Himmler was telling him, that much was obvious. He lit another cigarette and left, losing his way at the end of the corridor. He hesitated, uncertain, then realized that the archway at the end led onto the balcony above the great hall. He was about to turn and go the other way when he heard voices. Intrigued, he moved forward onto the balcony and peered down cautiously. Himmler was standing at the head of the great table flanked by Rossman and Berger. The Reichsführer was speaking.

"There are those, Berger, who are more concerned with people than ideas. They become sentimental too easily. I do not think you are one of them."

"No, Reichsführer," Berger said.

"Unfortunately, General Schellenberg is. That's why I'm sending you with him to Lisbon. The man Devlin comes whether he likes it or not. I look to you to see to it."

"Is the Reichsführer doubting General Schellenberg's loyalty?" Rossman asked.

"He has been of great service to the Reich," Himmler said. "Probably the most gifted officer to serve under my command, but I've always doubted his loyalty to the Party. But there is no problem here, Rossman. He is too useful for me to discard at the present time. We must put all our energies into the preparation for Belle-Île while Schellenberg busies himself with the Steiner affair." He turned to Berger. "You'd better be off."

"Reichsführer." Berger clicked his heels and turned away. When he was halfway across the hall, Himmler called, "Show me what you can do, Sturmbannführer."

Berger had the flap of his holster open, turned with incredible speed, arm extended. There was a fresco of knights on the far wall done in medieval style in plaster. He fired three times very fast and three heads disintegrated. The shots echoed through the hall as he replaced his weapon.

"Excellent," Himmler said.

Schellenberg was already on his way. He was good himself, maybe as good as Berger, but that wasn't the point. In the hall he retrieved his greatcoat and cap and was sitting in the rear of the Mercedes when Berger joined him five minutes later.

"Sorry if I've kept you waiting, General," he said as he got in.

"No problem," Schellenberg said and nodded to the driver, who drove away. "Smoke if you like."

"No vices, I'm afraid," Berger said.

"Really? Now that is interesting." Schellenberg turned up the collar of his greatcoat and leaned back in the corner pulling the peak of his cap over his eyes. "A long way to Berlin. I don't know about you, but I'm going to get some sleep."

He did just that. Berger watched him for a while, and then he also pulled up the collar of his greatcoat and turned into the corner.

Schellenberg's office at Prinz Albrechtstrasse had a military camp bed in one corner, for he often spent the night there. He was in the small bathroom adjacent to it shaving when his secretary, Ilse Huber, entered. She was forty-one at that time, already a war widow, a sensual, attractive woman in white blouse and black skirt. She had once been Heydrich's secretary, and Schellenberg, to whom she was devoted, had inherited her.

"He's here," she said.

"Rivera?" Schellenberg wiped soap from his face. "And Canaris?"

"The Herr Admiral will be riding in the Tiergarten at ten o'clock as usual. Will you join him?"

Schellenberg frequently did, but when he went to the window and saw the powdering of snow in the streets he laughed. "Not this morning, thank you, but I must see him."

Dedicated as she was to Schellenberg's

welfare, she had an instinct about things. She went and poured coffee from the pot on the tray she had put on his desk. "Trouble, General?"

"In a way, my love." He drank some of the coffee and smiled that ruthless, dangerous smile of his that made the heart turn over in her. "But don't worry. Nothing I can't handle. I'll fill you in on the details before I leave. I'm going to need your help with this one. Where's Berger, by the way?"

"Downstairs in the canteen, last I saw of him."

"All right. I'll see Rivera now."

She paused at the door and turned. "He frightens me that one. Berger, I mean."

Schellenberg went and put an arm around her. "I told you not to worry. After all, when has the great Schellenberg ever failed to manage?"

His self-mockery, as always, made her laugh. He gave her a squeeze, and she was out of the door smiling. Schellenberg buttoned his tunic and sat down. A moment later the door opened and Rivera came in.

He wore a dark brown suit, an overcoat over one arm, a small man, sallow skin, black hair carefully parted. Just now he looked decidedly anxious.

"You know who I am?" Schellenberg asked him.

"Of course, General. An honor to meet you."

Schellenberg held up a piece of paper which was actually some stationery from the hotel he'd stayed at in Vienna the previous week. "This message you received from your cousin Vargas at the London Embassy concerning the whereabouts of a certain Colonel Steiner. Have you discussed it with anyone?"

Rivera seemed genuinely shocked. "Not a living soul, General. Before God I swear this." He spread his hands dramatically. "On my mother's life."

"Oh, I don't think we need to bring her into it. She's quite comfortable in that little villa you bought her in San Carlos." Rivera looked startled, and Schellenberg said, "You see, there is nothing about you I don't know. There is no place you could go where I couldn't reach you. Do you understand me?"

"Perfectly, General." Rivera was sweating.

"You belong to the SD now and Reichsführer Himmler, but it is me you answer to and no one else, so to start with: This message from your cousin in London. Why did you also send it to Admiral Canaris?"

"My cousin's orders, General. In these matters there is always the question of payment and in this case . . ." He shrugged.

"He thought you might get paid twice?" Schellenberg nodded. It made sense, and yet he had learned never to take anything for granted in this game. "Tell me about your cousin."

"What can I say that the general doesn't know? José's parents died in the influenza epidemic just after the First World War. My parents raised him. We were like brothers. Went to the University of Madrid together. Fought in the same regiment in the Civil War. He's one year older than me, thirty-three."

"He isn't married, you are," Schellenberg said. "Does he have a girlfriend in London?"

Rivera spread his hands. "As it happens, José's tastes do not run to women, General."

"I see." Schellenberg brooded about it for a moment. He had nothing against homosexuals, but such people were susceptible to blackmail, and that was a weakness for anyone engaged in intelligence work. A point against Vargas, then.

"You know London?"

Rivera nodded. "I served at the Embassy there with José in nineteen thirty-nine for one year. I left my wife in Madrid."

"I know London also," Schellenberg said. "Tell me about his life. Does he live at the Embassy?"

"Officially he does, General, but for the purposes of his private life he has a small apartment, a 'flat' as the English call it. He took a seven-year lease on the place while I was there, so he must still have it."

"Where would that be?"

"Stanley Mews, quite close to Westminster Abbey."

"And convenient for the Houses of Parliament. A good address. I'm impressed."

"José always did like the best."

"Which must be paid for." Schellenberg got up and went to the window. It was snowing lightly. He said, "Is he reliable, this cousin of yours? Any question of him ever having had any dealings with our British friends?"

Rivera looked shocked again. "General Schellenberg, I assure you. José, like me, is a good Fascist. We fought together with General Franco in the Civil War. We—"

"All right, I was just making the point.

Now listen to me carefully. We may well decide to attempt to rescue Colonel Steiner."

"From the Tower of London, señor?" Rivera's eyes bulged.

"In my opinion, they'll move him to some sort of safe house. May well have done so already. You will send a message to your cousin today asking for all possible information."

"Of course, General."

"Get on with it then." As Rivera reached the door, Schellenberg added, "I need hardly say that if one word of this leaks out you will end up in the river Spree, my friend, and your cousin in the Thames. I have an extraordinarily long arm."

"General, I beg of you." Rivera started to protest again.

"Spare me all that stuff about what a good Fascist you are. Just think about how generous I'm going to be. A much sounder basis for our relationship."

Rivera departed and Schellenberg phoned down for his car, pulled on his overcoat and went out.

Admiral Wilhelm Canaris was fifty-six, a U-boat captain of distinction in the First World War. He had headed the Abwehr since 1935

57

and despite being a loyal German had always been unhappy with National Socialism. Although he was opposed to any plan to assassinate Hitler, he had been involved with the German Resistance movement for some years, treading a dangerous path that was eventually to lead to his downfall and death.

That morning, as he galloped along the path between the trees in the Tiergarten, his horse's hooves kicked up the powdered snow, filling him with a fierce joy. The two dachshunds which accompanied him everywhere followed with surprising speed. He saw Schellenberg standing beside his Mercedes, waved and turned toward him.

"Good morning, Walter. You should be with me."

"Not this morning," Schellenberg told him. "I'm off on my travels again."

Canaris dismounted, and Schellenberg's driver held the horse's reins. Canaris offered Schellenberg a cigarette, and they went and leaned on a parapet overlooking the lake.

"Anywhere interesting?" Canaris asked.

"No, just routine," Schellenberg said.

"Come on, Walter, out with it. There's something on your mind."

"All right. The Operation Eagle affair."

"Nothing to do with me," Canaris told

him. "The Führer came up with the idea. What nonsense! Kill Churchill when we've already lost the war."

"I wish you wouldn't say that sort of thing out loud," Schellenberg said gently.

Canaris ignored him. "I was ordered to prepare a feasibility study. I knew the Führer would forget it within a matter of days and he did, only Himmler didn't. Wanted to make life disagreeable for me as usual. Went behind my back, suborned Max Radl, one of my most trusted aides. And the whole thing turned out to be the shambles I knew it would."

"Of course Steiner almost pulled it off," Schellenberg said.

"Pulled what off? Come off it, Walter, I'm not denying Steiner's audacity and bravery, but the man they were after wasn't even Churchill. Would have been quite something if they'd brought him back. The look on Himmler's face would have been a joy to see."

"And now we hear that Steiner didn't die," Schellenberg said. "That they have him in the Tower of London."

"Ah, so Rivera has passed on his dear cousin's message to the Reichsführer also."

Canaris smiled cynically. "Doubling up their reward as usual."

"What do you think the British will do?"

"With Steiner? Lock him up tight until the end of the war like Hess, only they'll keep quiet about it. Wouldn't look too good, just as it wouldn't look too good to the Führer if the facts came to his attention."

"Do you think they're likely to?" Schellenberg asked.

Canaris laughed out loud. "You mean from me? So that's what all this is about? No, Walter, I'm in enough trouble these days without looking for more. You can tell the Reichsführer that I'll keep quiet if he will."

They started to walk back to the Mercedes. Schellenberg said, "I suppose he's to be trusted, this Vargas. We can believe him?"

Canaris took the point seriously. "I'm the first to admit our operations in England have gone badly. The British secret service came up with a stroke of some genius when they stopped having our operatives shot when they caught them and simply turned them into double agents."

"And Vargas?"

"One can never be sure, but I don't think so. His position at the Spanish Embassy, the fact that he has only worked occasionally and as a free-lance. No contacts with any other agents in England, you see." They had reached the car. He smiled. "Anything else?"

Schellenberg couldn't help saying it, he liked the man so much. "As you well know, there was another attempt on the Führer's life at Rastenburg. As it happened, the bombs the young officer involved was carrying went off prematurely."

"Very careless of him. What's your point, Walter?"

"Take care, for God's sake. These are dangerous times."

"Walter, I have never condoned the idea of assassinating the Führer." The admiral climbed back into the saddle and gathered his reins. "However desirable that possibility may seem to some people. And shall I tell you why, Walter?"

"I'm sure you're going to."

"Stalingrad, thanks to the Führer's stupidity, lost us more than three hundred thousand dead. Ninety-one thousand taken prisoner, including twenty-four generals. The greatest defeat we've ever known. One balls-up after another, thanks to the Führer." He laughed harshly. "Don't you realize

61

the truth of it, my friend? His continued existence actually shortens the war for us."

He put his spurs to his horse, the dachshunds yapping at his heels, and galloped into the trees.

Back at the office, Schellenberg changed into a light gray flannel suit in the bathroom, speaking through the other door to Ilse Huber as he dressed, filling her in on the whole business.

"What do you think?" he asked as he emerged. "Like a fairy tale by the Brothers Grimm?"

"More like a horror story," she said as she held his black leather coat for him.

"We'll refuel in Madrid and carry straight on. Should be in Lisbon by late afternoon."

He pulled on the coat, adjusted a slouch hat and picked up the overnight bag she had prepared. "I expect news from Rivera within two days at the outside. Give him thirty-six hours, then apply pressure." He kissed her on the cheek. "Take care, Ilse. See you soon." And he was gone.

The plane was a Ju-52 with its famous three engines and corrugated metal skin. As it lifted from the Luftwaffe fighter base outside

Berlin, Schellenberg undid his seat belt and reached for his briefcase.

Berger, on the other side of the aisle, smiled. "The Herr Admiral was well, General?"

Now that isn't very clever, Schellenberg thought. You weren't supposed to know I was seeing him.

He smiled back. "He seemed his usual self."

He opened his briefcase, started to read Devlin's background report and examined a photo of him. After a while he stopped and looked out of the window, remembering what Canaris had said about Hitler.

His continued existence actually shortens the war for us.

Strange how that thought went around and around in his brain and wouldn't go away.

3

BARON OSWALD VON HOYNINGEN-HEUNE, the minister to the German Legation in Lisbon, was a friend and an aristocrat of the old school who was also no Nazi. He was delighted to see Schellenberg and showed it.

"My dear Walter. Good to see you. How's Berlin at the moment?"

"Colder than this," Schellenberg told him as they moved out through French windows and sat at a table on the pleasant terrace. The garden was a sight to see, winter flowers everywhere. A houseboy in white jacket brought coffee on a tray, and Schellenberg sighed. "Yes, I can understand you hanging on here instead of coming back to Berlin. The best place to be these days, Lisbon."

"I know," the baron told him. "The constant worry all my staff have is of being transferred." He poured the coffee. "A strange time to arrive, Walter, Christmas Eve."

"You know Uncle Heini when he gets the bit between his teeth," Schellenberg told him, using the nickname common in the SS behind Himmler's back.

"It must be important," the baron said. "Especially if he sends you."

"There's a man we want, an Irishman—Liam Devlin." Schellenberg took Devlin's photo from his wallet and passed it across. "He worked for Abwehr for a while. The IRA connection. Walked out of a hospital in Holland the other week. Our information is that he's here, working as a waiter at a club in Alfama."

"The old quarter." The baron nodded. "If he's Irish, this man, I hardly need point out that makes him officially a neutral. A situation of some delicacy."

"No rough stuff needed," Schellenberg said. "I hope we can persuade him to come back peaceably. I have a job to offer him that could be rather lucrative."

"Fine," the baron said. "Just remember that our Portuguese friends really do value their neutrality. Even more so now that victory seems to be slipping away from us. However, Captain Eggar, my police attaché here, should be able to assist you." He picked up his phone and spoke to an aide. As he put it down he said, "I caught a glimpse of your companion."

"Sturmbannführer Horst Berger—Gestapo," Schellenberg said.

"Doesn't look your sort."

"A Christmas present from the Reichsführer. I didn't have much choice."

"Like that, is it?"

There was a knock at the door and a man in his forties slipped in. He had a heavy mustache and wore a brown gabardine suit that didn't fit too well. A professional policeman. Schellenberg recognized the type.

"Ah, there you are, Eggar. You know General Schellenberg, don't you?"

"Of course. A great pleasure to see you again. We met during the course of the Windsor affair in nineteen forty."

"Yes, well we prefer to forget all about that these days." Schellenberg passed Devlin's photo across. "Have you seen this man?"

Eggar examined it. "No, General."

"He's Irish, ex-IRA, if you ever can be ex-IRA, age thirty-five. He worked for Abwehr for a while. We want him back. Our latest information is that he's been working as a waiter at a bar called Flamingo."

"I know the place."

"Good. You'll find my aide, Major Berger of the Gestapo, outside. Bring him in." Eggar went out and returned with Berger, and Schellenberg made the introductions. "Baron von Hoyningen-Heune, minister to the Legation, and Captain Eggar, police attaché. Sturmbannführer Berger." Berger, in his dark suit with that ravaged face of his, was a chilling presence as he nodded formally and clicked his heels. "Captain Eggar knows this Flamingo place. I want you to go there with him and check if Devlin still works there. If he does, you will not, I repeat *not*, contact him in any way. Simply report to me." Berger showed no emotion and turned to the door. As he opened it, Schellenberg called, "During the nineteen thirties Liam Devlin was one of the most notorious gunmen in the IRA. You gentlemen would do well to remember that fact."

The remark, as Berger immediately knew, was aimed at him. He smiled faintly. "We will, General." He turned and went out, followed by Eggar.

"A bad one that. You're welcome to him. Still . . ." The baron checked his watch. "Just after five, Walter. How about a glass of champagne?"

Major Arthur Frear was fifty-four and looked older with his crumpled suit and white hair. He'd have been retired by now on a modest pension leading a life of genteel poverty in Brighton or Torquay. Instead, thanks to Adolf Hitler, he was employed as military attaché at the British Embassy in Lisbon, where he unofficially represented SOE.

The Lights of Lisbon at the southern edge of the Alfama district was one of his favorite places. How convenient that Devlin was playing piano there, although there was no

67

sign of him at the moment. Devlin, in fact, was watching him through a bead curtain at the rear. He wore a linen suit in off-white, dark hair falling across his forehead, the vivid blue eyes full of amusement as they surveyed Frear. The first Frear knew of his presence was when Devlin slid onto the stool next to him and ordered a beer.

"Mr. Frear, isn't it?" He nodded to the barman. "Miguel here tells me you're in the Port business."

"That's right," Frear said jovially. "Been exporting it to England for years, my firm."

"Never been my taste," Devlin told him. "Now if it was Irish whiskey you were talking about."

"Can't help you there, I'm afraid." Frear laughed again. "I say, old man, do you realize you're wearing a Guards Brigade tie?"

"Is that a fact? Fancy you knowing that." Devlin smiled amiably. "And me buying it from a stall in the flea market only last week."

He slid off the stool, and Frear said, "Aren't you going to give us a tune?"

"Oh, that comes later." Devlin moved to the door and grinned. "Major," he added, and was gone.

The Flamingo was a shabby little bar and restaurant. Berger was forced to leave things to Eggar, who spoke the language fluently. At first they drew a blank. Yes, Devlin had worked there for a while, but he'd left three days ago. And then a woman who had come in to sell flowers to the customers overheard their conversation and intervened. The Irishman was working another establishment she called at, the Lights of Lisbon, only he was employed not as a waiter but as a pianist in the bar. Eggar tipped her and they moved outside.

"Do you know the place?" Berger said.

"Oh, yes, quite well. Also in the old quarter. I should warn you, the customers tend to the rougher side. Rather common round here."

"The scum of this life never give me a problem," Berger said. "Now show me the way."

The high walls of the Castelo de São Jorge lifted above them as they worked their way through a maze of narrow alleys, and then, as they came into a small square in front of a church, Devlin emerged from an alley and crossed the cobbles before them toward a café.

"My God, it's him," Eggar muttered. "Exactly like his photo."

"Of course it is, you fool," Berger said. "Is this the Lights of Lisbon?"

"No, Major, another café. One of the most notorious in Alfama. Gypsies, bullfighters, criminals."

"A good job we're armed then. When we go in, have your pistol in your right pocket and your hand on it."

"But General Schellenberg gave us express instructions to—"

"Don't argue. I've no intention of losing this man now. Do as I say and follow me." And Berger led the way toward the café where they could hear guitar music.

Inside, the place was light and airy in spite of the fact that dusk was falling. The bar top was marble, bottles ranged against an old-fashioned mirror behind it. The walls were whitewashed and covered with bullfighting posters. The bartender, squat and ugly with one white eye, wore an apron and soiled shirt and sat at a high stool reading a newspaper. Four other men played poker at a table, swarthy, fierce-looking gypsies. A younger man leaned against the wall and fingered a guitar.

The rest of the place was empty except for

Devlin, who sat at a table against the far wall reading a small book, a glass of beer at his hand. The door creaked open and Berger stepped in, Eggar at his back. The guitarist stopped playing, and all conversation died as Berger stood just inside the door, death come to visit them. Berger moved past the men who were playing cards. Eggar went closer as well, standing to the left.

Devlin glanced up, smiling amiably, and picked up the glass of beer in his left hand. "Liam Devlin?" Berger asked.

"And who might you be?"

"I am Sturmbannführer Horst Berger of the Gestapo."

"Jesus and why didn't they send the devil? I'm on reasonable terms there."

"You're smaller than I thought you'd be," Berger told him. "I'm not impressed."

Devlin smiled again. "I get that all the time, son."

"I must ask you to come with us."

"And me only halfway through my book. *The Midnight Court*, and in Irish. Would you believe I found it on a stall in the flea market only last week?"

"Now!" Berger said.

Devlin drank some more beer. "You remind me of a medieval fresco I saw on a church in Donegal once. People running in terror from a man in a hood. Everyone he touched got the Black Death, you see."

"Eggar!" Berger commanded.

Devlin fired through the tabletop, chipping the wall beside the door. Eggar tried to get the pistol out of his pocket. The Walther Devlin had been holding on his knee appeared above the table now and he fired again, shooting Eggar through the right hand. The police attaché cried out, falling against the wall, and one of the gypsies grabbed for his gun as he dropped it.

Berger's hand went inside his jacket, reaching for the Mauser he carried in a shoulder holster there. Devlin tossed the beer in his face and upended the table against him, the edge catching the German's shins so that he staggered forward. Devlin rammed the muzzle of the Walther into his neck and reached inside Berger's coat, removing the Mauser, which he tossed onto the bar.

"Present for you, Barbosa." The barman grinned and picked the Mauser up. The gypsies were on their feet, two of them with knives in their hands. "Lucky for you you picked on the sort of place where they don't call the peelers," Devlin said. "A real bad lot, these fellas. Even the man in the hood doesn't count for much with them. Barbosa there used to meet him most afternoons in the bullrings in Spain. That's where he got the horn in the eye."

The look on Berger's face was enough. Devlin slipped his book into his pocket, stepped around him, holding the Walther against his leg, and reached for Eggar's hand. "A couple of knuckles gone. You're going to need a doctor." He slipped the Walther into his pocket and turned to go.

Berger's iron control snapped. He ran at him, hands outstretched. Devlin swayed, his right foot flicking forward, catching Berger under the left kneecap. As the German doubled over, he raised a knee in his face, sending him back against the bar. Berger pulled himself up, hanging on to the marble top, and the gypsies started to laugh.

Devlin shook his head, "Jesus, son, but I'd say you should find a different class of work, the both of you." And he turned and went out.

When Schellenberg went into the small medical room, Eggar was sitting at the desk while the Legation's doctor taped his right hand.

"How is he?" Schellenberg asked.

"He'll live." The doctor finished and cut

73

off the end of the tape neatly. "He may well find it rather stiffer in future. Some knuckle damage."

"Can I have a moment?" The doctor nodded and went out and Schellenberg lit a cigarette and sat on the edge of the desk. "I presume you found Devlin?"

"Hasn't the Herr General been told?" Eggar asked.

"I haven't spoken to Berger yet. All I heard was that you'd come back in a taxi the worse for wear. Now tell me exactly what happened."

Which Eggar did, for as the pain increased, so did his anger. "He wouldn't listen, Herr General. Had to do it his way."

Schellenberg put a hand on his shoulder. "Not your fault, Eggar. I'm afraid Major Berger sees himself as his own man. Time he was taught a lesson."

"Oh, Devlin took care of that," Eggar said. "When I last saw it, the major's face didn't look too good."

"Really?" Schellenberg smiled. "I didn't think it could look worse."

Berger stood stripped to the waist in front of the washbasin in the small bedroom he had been allocated and examined his face in the mirror. A bruise had already appeared around his left eye and his nose was swollen. Schellenberg came in, closed the door and leaned against it.

"So, you disobeyed my orders."

Berger said, "I acted for the best. I didn't want to lose him."

"And he was better than you are. I warned you about that."

There was rage on Berger's face in the mirror as he touched his cheek. "That little Irish swine. I'll fix him next time."

"No you won't, because from now on I'll handle things myself," Schellenberg said. "Unless, of course, you'd prefer me to report to the Reichsführer that we lost this man because of your stupidity."

Berger swung around. "General Schellenberg, I protest."

"Get your feet together when you speak to me, Sturmbannführer," Schellenberg snapped. Berger did as he was told, the iron discipline of the SS taking control. "You took an oath on joining the SS. You vowed total obedience to your Führer and to those appointed to lead you. Is this not so?"

"*Jawohl, Brigadeführer.*"

"Excellent," Schellenberg told him. "You're remembering. Don't forget again.

The consequences could be disastrous." He moved to the door, opened it and shook his head. "You look awful, Major. Try and do something about your face before going down to dinner."

He went out and Berger turned back to the mirror. "Bastard!" he said softly.

Liam Devlin sat at the piano in the Lights of Lisbon, a cigarette dangling from the corner of his mouth, a glass of wine on one side. It was ten o'clock, only two hours till Christmas Day, and the café was crowded and cheerful. He was playing a number called "Moonlight on the Highway," a particular favorite, very slow, quite haunting. He noticed Schellenberg the moment he entered, not because he recognized him, only the kind of man he was. He watched him go to the bar and get a glass of wine, then looked away, aware that he was approaching.

Schellenberg said, "'Moonlight on the Highway.' I like that. One of Al Bowlly's greatest numbers," he added, mentioning the name of the man who had been England's most popular crooner until his death.

"Killed in the London Blitz, did you know that?" Devlin asked. "Would never go down to the cellars like everyone else when the air-raid siren went. They found him dead in bed from the bomb blast."

"Unfortunate," Schellenberg said.

"I suppose it depends on which side you're on."

Devlin moved into "A Foggy Day in London Town" and Schellenberg said, "You are a man of many talents, Mr. Devlin."

"A passable barroom piano, that's all," Devlin told him. "Fruits of a misspent youth." He reached for his wine, continuing to play one-handed. "And who might you be, old son?"

"My name is Schellenberg—Walter Schellenberg. You may have heard of me."

"I certainly have." Devlin grinned. "I lived long enough in Berlin for that. General now, is it, and the SD at that? Are you something to do with the two idiots who had a try at me earlier this evening?"

"I regret that, Mr. Devlin. The man you shot is the police attaché at the Legation. The other, Major Berger, is Gestapo. He's with me only because the Reichsführer ordered it."

"Jesus, are we into old Himmler again? Last time I saw him he didn't exactly approve of me."

"Well he needs you now."

"For what?"

"To go to England for us, Mr. Devlin. To London, to be more precise."

"No, thanks. I've worked for German intelligence twice in this war. The first time in Ireland, where I nearly got my head blown off." He tapped the bullet scar on the side of his forehead.

"And the second time, in Norfolk, you took a bullet in the right shoulder and only got away by the skin of your teeth, leaving Kurt Steiner behind."

"Ah, so you know about that?"

"Operation Eagle? Oh, yes."

"A good man, the colonel. He wasn't much of a Nazi—"

"Did you hear what happened to him?"

"Sure, they brought Max Radl into the hospital I was in in Holland after his heart attack. He got some sort of report from intelligence sources in England that Steiner was killed at a place called Meltham House trying to get at Churchill."

"Two things wrong about that," Schellenberg told him. "Two things Radl didn't know. It wasn't Churchill that weekend. He was on his way to the Tehran conference. It was his double. Some music-hall actor."

"Jesus, Joseph and Mary!" Devlin stopped playing.

"And more importantly, Kurt Steiner didn't die. He's alive and well and at present in the Tower of London, which is why I want you to go to England for me. You see I've been entrusted with the task of getting him safely back to the Reich, and I've little more than three weeks to do it in."

Frear had entered the café a couple of minutes earlier and had recognized Schellenberg instantly. He retreated to a side booth where he summoned a waiter, ordered a beer, and watched as the two men went out into the garden at the rear. They sat at a table and looked down at the lights of the shipping in the Tagus River.

"General, you've lost the war," Devlin said. "Why do you keep trying?"

"Oh, we all have to do the best we can until the damn thing is over. As I keep saying, it's difficult to jump off the merry-go-round once it's in motion. A game we play."

"Like the old sod with the white hair in the end booth watching us now," Devlin observed.

Schellenberg looked around casually. "And who might he be?"

"Pretends to be in the Port business. Name of Frear. My friends tell me he's military attaché at the Brit Embassy here."

"Indeed." Schellenberg carried on calmly. "Are you interested?"

"Now why would I be?"

"Money. You received twenty thousand pounds for your work on Operation Eagle paid into a Geneva account."

"And me stuck here without two pennies to scratch myself with."

"Twenty-five thousand pounds, Mr. Devlin. Paid anywhere you wish."

Devlin lit another cigarette and leaned back. "What do you want him for? Why go to all the trouble?"

"A matter of security is involved."

Devlin laughed harshly. "Come off it, General. You want me to go jumping out of Dorniers again at five thousand feet in the dark like that last time over Ireland, and you try to hand me that kind of bollocks."

"All right." Schellenberg put up a hand defensively. "There's a meeting in France on the twenty-first of January. The Führer, Rommel, Canaris and Himmler. The Führer doesn't know about Operation Eagle. The Reichsführer would like to produce Steiner at that meeting. Introduce him."

"And why would he want to do that?"

"Steiner's mission ended in failure, but he led German soldiers in battle on English soil. A hero of the Reich."

"And all that old balls?"

"Added to which the Reichsführer and Admiral Canaris do not always see eye to eye. To produce Steiner." He shrugged. "The fact that his escape had been organized by the SS—"

"Would make Canaris look bad." Devlin shook his head. "What a crew. I don't much care for any of them or that old crow Himmler's motives, but Kurt Steiner's another thing. A great man, that one. But the bloody Tower of London!"

He shook his head again, and Schellenberg said, "They won't keep him there. My guess is they'll move him to one of their London safe houses."

"And how can you find that out?"

"We have an agent in London working out of the Spanish Embassy."

"Can you be sure he's not a double?"

"Pretty sure in this case." Devlin sat there frowning, and Schellenberg said, "Thirty thousand pounds." He smiled. "I'm good at my job, Mr. Devlin. I'll prepare a plan for you that will work."

Devlin nodded. "I'll think about it." He stood up.

"But time is of the essence. I need to get back to Berlin."

"And I need time to think, and it's Christmas. I've promised to go up country to a bull ranch a friend of mine called Barbosa runs. Used to be a great torero in Spain, where they like sharp horns. I'll be back in three days."

"But, Mr. Devlin," Schellenberg tried again.

"If you want me, you'll have to wait." Devlin clapped him on the shoulder. "Come on now, Walter, Christmas in Lisbon. Lights, music, pretty girls. At this present moment they've got a blackout in Berlin, and I bet it's snowing. Which would you rather have?"

Schellenberg started to laugh helplessly, and behind them Frear got up and went out.

Urgent business had kept Dougal Munro at his office at SOE headquarters on the morning of Christmas Day. He was about to leave when Jack Carter limped in. It was just after noon.

Munro said, "I hope it's urgent, Jack. I'm due for Christmas lunch with friends at the Garrick."

"I thought you'd want to know about this, sir." Carter held up a signal flimsy. "From Major Frear, our man in Lisbon. Friend Devlin."

Munro asked, "What about him?"

"Guess who he was locked in conversation with last night at a Lisbon club. Walter Schellenberg."

Munro sat down at his desk. "Now what in the hell is the good Walter playing at?"

"God knows, sir."

"The devil, more like. Signal Frear most immediate. Tell him to watch what Schellenberg gets up to. If he and Devlin leave Portugal together, I want to know at once."

"I'll get right onto it, sir," Carter told him and hurried out.

It had tried to snow over Christmas, but in London on the evening of the twenty-seventh it was raining when Jack Carter turned into a small mews near Portman Square not far from SOE headquarters; which was why he had chosen it when he'd received a phone call from Vargas. The café was called Mary's Pantry, blacked-out, but when he went in, the place was bright with Christmas decorations and holly. It was early evening and there were only three or four customers.

Vargas sat in the corner drinking coffee and reading a newspaper. He wore a heavy blue overcoat and there was a hat on the table. He had olive skin and hollow cheeks and a pencil mustache, his hair brilliantined and parted in the center.

Carter said, "This had better be good."

"Would I bother you if it were not, señor?" Vargas asked. "I've heard from my cousin in Berlin."

"And?"

"They want more information about Steiner. They're interested in mounting a rescue operation."

"Are you certain?"

"That was the message. They want all possible information as to his whereabouts. They seem to think you will move him from the Tower."

"Who's they? The Abwehr?"

"No. General Schellenberg of the SD is in charge. At least that is who my cousin is working for."

Carter nodded, fiercely excited, and got up. "I want you to phone me at the usual number at eleven, old chum, and don't fail." He leaned forward. "This is the big one, Vargas. You'll make a lot of cash if you're smart."

He turned and went out and hurried along Baker Street as fast as his game leg would allow.

In Lisbon at that precise moment Walter Schellenberg was climbing the steep cobbled alley in Alfama toward the Lights of Lisbon. He could hear the music even before he got there. When he went inside, the place was deserted except for the barman and Devlin at the piano.

The Irishman stopped to light a cigarette and smiled. "Did you enjoy your Christmas, General?"

"It could have been worse. And you?"

"The bulls were running well. I got trampled. Too much drink taken."

"A dangerous game."

"Not really. They tip the ends of the horns in Portugal. Nobody dies."

"It hardly seems worth the candle," Schellenberg said.

"And isn't that the fact? Wine, grapes, bulls and lots and lots of sun, that's what I had for Christmas, General." He started to play "Moonlight on the Highway." "And me thinking of old Al Bowlly in the Blitz, London, fog in the streets. Now isn't that the strange thing?"

Schellenberg felt the excitement rise inside him. "You'll go?"

"On one condition. I can change my mind at the last minute if I think the thing isn't watertight."

"My hand on it."

Devlin got up and they walked out to the terrace. Schellenberg said, "We'll fly out to Berlin in the morning."

"You will, General, not me."

"But, Mr. Devlin."

"You have to think of everything in this game, you know that. Look down there."

Over the wall they could see that Frear had come in and was talking to one of the waiters as he wiped down the outside tables. "He's been keeping an eye on me, old Frear. He's seen me talking to the great Walter Schellenberg. I should think that would figure in one of his reports to London."

"So what do you suggest?"

"You fly back to Berlin and get on with the preparations. There'll be plenty to do. Arrange the right papers for me at the Legation, traveling money and so on, and I'll come the low-risk way by rail. Lisbon to Madrid, then the Paris Express. Fix it up for me to fly from there if it suits, or I could carry on by train."

"It would take you two days at least."

"As I say, you'll have things to do. Don't tell me the work won't be piling up."

Schellenberg nodded. "You're right. So, let's have a drink on it. To our English enterprise."

"Holy Mother of God, not that, General. Someone used that phrase to me last time. They didn't realize that's how the Spanish Armada was described, and look what happened to that lot."

"Then to ourselves, Mr. Devlin," Schellenberg said. "I will drink to you and you will drink to me." And they went back inside.

Munro sat at his desk in the Haston Place flat and listened intently as Carter gave him the gist of his conversation with Vargas.

He nodded. "Two pieces of the jigsaw puzzle, Jack. Schellenberg's interested in rescuing Steiner, and where is Schellenberg right now? In Lisbon hobnobbing with Liam Devlin. Now, what conclusion does that lead you to?"

"That he wants to recruit Devlin to the cause, sir."

"Of course. The perfect man." Munro

nodded. "This could lead to interesting possibilities."

"Such as?"

Munro shook his head. "Just thinking out loud. Time to think of moving Steiner anyway. What would you suggest?"

"There's the London Cage in Kensington," Carter said.

"Come off it, Jack. That's only used for processing transients, isn't it? Prisoners of war such as Luftwaffe aircrews."

"There's Cockfosters, sir, but that's just a cage, too, and the school opposite Wandsworth Prison. A number of German agents have been held there." Munro wasn't impressed, and Carter tried again. "Of course there's Mytchett Place in Hampshire. They've turned that into a miniature fortress for Hess."

"Who lives there in splendor so solitary that in June nineteen forty-one he jumped from a balcony and tried to kill himself. No, that's no good." Munro went to the window and looked out. The rain had turned to sleet now. "Time I spoke with friend Steiner, I think. We'll try and make it tomorrow."

"Fine, sir. I'll arrange it."

Munro turned. "Devlin—there is a photo on file?"

"Passport photo, sir. When he was in Norfolk he had to fill in an alien's registration form. That's a must for Irish citizens and it requires a passport photo. Special Branch ran it down. It's not very good."

"They never are, those things." Munro suddenly smiled. "I've got it, Jack. Where to hold Steiner. That place in Wapping. St. Mary's Priory."

"The Little Sisters of Pity, sir? But that's a hospice for terminal cases."

"They also look after chaps who've had breakdowns, don't they? Gallant RAF pilots who've cracked up."

"Yes, sir."

"And you're forgetting that Abwehr agent Baum in February. The one who got shot in the chest when Special Branch and MI-Five tried to pick him up in Bayswater. They nursed him at the priory and interrogated him there. I've seen the reports. MI-Five don't use it regularly, I know that for a fact. It would be perfect. Built in the seventeenth century. They used to be an enclosed order, so the whole place is walled. Built like a fortress."

"I've never been, sir."

"I have. Strange sort of place. Protestant for years when Roman Catholics were proscribed, then some Victorian industrialist who was a religious crank turned it into a hostel for people off the street. It stood empty for years, and then in nineteen ten some benefactor purchased it. The place was reconsecrated Roman Catholic, and the Little Sisters of Pity were in business." He nodded, full of enthusiasm. "Yes, I think the priory will do nicely."

"There is one thing, sir. I would remind you that this is a counterespionage matter, which means it's strictly an MI-Five and Special Branch affair."

"Not if they don't know about it." Munro smiled. "When Vargas phones, see him at once. Tell him to leave it three or four days, then to notify his cousin that Steiner is being moved to St. Mary's Priory."

"Are you actually inviting them to try and mount this operation, sir?"

"Why not, Jack? We'd bag not only Devlin but any contacts he would have. He couldn't work alone. No, there are all sorts of possibilities to this. Off you go."

"Right, sir."

Carter limped to the door, and Munro said, "Silly me, I'm forgetting the obvious. Walter Schellenberg is going to want a source for this information. It's got to look good."

"May I make a suggestion, sir?"

"By all means."

"José Vargas is a practicing homosexual, sir, and there's a company of Scots Guards on duty at the Tower at the moment. Let's say Vargas has picked one of them up in one of those pubs the soldiers frequent round the Tower."

"Oh, very good, Jack. Excellent," Munro said. "Get on with it then."

From a discreet vantage point on the concourse at the airport outside Lisbon, Frear watched Schellenberg and Berger walk across the apron and board the Junkers. He stayed there, watching it taxi away, and only went out to the cab rank when the plane had actually taken off.

Half an hour later he went into the Lights of Lisbon and sat at the bar. He ordered a beer and said to the barman, "Where's our Irish friend today?"

"Oh, him? Gone." The barman shrugged. "Nothing but trouble. The boss sacked him. There was a guest here last night. Nice man. A German, I think. This Devlin had a row with him. Nearly came to blows. Had to be dragged off."

"Dear me," Frear said. "I wonder what he'll do now."

"Plenty of bars in Alfama, senhor," the barman said.

"Yes, you're certainly right there." Frear swallowed his beer. "I'll be off then."

He went out, and Devlin stepped through the bead curtain at the back of the bar. "Good man yourself, Miguel. Now let's have a farewell drink together."

It was late afternoon and Munro was at his desk in his office at SOE headquarters when Carter came in.

"Another signal from Frear, sir. Schellenberg left for Berlin by plane this morning, but Devlin didn't go with him."

"If Devlin is as smart as I think he is, Jack, he's been onto Frear from the start. You can't be a military attaché at any embassy in a place like Lisbon without people knowing."

"You mean he's gone to Berlin by another route, sir?"

"Exactly. Twisting and turning like the fox he is, and all to no avail." Munro smiled. "We have Rivera and Vargas in our pockets, and that means we'll always be one step ahead."

"So what happens now, sir?"

"We wait, Jack, we just wait and see what their next move is. Did you arrange the meeting with Steiner?"

"Yes, sir."

Munro went to the window. The sleet had turned to rain, and he snorted. "Looks as if we're going to get some fog now. Bloody weather." He sighed. "What a war, Jack, what a war."

4

As THE car went along Tower Hill, fog rolled in from the Thames. Munro said, "What's the situation here now?"

"The whole place is guarded, Brigadier. Public aren't allowed in like they used to be before the war. I understand they run sightseeing trips for Allied servicemen in uniform some days."

"And the Yeomen?"

"Oh, they still function and still live in the married quarters with their families. The whole place has been bombed more than once. Three times while Rudolf Hess was there, remember?"

They were stopped at a sentry post to have passes checked and moved on through the wool of the fog, traffic sounds muted, an anguished cry from the Thames as a ship sounded its foghorn on the way down to the sea.

They were checked again, then drove on over the drawbridge and through the gate. "Not exactly a day to fill the heart with joy," Munro observed.

There wasn't much to see with the fog, only gray stone walls as they moved on, eventually reaching the Inner Ward, everything cut off around them.

"The hospital's over there, sir," Carter said.

"You've made the arrangements as I ordered?"

"Yes, sir, but with some reluctance."

"You're a nice man, Jack, but this isn't a nice war. Come on, we'll get out here and walk across."

"Right, sir."

Carter struggled to follow him, his leg the usual problem. The fog was yellow and acrid and bit at the back of the throat like acid.

"Shocking, isn't it?" Munro said. "Real pea-souper. What was it Dickens called it? A London Particular?"

"I believe so, sir."

They started to walk. "What a bloody

94

place, Jack. Supposed to be haunted by ghosts. That wretched little girl Lady Jane Grey and Walter Raleigh ceaselessly prowling the walls. I wonder what Steiner makes of it."

"I shouldn't think it exactly helps him to sleep, sir."

One of the Tower's famous black ravens emerged from the fog, enormous wings flapping as it cawed at them.

Munro started violently. "Get away, you filthy great creature." He shuddered. "There, what did I tell you, spirits of the dead."

The small hospital room was painted dark green. There was a narrow bed, a cupboard and a wardrobe. There was also a bathroom adjacent to it. Kurt Steiner, in pajamas and terry-cloth robe, sat by the window reading. The window was barred, although it was possible to reach through and open the casement. He preferred to sit there because in better weather he could see out into the Inner Ward and the White Tower. It gave an illusion of space, and space meant freedom.

There was a rattle of bolts at the stout door. It opened and a military policeman stepped in. "Visitors for you, Colonel."

Munro moved in followed by Carter. "You may leave us, Corporal," he told the MP.

"Sir." The man went out, locking the door.

Munro, more for the effect than anything else, was in uniform. He shrugged off his British Warm greatcoat, and Steiner took in the badges of rank and red tabs of a staff officer.

"Oberstleutnant Kurt Steiner?"

Steiner stood up. "Brigadier?"

"Munro, and this is my aide, Captain Jack Carter."

"Gentlemen, I gave my name, my rank and my number some time ago," Steiner said. "I've nothing to add except to say I'm surprised no one's tried to squeeze more out of me since, and I apologize for the fact that there's only one chair here, so I can't ask you to sit down."

His English was perfect, and Munro found himself warming to him. "We'll sit on the bed if we may. Jack, give the colonel a cigarette."

"No, thanks," Steiner said. "A bullet in the chest was a good excuse to give it up."

They sat down. Munro said, "Your English is really excellent."

"Brigadier"—Steiner smiled—"I'm sure you're aware that my mother was American and that I lived in London for many years as a boy when my father was military attaché at the German Embassy. I was educated at St. Paul's."

He was twenty-seven and in good shape except for a slight hollowing in the cheeks, obviously due to his hospitalization. He was quite calm, a slight smile on his lips, a kind of self-sufficiency there that Munro had noticed in many airborne soldiers.

"You haven't been pressured into any further interrogation, not only because of the condition you were in for so long," Munro said, "but because we know everything there is to know about Operation Eagle."

"Really?" Steiner said dryly.

"Yes. I work for Special Operations Executive, Colonel. Knowing things is our business. I'm sure you'll be surprised to discover that the man you tried to shoot that night at Meltham House wasn't Mr. Churchill."

Steiner looked incredulous. "What are you trying to tell me now? What nonsense is this?"

"Not nonsense," Jack Carter said. "He was one George Howard Foster, known in the music halls as the Great Foster. An impressionist of some distinction."

Steiner laughed helplessly. "But that's wonderful. So bloody ironic. Don't you see? If it had all succeeded and we'd taken him back . . . My God, a music-hall artist. I'd love to have seen that bastard Himmler's face." Concerned that he was going too far, he took a deep breath and pulled himself together. "So?"

"Your friend Liam Devlin was wounded but survived," Carter said. "Walked out of a Dutch hospital and escaped to Lisbon. As far as we know, your second-in-command, Neumann, still survives and is hospitalized."

"As is Colonel Max Radl, your organizer," Munro put in. "Had a heart attack."

"So, not many of us left," Steiner said lightly.

"Something I've never understood, Colonel," Carter said. "You're no Nazi, we know that. You ruined your career trying to help a Jewish girl in Warsaw, and yet that last night in Norfolk you still tried to get Churchill."

"I'm a soldier, Captain. The game was in play, and it is a game, wouldn't you agree?"

"And in the end the game was playing you," Munro said shrewdly.

"Something like that."

"Nothing to do with the fact that your father, General Karl Steiner, was being held at Gestapo headquarters at Prinz Albrecht-strasse in Berlin for complicity in a plot against the Führer?" Carter asked.

Steiner's face shadowed. "Captain Carter, Reichsführer Himmler is noted for many things, but charity and compassion are not among them."

"And it was Himmler behind the whole business," Munro told him. "He pressured Max Radl into working behind Admiral Canaris's back. Even the Führer had no idea that was going on. Still hasn't."

"Nothing would surprise me," Steiner said. He stood up and paced to the wall. He turned. "Now, gentlemen, what is this all about?"

"They want you back," Munro told him.

Steiner stared at him, incredulous. "You're joking. Why would they bother?"

"All I know is that Himmler wants you out of here."

Steiner sat down again. "But this is nonsense. With all due respect to my fellow countrymen, German prisoners of war have not been noted for escaping from England, not since the First World War."

"There has been one," Carter told him. "Luftwaffe pilot, but even he had to do it from Canada into the States before they were in the war."

"You miss the point," Munro said. "We're not talking of a prisoner simply making a run for it. We're talking about a plot, if you like. A meticulously mounted operation masterminded by General Walter Schellenberg of the SD. Do you know him?"

"Of him only," Steiner replied automatically.

"Of course it would require the right man to pull it off, which is where Liam Devlin comes in," Carter added.

"Devlin?" Steiner shook his head. "Nonsense. Devlin is one of the most remarkable men I have ever known, but even he couldn't get me out of this place."

"Yes, well it wouldn't be from here. We're moving you to a safe house in Wapping. St. Mary's Priory. You'll be given the details later."

"No, I can't believe it. This is some trick," Steiner said.

"Good God, man, what profit would there be in it for us?" Munro demanded. "There's a man at the Spanish Embassy here in London called José Vargas, a commercial attaché. He works for your side on occasion for money. Operates via his cousin at the Spanish Embassy in Berlin using a diplomatic pouch."

"He works for us, you see, also for money," Carter said. "And they have been in touch, indicated their interest in pulling you out, and requesting more information as to your whereabouts."

"And we've told him what he needs to know," Munro put in. "Even your new home at the priory."

"So, now I understand," Steiner said. "You allow the plan to proceed, Devlin comes to London. He will need help, of course, other agents or what have you, and at the appropriate moment you arrest the lot."

"Yes, that is one way," Munro said. "There is another possibility, of course."

"And what would that be?"

"That I simply allow it all to happen. You escape to Germany—"

"Where I work for you?" Steiner shook his head. "Sorry, Brigadier. Carter was right. I'm no Nazi, but I'm still a soldier—a German soldier. I'd find the word traitor difficult to handle."

"Would you say your father and others

were traitors because they tried to remove the Führer?" Munro asked.

"In a sense that's different. Germans trying to handle their own problem."

"A neat point." Munro turned and said, "Jack."

Carter went and knocked on the door. It opened and the MP appeared. Munro got up. "If you'd be kind enough to follow me, Colonel, there's something I'd like you to see."

As far as Adolf Hitler was concerned there was to be no possibility of an honorable death for a traitor. No officer convicted of plotting against him met his end at the hands of a firing squad. The punishment was statutory, death by hanging, usually from a meat hook, and often piano wire was employed. Victims frequently took a long time to die, often very unpleasantly. The Führer had ordered all such executions to be recorded on film. Many were so appalling that even Himmler had been known to walk out of the showings sick to the stomach.

The one which was being shown now in the large stockroom at the end of the corridor was flickering and rather grainy. The young intelligence sergeant, anonymous behind the film projector in the darkness, was using the white-painted wall as a screen. Steiner sat on a chair alone, Munro and Carter behind him.

General Karl Steiner, carried in by two SS men, was already dead from a heart attack, the only good thing about the entire proceedings. They hung him to the hook anyway and moved away. For a little while the camera stayed on that pathetic figure, swaying slightly from side to side, then the screen went blank.

The projectionist switched on the light. Kurt Steiner stood, turned and moved to the door without a word. He opened it, went past the MP and walked down the corridor to his room. Munro and Carter followed. When they went into the room, Steiner was standing at the window gripping the bars and looking out. He turned, his face very pale.

"You know I really think it's about time I took up smoking again, gentlemen."

Jack Carter fumbled a cigarette out of a packet of Players and gave him a light.

"I'm sorry about that," Munro said, "but it was important you knew that Himmler had broken his promise."

"Come off it, Brigadier," Steiner said. "You're not sorry about anything. You wanted to make your point, and you've made it. I never thought my father stood much of a chance of survival whatever I did. As far as Himmler is concerned, keeping promises is a low priority."

"And what do you think now?" Munro asked.

"Ah, so we come to the purpose of the exercise? Will I now, in a white hot rage, offer my services to the Allies? Allow myself to be spirited off to Germany, where I assassinate Hitler at the first opportunity?" He shook his head. "No, Brigadier. I'll have some bad nights over this. I may even ask to see a priest, but the essential point remains the same. My father's involvement in a plot on Hitler's life was as a German. He was doing it for Germany."

It was Carter who said, "Yes, one sees that."

Steiner turned to him. "Then you must also realize that for me to do what the brigadier suggests would be a betrayal of everything my father stood for and gave his life for."

"All right." Munro stood up. "We're wasting our time. You'll be transferred to St. Mary's Priory in the New Year, Colonel. Your friend Devlin hasn't a hope of getting you out, of course, but we'd love him to try." He turned to Carter. "Let's get moving, Jack."

Steiner said, "One thing, Brigadier, if I may."

"Yes?"

"My uniform. I would remind you that under the Geneva Convention I am entitled to wear it."

Munro glanced at Carter, who said, "It has been repaired, Colonel, and cleaned. I'll arrange for you to have it later today together with all your medals, naturally."

"That's all right then," Munro said and went out. Carter took out his packet of cigarettes and a box of matches and laid them on the locker. "You mentioned a priest. I'll arrange for one if you like."

"I'll let you know."

"And a supply of cigarettes?"

"Better not. This one tasted terrible." Steiner managed a smile.

Carter went to the door, hesitated and turned. "If it helps at all, Colonel, it was apparently a heart attack your father died of. I don't know the circumstances."

"Oh, I can imagine them well enough, but my thanks anyway," Steiner answered.

He stood there, hands thrust into the

pockets of his robe, quite calm, and Carter, unable to think of anything else to say, stepped into the corridor and went after Munro.

As they drove through the fog along Tower Hill, Munro said, "You don't approve, do you, Jack?"

"Not really, sir. An unnecessary cruelty in my opinion."

"Yes, well, as I told you before, it's not a nice war. At least we know where we stand with friend Steiner now."

"I suppose so, sir."

"As for Devlin, if he's mad enough to try, let him come whenever he wants. With Vargas tipping us off on every move he makes, we can't go wrong."

He settled back in the seat and closed his eyes.

It was actually New Year's Day when Devlin finally arrived in Berlin. It had taken him two days to get a seat on the Paris Express from Madrid. In Paris itself, his priority, thanks to Schellenberg, had got him on the Berlin Express, but B-17 bombers of the American 8th Air Force operating out of England had inflicted severe damage on the Frankfurt railway marshaling yards. This had necessitated a rerouting of most rail traffic from France and the Netherlands into Germany.

The weather was bad in Berlin, the kind of winter that couldn't make up its mind, a thin snow changing to sleet and driving rain. Devlin, still wearing a suit more apt for Portugal, had managed to procure a raincoat in Paris, but he was freezing and quite miserable as he trudged through the crowds in the railway station in Berlin.

Ilse Huber recognized him at once from his file photo as she stood at the barrier beside the security police. She had already made arrangements with the sergeant in charge, and when Devlin appeared, bag in hand, his papers ready, she intervened at once.

"Herr Devlin? Over here, please." She held out her hand. "I am Ilse Huber, General Schellenberg's secretary. You look awful."

"I feel bloody awful."

"I have transport waiting," she said.

The car was a Mercedes saloon with an SS pennant conspicuously on display. Devlin said, "I suppose that thing makes people get out of the way fast."

"It certainly helps," she said. "It occurred

to General Schellenberg that you might be caught out by the weather."

"You can say that again."

"I've made arrangements to take you to a secondhand shop. We'll get everything you need there. And you'll need someplace to stay. I have an apartment not too far from headquarters. There are two bedrooms. If it suits, you can have one of them while you're here."

"More to the point, does it suit you?" he asked.

She shrugged. "Mr. Devlin, my husband was killed in the Winter War in Russia. I have no children. My mother and father died in an RAF raid on Hamburg. Life could be difficult except for one thing. Working for General Schellenberg usually takes at least sixteen hours out of my day, so I'm hardly ever home."

She smiled and Devlin warmed to her. "It's a deal, then. Ilse, is it? Let's get on with the clothes. I feel as if some of my more particular parts have frozen solid."

When they emerged forty minutes later from the secondhand shop she'd taken him to, he wore a tweed suit, laced boots, a heavy overcoat almost ankle-length, gloves and a trilby hat.

"So, you are equipped to handle Berlin in January," she said.

"Where to now, your apartment?"

"No, we can go there later. General Schellenberg wants to see you as soon as possible. He's at Prinz Albrechtstrasse now."

Devlin could hear the sounds of shooting as they descended the steep stairway. "And what's all this then?"

Ilse said, "The basement firing range. The general likes to keep in practice."

"Is he any good?"

She looked almost shocked. "The best. I've never seen anyone shoot better."

"Really?" Devlin was unconvinced.

But he had cause to revise his opinion a moment later when they opened the door and went in. Schellenberg was firing at a series of cardboard Russian soldiers, watched by an SS sergeant major who was obviously in charge. He worked his way across three targets, placing two rounds neatly in each heart. As he paused to reload, he noticed their presence.

"Ah, Mr. Devlin, so you finally got here."

"A hell of a journey, General."

"And Ilse's taken care of your wardrobe I see."

"And how did you guess?" Devlin said. "It can only have been the smell of the mothballs."

Schellenberg laughed and reloaded his Mauser. "Schwarz," he said to the sergeant major, "something for Mr. Devlin. I believe he's quite a marksman."

Schwarz rammed a magazine into the butt of a Walther PPK and handed it to the Irishman.

"All right?" Schellenberg asked.

"Your shout, General."

Fresh targets sprang up, and Schellenberg fired six times very fast, again two holes in the heart area on three separate targets.

"Now isn't that something?" Devlin's hand swung up, he fired three rounds so close together that they might almost have been one. A hole appeared between the eyes of all three targets.

He laid the Walther down, and Ilse Huber said, "My God!"

Schellenberg handed his pistol to Schwarz. "A remarkable talent, Mr. Devlin."

"Remarkable curse more like. Now what happens, General?"

"The Reichsführer has expressed a desire to see you."

Devlin groaned. "He didn't like me the

last time around. A glutton for punishment that man. All right, let's get it over with."

The Mercedes turned out of Wilhelmplatz and into Vosstrasse and drove toward the Reich Chancellery.

"What's all this?" Devlin demanded.

"Times have changed since Göring said that if a single bomb fell on Berlin you could call him Meier."

"You mean he got it wrong?"

"I'm afraid so. The Führer has had a bunker constructed below the Chancellery. Subterranean headquarters. Thirty meters of concrete, so the RAF can drop as many bombs as they like."

"Is this where he intends to make his last stand then?" Devlin inquired. "Wagner playing over the loudspeakers?"

"Yes, well we don't like to think about that," Schellenberg said. "The important people have secondary accommodation down there, which obviously includes the Reichsführer."

"So what goes on now? Are they expecting the RAF to plaster the city tonight or what?"

"Nothing so exciting. The Führer likes to have staff meetings now and then in the map room. He gives them dinner afterwards."

"Down there?" Devlin shuddered. "I'd rather have a corned-beef sandwich."

The Mercedes drew into the car ramp, and an SS sentry approached. In spite of Schellenberg's uniform the sentry checked their identities thoroughly before allowing them through.

Devlin followed Schellenberg down a seemingly endless passage, concrete walls, dim lighting. There was a soft humming from electric fans in the ventilating system, the occasional blast of cold air. There were SS guards here and there, but no great evidence of people, and then a door opened, a young corporal emerged, and behind him Devlin saw a room crammed with radio equipment and a number of operatives.

"Don't make the mistake of thinking there's no one here," Schellenberg said. "Rooms everywhere. A couple of hundred people tucked in all over the place like that radio room."

A door opened farther along the passage, and to Devlin's astonishment, Hitler emerged followed by a broad, rather squat man in a nondescript uniform. As they approached, Schellenberg pulled Devlin to one side and stood at attention. The Führer was talking to the other man in a low voice and totally ignored them as he passed and descended the stairs at the other end of the passage.

"The man with him was Bormann," Schellenberg said. "Reichsleiter Martin Bormann. Head of the Nazi Party Chancellery. A very powerful man."

"So that was the Führer," Devlin said. "And me almost getting to touch the hem of his robe."

Schellenberg smiled. "Sometimes, my friend, I wonder how you've managed to last as long as you have."

"Ah, well it must be my good looks, General."

Schellenberg tapped on a door, opened it and led the way in. A young woman, an SS auxiliary in uniform, sat at a typewriter in the corner. The rest of the room was mainly taken up by filing cabinets and the desk behind which Himmler sat, working through a file. He glanced up and removed his pince-nez.

"So, General, he's arrived."

"God bless all here," Devlin said cheerfully.

Himmler winced and said to the girl, "Leave us. Come back in fifteen minutes."

She went out and he carried on. "I expected you in Berlin sooner, Herr Devlin."

"Your railway system seemed to be having trouble with the RAF," Devlin told him and lit a cigarette, mainly because he knew Himmler detested the habit.

Himmler was annoyed but didn't tell him to stop. Instead, he said to Schellenberg, "You seem to have wasted an inordinate amount of time so far, General. Why didn't Herr Devlin return from Lisbon with you?"

"Ah, the general did a fine job," Devlin said. "It was me had plans for Christmas, you see. No, the general was very reasonable. More than I can say for the other fella, Berger. We didn't get on at all."

"So I understand," Himmler said. "But that scarcely matters, as Sturmbannführer Berger has other duties to take care of." He leaned back. "So, you think this thing can be done? You believe you could get Steiner out?"

"Depends on the plan," Devlin said, "but anything's possible."

Himmler nodded. "It would be a remarkable coup for all of us."

"That's as may be," Devlin said. "It's getting back in one piece that worries me. I only just made it last time."

"You were well paid then, and I would remind you that you're being well paid this time."

"And that's a fact," Devlin said. "As my old mother used to say, money will be the death of me."

Himmler looked extremely annoyed. "Can't you take anything seriously, you Irish?"

"When I last had the pleasure of meeting your honor, I gave you the answer to that one. It's the rain."

"Oh, get him out of here," Himmler said. "And get on with it, General. Needless to say I expect a regular progress report."

"Reichsführer." Schellenberg ushered Devlin out.

The Irishman was grinning hugely. "I enjoyed that." He dropped his cigarette on the floor and stamped on it as Berger came around the corner, a rolled-up map under his arm.

He was in uniform and wore Iron Crosses First and Second Class. He stiffened when he saw them, and Devlin said cheerfully, "Very pretty, son, but it looks to me as if someone's been spoiling your good looks."

Berger's face was very pale, and although the swelling had subsided it was obvious his nose was broken. He ignored Devlin and nodded formally to Schellenberg. "General." He passed on and knocked at Himmler's door.

"He must be well in there," Devlin observed.

"Yes." Schellenberg nodded. "Interesting."

"Where to now? Your office?"

"No, tomorrow will be soon enough. I'll take you for a meal and drop you at Ilse's place afterwards. You'll get a good night's sleep and we'll go over things in the morning."

As they reached the mouth of the tunnel, fresh air drifted in and Devlin took a deep breath. "Thank God for that." And then he started to laugh.

"What is it?" Schellenberg demanded.

Devlin pointed to a poster on the wall that carried a picture of a rather idealized SS soldier that underneath it said, *At the end stands victory*.

Devlin laughed again. "God save us, General, but some people will believe anything."

Berger clicked his heels in front of Himmler's desk. "I have the plan of the Château de Belle-Île here, Reichsführer."

116

"Excellent," Himmler said. "Let me see."

Berger unrolled the plan, and the Reichsführer examined it. "Good. Very good." He looked up. "You will be in sole charge, Berger. How many men would you suggest for the honor guard?"

"Twenty-five. Thirty at the most, Reichsführer."

"Have you visited the place yet?" Himmler asked.

"I flew down to Cherbourg the day before yesterday and drove out to the château. It's quite splendid. The owners are French aristocrats who fled to England. There is at the moment only a caretaker and his wife. I've informed him that we'll be taking the place over in the near future, but not why, naturally."

"Excellent. No need to go near the place again for another couple of weeks. In other words, wait as long as possible before you and your men take over. You know what this so-called French Resistance is like. Terrorists, all of them. They bomb—murder." He rolled the plan up and returned it to Berger. "After all, the Führer will be our direct responsibility at this conference, Major. A sacred responsibility."

"Of course, Reichsführer."

Berger clicked his heels and went out. Himmler picked up his pen and started to write again.

The Mercedes moved along the Kurfursten-damm as snow started to fall again. There was evidence of bomb damage everywhere, and with the blackout and dusk falling, the prospect was less than pleasing.

"Look at it," Schellenberg said. "Used to be a great city this. Art, music, theater. And the clubs, Mr. Devlin. The Paradise and the Blue Nile. Always filled with the most beautifully dressed transvestites you've ever seen."

"My tastes never ran that way," Devlin told him.

"Nor mine." Schellenberg laughed. "I always think they're missing out on a good thing. Still, let's eat. I know a little restaurant in a back street not far from here where we'll do reasonably well. Black market, but then they do know me, which helps."

The place was homely enough with no more than a dozen tables. It was run by a man and his wife who obviously did know Schellenberg well. The general apologized for the dearth of corned-beef sandwiches, but was able to produce a mutton broth, lamb, potatoes and cabbage and a bottle of hock to go with it.

The booth they sat in was quite private, and as they finished the meal Schellenberg said, "Do you really think it is possible, this thing?"

"Anything's possible. I remember a case during the Irish Revolution. Nineteen twenty, it was. The Black and Tans had captured a fella called Michael Fitzgerald, an important IRA leader. Held him in Limerick Prison. A man called Jack O'Malley who served in the British army in Flanders as a captain got his old uniform out, dressed up half a dozen of his men as soldiers and went to Limerick Prison with a fake order that said they wanted Fitzgerald at Dublin Castle."

"And it worked?"

"Like a charm." Devlin poured the last of the wine into both their glasses. "There is one problem here though, a very important problem."

"And what's that?"

"Vargas."

"But that's taken care of. We've told him we must have firm information as to where they intend to move Steiner."

"You're convinced they will move him?"

"Certain of it. They won't continue to keep him in the Tower. It's too absurd."

"So you think Vargas will come up with the right information?" Devlin shook his head. "He must be good."

"He always has been in the past, so the Abwehr have found. This is a Spanish diplomat, Mr. Devlin, a man in a privileged position. No ordinary agent. I have had his cousin, this Rivera fellow, thoroughly vetted."

"All right, I accept that. Let's say Rivera's as clean as a whistle, but who checks out Vargas? There is no one. Rivera is just a conduit through which the messages come and go, but what if Vargas is something else?"

"You mean a neat British intelligence plot to entice us in?"

"Well, let's look at the way they would see it. Whoever drops in needs friends in London, some sort of organization. If I was in charge on the Brit side, I'd give a little rope, let things get started, then arrest everybody in sight. From their point of view, quite a coup."

"Are you telling me you're having second thoughts? That you don't want to go?"

"Not at all. What I'm saying is that if I do, I have to go on the supposition that I'm

120

expected. That Vargas has sold us out. Now that's a very different thing."

"Are you serious?" Schellenberg demanded.

"I'd look a right idiot if we organize things on the basis that Vargas is on our side and I get there and he isn't. Tactics, General, that's what's needed here. Just like chess. You've got to think three moves ahead."

"Mr. Devlin, you are a remarkable man," Schellenberg told him.

"A genius on my good days," Devlin replied solemnly.

Schellenberg settled the account and they went outside. It was still snowing lightly as they walked to the Mercedes.

"I'll take you to Ilse's now and we'll meet up in the morning." At that moment the sirens started. Schellenberg called to his driver, "Hans, this way." He turned to Devlin. "On second thought, I think we'll go back to the restaurant and sit in their cellar with the other sensible people. It's quite comfortable. I've been there before."

"Why not," Devlin said and turned with him. "Who knows—they might find us a bottle of something in there."

Behind them, gunfire was already rumbling like thunder on the edge of the city.

5

As THEY approached Schellenberg's office at Prinz Albrechtstrasse, the morning air was tainted with smoke. "They certainly hit the target last night," he said.

"You can say that again," Devlin replied.

The door opened and Ilse Huber nodded good morning. "There you are, General. I was a little worried."

"Mr. Devlin and I spent the night in the cellar of that restaurant in Marienstrasse."

"Rivera's on his way," she told him.

"Oh, good. Send him in when he arrives."

She went out and ten minutes later ushered Rivera in. The Spaniard stood there clutching his hat, nervously glancing at Devlin.

"You may speak freely," Schellenberg said.

"I've had another message from my cousin, General. He says they are moving Steiner from the Tower of London to a place called St. Mary's Priory."

"Did he give an address for that?"

"He just said it was in Wapping, by the river."

Devlin said, "A remarkable fella, your cousin, to come up with such a prime piece of information so easily."

Rivera smiled eagerly. "José is certain his information is correct, señor. He got it from a friend of his, a soldier in the Scots Guards. They have a company serving the Tower at the moment. They use the public houses nearby, and my cousin . . ." Rivera shrugged. "A matter of some delicacy."

"Yes, we understand, Rivera." Schellenberg nodded. "All right, you can go for now. I'll be in touch when I need you."

Ilse showed him out and came back. "Is there anything you'd like me to do, General?"

"Yes, find me one of those gazetteers from the files. You know the sort of thing. London street-by-street. See if this place is mentioned."

She went out. "I used to know Wapping well at one stage of my career," Devlin said.

"With the IRA?"

"The bombing campaign. They were always having a go, the hard men, those who'd blow up the Pope if they thought it would help the cause. Nineteen thirty-six, there was an active service unit who set a bomb or two off in London. You know the sort of thing. Women, kids, passersby. I was used as an enforcer in those days, and the men at the top wanted it stopped. Lousy publicity, you see."

"And this is when you knew Wapping?"

"A friend from my youth in County Down. Friend of my mother's actually."

"Who is this friend?"

"Michael Ryan. Ran a safe house. Not active at all. Very deep cover."

"And you took care of this active service unit?"

"There were only the three of them." Devlin shrugged. "They wouldn't be told. After that, I went to Spain. Joined the Lincoln-Washington Brigade. Did my bit against Franco till the Italians took me prisoner. Eventually the Abwehr pulled me out."

"And this friend of yours in Wapping, this Ryan—I wonder what happened to him."

"Still in deep, old Michael, I should imagine. He wouldn't want to know any more. That kind of man. Had doubts about the use of violence. When the Abwehr sent me to Ireland in forty-one, I met a friend of his in Dublin. From what he told me, I know for a fact the IRA didn't use Mick during their bombing campaign in England at the beginning of the war."

"Could this be of any use?" Schellenberg suggested.

"Jesus, General, you've got the cart running before the horse, haven't you?"

Ilse came in with an orange-colored book. "I've found it, General, St. Mary's Priory, Wapping. See, right on the edge of the Thames."

Schellenberg and Devlin examined the map. "That isn't going to tell us much," Devlin said.

Schellenberg nodded. "I've just had a thought. Operation Sea Lion, nineteen forty."

"You mean the invasion that never was?"

"Yes, but it was thoroughly planned. One task the SD was given was a comprehensive survey of London. Buildings, I'm talking about. Their usefulness if London were occupied."

"You mean which place was suitable for Gestapo headquarters? That sort of thing."

Schellenberg smiled amiably. "Exactly. There was a listing of many hundreds of such places on file and plans, where obtainable." He turned to Ilse Huber. "See what you can do."

"At once, General."

Devlin sat by the window, Schellenberg at his desk. They lit cigarettes. Schellenberg said, "You said last night you preferred to proceed with the notion of Vargas being a traitor."

"That's right."

"So what would you do? How would you handle it?"

"Easy. A stroke of genius hit me at the height of the bombing, General. We don't tell Vargas I'm going."

"I don't understand."

"We extract what information we need. In fact, we probably have enough already. Then, once a week, Rivera asks for more information on your behalf. Steiner's regime at the priory, the guard system, that sort of thing, only I'll already be in London. Now, Walter, my old son, you've got to admit that's good."

Schellenberg laughed helplessly, then got up. "Very good—bloody marvelous. Let's go down to the canteen and have a coffee on it."

Later, Schellenberg called for his Mercedes, and they drove to the Tiergarten and walked around the lake, feet crunching in the light powdering of snow.

"There's another difficulty," Devlin said. "The Special Branch managed to hunt me down when I was in Norfolk. A little late in the day, as it happened, but they did, and one of the things that helped was the fact that as an Irish citizen I had to be entered on the aliens' register by the local police, and that required a passport photo."

"I see. So what are you saying?"

"A complete change in appearance—a real change."

"You mean hair coloring and so on?"

Devlin nodded. "Add a few years as well."

"I think I can help there," Schellenberg said. "I have friends at the UFA film studios here in Berlin. Some of their makeup artists can achieve remarkable things."

"Another thing. No aliens' register this time. I was born in County Down, which is in Ulster, and that makes me officially a British citizen. We'll stick with that when it comes to false papers and so on."

"And your identity?"

"Last time I was a war hero. A gallant Irishman who'd been wounded at Dunkirk and invalided out." Devlin tapped the bullet scar on the side of his head. "This helped the story, of course."

"Good. Something like that then. What about method of entry?"

"Oh, parachute again."

"Into England?"

Devlin shook his head. "Too chancy, and if I'm seen, it's bound to be reported. No, make it Ireland like last time. If they see me there, no one gives a bugger. A stroll across the border into Ulster, the breakfast train to Belfast and I'm on British soil."

"And afterwards?"

"The boat. Belfast to Heysham in Lancashire. Last time, I had to take the other route from Larne to Stranraer in Scotland. The boats get full, just like the train." Devlin grinned. "There's a war on, General."

"So, you are in London. What happens then?"

Devlin lit a cigarette. "Well, if I keep away from Vargas, that means no help from any of your official sources."

Schellenberg frowned. "But you will need the help of others. Also weapons, a radio transmitter, because without the ability to communicate—"

"All right," Devlin said. "So a few things are going to have to be taken on trust. We were talking about my old friend in Wapping earlier, Michael Ryan. Now the odds are good that he's still around, and if he is, he'll help, at least with suitable contacts."

"Such as?"

"Michael ran a cab and he worked for the bookies on the side. He had a lot of under-world friends in the old days. The kind of crooks who'd do anything for money, deal in guns, that sort of thing. That IRA active service unit I had to knock off in London back in thirty-six—they used underworld contacts a lot, even to buy their explosives."

"So, this would be excellent. The help of your IRA friend and the assistance, when needed, of some criminal element. But for all you know, your friend could no longer be in London."

"Or killed in the Blitz, General. Nothing is guaranteed."

"And you're still willing to take a chance?"

"I reach London, I assess the situation because I have to do that however clever the plan looks that we put together here. If Michael Ryan isn't around, if it simply looks impossible, the whole thing, I'm on the next boat back to Belfast and over the border and safe in Dublin before you know it." Devlin grinned. "I'll give you the bad news from your Embassy there. Now could we go back to your office? It's so damn cold I think my bollocks are going to fall off."

In the office, after lunch, they started again. Ilse sitting in the corner taking notes.

Schellenberg said, "Say, for argument's sake, that you got Steiner out one dark evening in London."

"Broke him out of the priory, you mean?"

"Exactly. And that's only the first step. How do you get him back? Do you take him to Ireland? Return the way you came?"

"Not so healthy that," Devlin said. "De Valera, the Irish Prime Minister, has played it very cleverly. Kept Ireland out of the war, but that doesn't mean he's putting himself out for your people. All the Luftwaffe crews who've ended up in Ireland have been put in prison camps. On the other hand, if an RAF plane strays and crash-lands, they usually give them bacon and eggs for breakfast and send them home."

"And he's been imprisoning IRA members, I understand."

Devlin said, "In forty-one, I got back on a neutral boat, a Brazilian cargo ship from Ireland that put in at Lisbon, but that's a tricky one. Nothing guaranteed at all."

Ilse said diffidently, "Surely the moment the colonel is out they'll be looking for him."

"Exactly," Devlin said. "Police, army, Home Guard, the security services. Every port watched, especially the Irish routes." He shook his head. "No, once out we've got to leave England almost immediately. Be on our way before they know what's hit them."

Schellenberg nodded, thinking about it. "It occurs to me that one of the cleverest things about Operation Eagle was the way Colonel Steiner and his men were transported to England."

"The Dakota, you mean?" Devlin said.

"An RAF Dakota which had crash-landed in Holland and was put back into service. To all intents, a British plane flying home if anyone saw it, and all it had to do to make the drop was fly in under eight hundred feet, because many sections of the English coast have no low-level radar."

"Worked like a charm," Devlin said, "except on the way back. Gericke, the pilot, was in the same hospital as me. He was shot down by a Luftwaffe night fighter."

"Unfortunate, but an intriguing thought. A small plane flying in under radar. A British plane. A suitable landing place. It could have you and Steiner out and safely in France in no time at all."

"And pigs might fly, General. Not only would you need a suitable plane. You'd need the landing place. May I also point out you'd need an exceptional pilot."

"Come now, Mr. Devlin, anything is possible. We have what's called the Enemy Aircraft Flight where the Luftwaffe tests captured British and American planes of every kind. They even have a B-seventeen. I've seen it." He turned to Ilse. "Get in touch with them at once. Also extend your research on Operation Sea Lion to cover any sites in the general area of London that we intended to use for covert operations, landings by night, that sort of thing."

"And a pilot," Devlin told her. "Like I said, someone special."

"I'll get right on to it."

As she turned, there was a knock at the door and a young woman in SS auxiliary uniform came in carrying a large file. "St. Mary's Priory, Wapping. Was that what the general wanted?"

Ilse laughed triumphantly. "Good girl, Sigrid. Wait for me in the office. I've got something else for you." She turned and handed the file to Schellenberg. "I'll get her started on the other thing."

As she reached the door, Schellenberg said, "Another possibility, Ilse. Check the files on those British right-wing organizations that flourished before the war, the ones that sometimes had members of Parliament on their books."

She went out and Devlin asked, "And who in the hell would they be, General?"

"Anti-Semitics, people with Fascist sympathies. Many members of the British aristocracy and upper classes rather admired the Führer, certainly before the war."

"The kind who were disappointed not to see the Panzers driving up to Buckingham Palace?"

"Something like that." Schellenberg opened the bulky file, extracted the first plan and opened it. "So, Mr. Devlin, there you have it in all its glory. St. Mary's Priory."

Asa Vaughan was twenty-seven years of age. He was born in Los Angeles and his father was a film producer. Asa had been fascinated by flying from an early age, had taken his pilot's license even before going to West Point. Afterwards he had completed his training as a fighter pilot, performing so well that he was assigned to take an instructors' course with the navy at San Diego. And then came the night his whole world had collapsed, the night he'd got into a drunken brawl in a harborside bar and punched a major in the mouth.

October 5, 1939. The date was engraved on his heart. No scandal, no court-martial. No one wanted that. Just his resignation. One week at his parents' opulent home in Beverly Hills was all he could bear. He packed a bag and made for Europe.

The war had started in September, and the RAF were accepting a few Americans, but they didn't like his record. And then on November 30 the Russians invaded Finland. The Finns needed pilots badly, and volunteers from many nations flooded in to join the Finnish air force, Asa among them.

It was a hopeless war from the start, in spite of the gallantry of the Finnish army, and most of the fighter planes available were outdated. Not that the Russians were much better, but they did have a few of the new German FW-190s which Hitler had promised to Stalin as a goodwill gesture over the Poland deal.

Asa had flown biplanes like the Italian Fiat Falco and the British Gloucester Gladiator, hopelessly outclassed by the opposition, only his superior skill as a pilot giving him an edge. His personal score stood at seven, which made him an ace, and then came that morning of ferocious winds and driving snow when he'd come in at four hundred feet, flying blind, lost his engine at the last moment and crash-landed.

That was in March 1940, two days before the Finns capitulated. His pelvis fractured and back broken, he'd been hospitalized for eighteen months, was undergoing final therapy and still a lieutenant in the Finnish air force, when on June 25, 1941, Finland joined forces with Nazi Germany and declared war on Russia.

He'd returned to flying duties gradually, working as an instructor, not directly involved in any action. The months had gone by, and suddenly the roof had fallen in. First Pearl Harbor and then the declaration of war between Germany and Italy and the U.S.A.

They held him in a detention camp for three months, the Germans, and then the officers had come to see him from the SS. Himmler was extending the SS foreign legions—Scandinavian, French, the neutral Swedes, Indian prisoners of war from the British army in North Africa. There was even the Britisches Freikorps with their collar patches of three leopards instead of SS runes and the Union Jack on the left sleeve. Not that they'd had many takers, no more than fifty, mostly scum from prison camps attracted by the offer of good food, women and money.

The George Washington Legion was something else again. Supposedly for American sympathizers to the Nazi cause, as far as Asa knew, they never had more than half a dozen members, and he hadn't met the others. He had a choice. To join or be sent to a concentration camp. He argued as best he could. The final agreement was that he would serve only on the Russian Front. As it happened, he seldom flew in straight combat, for his skill as a pilot was so admired he was employed mainly on the courier service, ferrying high-ranking officers.

So here he was, not too far from the Russian border with Poland, at the controls of a Stork, forest and snow five thousand feet below, Hauptsturmführer Asa Vaughan from the U.S. of A. An SS Brigadeführer called Farber was sitting behind him examining maps.

Farber looked up. "How long now?"

"Twenty minutes," Asa told him. He spoke excellent German, although with an American accent.

"Good. I'm frozen to the bone."

How in the hell did I ever get into this? Asa

asked himself. *And how do I get out?* A great shadow swooped in. The Stork bucked wildly and Farber cried out in alarm. A fighter plane took station to starboard for a moment, the Red Star plain on its fuselage, then it banked away.

"Russian Yak fighter. We're in trouble," Asa said.

The Yak came in fast from behind, firing both cannon and machine guns, and the Stork staggered, pieces breaking from the wings. Asa banked and went down, the Yak followed, turning in a half-circle, and took up station again. The pilot, conscious of his superiority in every department, waved, enjoying himself.

"Bastard!" Asa said.

The Yak banked again, came in fast, cannon shell punching into the Stork, and Farber cried out as a bullet caught him in the shoulder. As the windscreen shattered, he screamed, "Do something, for God's sake."

Asa, blood on his cheek from a splinter, cried, "You want me to do something, I'll do something. Let's see if this bastard can fly."

He took the Stork straight down to two thousand, waited until the Yak came in, banked and went down again. The forest in the snow plain below seemed to rush toward them.

"What are you doing?" Farber cried.

Asa took her down to a thousand, then five hundred feet, and the Yak, hungry for the kill, stayed on his tail. At the right moment, the American dropped his flaps, the Yak banked to avoid the collision and plowed straight down into the forest at 350 miles an hour. There was a tongue of flame, and Asa pulled back the column and leveled out at two thousand feet.

"You okay, General?"

Farber clutched his arm, blood pumping through. "You're a genius—a genius. I'll see you get the Iron Cross for this."

"Thanks." Asa wiped blood from his cheek. "That's all I need."

At the Luftwaffe base outside Warsaw, Asa walked toward the officers' mess feeling unaccountably depressed. The medical officer had put two stitches in his cheek but had been more concerned with Brigadeführer Farber's condition.

Asa went into the mess and took off his flying jacket. Underneath he wore a beautifully tailored uniform in field gray, SS runes on his collar patch. On his left sleeve was a Stars and Stripes shield, and the cuff title on his left wrist said, *George Washington Legion.* He had the ribbon of the Iron Cross Second Class on his tunic and the Finnish Gold Cross of Valor.

His very uniqueness made most other pilots avoid him. He ordered a cognac, drank it quickly, and ordered another.

A voice said, "And it's not even lunchtime."

As Asa turned, the Gruppenkommandant, Colonel Erich Adler, sat on the stool next to him. " 'Champagne," he told the barman.

"And what's the occasion?" Asa demanded.

"First, my miserable Yankee friend, the good Brigadeführer Farber has recommended you for an immediate Iron Cross First Class, which, from what he says, you deserve."

"But Erich, I've got a medal," Asa said plaintively.

Adler ignored him, waiting for the champagne, then passed him a glass. "Second, you're out of it. Grounded immediately."

"I'm what?"

"You fly out to Berlin on the next available transport, priority one. That's usually Göring. You report to General Walter Schellenberg at SD headquarters in Berlin."

"Just a minute," Asa told him. "I only fly on the Russian Front. That was the deal."

"I wouldn't argue if I were you. This order comes by way of Himmler himself." Adler raised his glass. "Good luck, my friend."

"God help me, but I think I'm going to need it," Asa Vaughan told him.

Devlin came awake about three in the morning to the sound of gunfire in the distance. He got up and padded into the living room and peered out through a chink in the blackout curtains. He could see the flashes on the far horizon beyond the city.

Behind him, Ilse switched on the light in the kitchen. "I couldn't sleep either. I'll make some coffee."

She was wearing a robe against the cold, her hair in two pigtails that made her look curiously vulnerable. He went and got his overcoat and put it on over his pajamas and sat at the table smoking a cigarette.

"Two days and no suitable landing site for a plane," he said. "I think the general's getting impatient."

"He likes to do things yesterday," Ilse said. "At least we've found a suitable base on the French coast, and the pilot looks promising."

"You can say that again," Devlin told her. "A Yank in the SS, not that the poor sod had much choice from what the record says. I can't wait to meet him."

"My husband was SS, did you know that? A sergeant major in a Panzer regiment."

"I'm sorry," Devlin said.

"You must think we're all very wicked sometimes, Mr. Devlin, but you must understand how it started. After the First War, Germany was on her knees, ruined."

"And then came the Führer."

"He seemed to offer so much. Pride again—prosperity. And then it started—so many bad things, the Jews most of all." She hesitated. "One of my great-grandmothers was Jewish. My husband had to get special permission to marry me. It's there on my record, and sometimes I wake in the night and think what would happen to me if someone decided to do something about it."

Devlin took her hands. "Hush now, girl, we all get that three-o'clock-in-the-morning feeling when everything looks bad." There were tears in her eyes. "Here, I'll make you smile. My disguise for this little jaunt I'm taking. Guess what?"

She was smiling slightly already. "No, tell me."

"A priest."

Her eyes widened. "You, a priest?" She started to laugh. "Oh, no, Mr. Devlin."

"Wait now while I explain. You'd be surprised at the religious background I have. Oh, yes." He nodded solemnly. "Altar boy, then after the British hanged my father in nineteen twenty-one, my mother and I went to live with my old uncle, who was a priest in Belfast. He sent me to a Jesuit boarding school. They beat religion into you there, all right." He lit another cigarette. "Oh, I can play the priest as well as any priest, if you follow me."

"Well, let's hope you don't have to celebrate Mass or hear Confession." She laughed. "Have another coffee."

"Dear God, woman, you've given me an idea there. Where's your briefcase? The file we were looking at earlier—the general file?"

She went into her bedroom and came back with it. "Here it is."

Devlin leafed through it quickly, then nodded. "I was right. It's here in his record. The Steiners are an old Catholic family."

"What are you getting at?"

"This St. Mary's Priory. It's the sort of

142

place priests visit all the time to hear the Confessions. The Little Sisters of Pity are saints compared to the rest of us, but they need Confession before they partake of Communion, and both functions need a priest. Then there would be those patients who were Catholic."

"Including Steiner, you mean?"

"They couldn't deny him a priest, and him in a place like that." He grinned. "It's an idea."

"Have you thought any more about your appearance?" she asked.

"Ah, we can leave that for another few days, then I'll see one of these film people the general mentioned. Put myself in their hands."

She nodded. "Let's hope we come up with something in those Sea Lion files. The trouble is there's so much to wade through." She got up. "Anyway, I think I'll go back to bed."

Outside, the air-raid siren sounded. Devlin smiled wryly. "No you won't. You'll get dressed like a good girl, and we'll go down and spend another jolly night in the cellars. I'll see you in five minutes."

Schellenberg said, "A priest? Yes, I like that."

"So do I," Devlin said. "It's like a uniform, you see. A soldier, a postman, a railway porter—it's the appearance of things you remember, not the face. As I say, the uniform. Priests are like that. Nice and anonymous."

They were standing at a collapsible map table Schellenberg had erected, the plans of St. Mary's Priory spread before them.

"Having studied these on and off for some days, what is your opinion?" Schellenberg asked.

"The most interesting thing is this plan." Devlin tapped it with a finger. "The architect's plans for the changes made in nineteen hundred and ten when the priory was reconsecrated Roman Catholic and the Little Sisters took over."

"What's your point?"

"Underneath, London is a labyrinth, a subterranean world of sewers. I read once there's over a hundred miles of rivers under the city, like the Fleet, which rises in Hampstead and comes out into the Thames at Blackfriars, all underground."

"So?"

"Seven or eight hundred years of sewers,

underground rivers, tunnels, and nobody knows where half of them are until they're excavating or making changes, as they were at the priory. Look at the architect's plan here. Regular flooding of the crypt beneath the chapel. They were able to deal with the problem because they discovered a stream running through an eighteenth-century tunnel next door. See, it's indicated there on the plan running into the Thames."

"Very interesting," Schellenberg said.

"They built a grille in the wall of the crypt to allow water to draw into that tunnel. There's a note here on the plan."

"A way out, you mean?"

"It's a possibility. Would have to be checked." Devlin threw down his pencil. "It's knowing what goes on in that place that's the thing, General. For all we know, it could be dead easy. A handful of guards, slack discipline."

"On the other hand, they could be waiting for you."

"Ah, but not if they think I'm still in Berlin," Devlin reminded him.

At that moment Ilse Huber came in, very excited. "You were right to recommend me to check on British right-wing organizations,

General. I found details of a man in there cross-referenced to Sea Lion."

"What's his name?" Schellenberg demanded.

"Shaw," she said. "Sir Maxwell Shaw." She laid two bulky files on the table.

6

ROMNEY MARSH, some forty-five miles southeast of London on the coast of Kent, is a two-hundred-square-mile area reclaimed from the sea by a system of dikes and channels started as far back as Roman times. Much of it is below sea level, and only innumerable drainage ditches prevent it from reverting to its natural state.

Charbury was not even a village. A hamlet of no more than fifteen houses, a church and a village store. There wasn't even a pub any longer, and half the cottages were empty, only the old folk left. The younger people had departed long ago for war work or service in the armed forces.

It was raining that morning as Sir Maxwell Shaw walked down the village street, a black Labrador at his heels. He was a heavily built man of medium height, face craggy, the evidence of heavy drinking there, and the black mustache didn't help. He looked morose and angry much of the time, ready for trouble, and most people avoided him.

He wore a tweed hat, the brim turned down, a waterproof shooting jacket and Wellingtons. He carried a double-barreled twelve-bore shotgun under one arm. When he reached the store, he bent down and fondled the Labrador's ears, his face softening.

"Good girl, Nell. Stay."

A bell tinkled as he went in the shop. There was an old man in his seventies leaning against the counter talking to a woman behind who was even older.

"Morning, Tinker," Shaw said.

"Morning, Sir Maxwell."

"You promised me some cigarettes, Mrs. Dawson."

The old lady produced a package from beneath the counter. "Managed to get you two hundred Players from my man in Dymchurch, Sir Maxwell. Black market, I'm afraid, so they come expensive."

"Isn't everything these days? Put it on my bill."

He placed the package in one of his game pockets and went out. As he closed the door, he heard Tinker say, "Poor sod."

He took a deep breath to contain his anger and touched the Labrador. "Let's go, girl," he said and went back along the street.

It was Maxwell Shaw's grandfather who had made the family's fortune, a Sheffield ironmaster who had risen on the high tide of Victorian industrialization. It was he who had purchased the estate, renamed Shaw Place, where he had retired, a millionaire with a baronetcy, in 1885. His son had shown no interest in the family firm, which had passed into other hands. A career soldier, he had died leading his men into battle at Spion Kop during the Boer War.

Maxwell Shaw, born in 1890, had followed in his father's footsteps. Eton, Sandhurst, a commission in the Indian army. He served in Mesopotamia during the First World War, came home in 1916 to transfer to an infantry regiment. His mother was still alive. Lavinia, his younger sister, was married to a pilot in the Royal Flying Corps and was serving as a nurse. In 1917 he returned from France badly wounded and with an MC. During his convalescence he met the girl who was to become his wife at the local hunt ball and married her before returning to France.

It was in 1918, the last year of the war,

when everything seemed to happen at once. His mother died, then his wife, out with the local hunt, when she took a bad fall. She'd lasted ten days, long enough for Shaw to rush home on compassionate leave to be with her when she died. It was Lavinia who had supported him every step of the way, kept him upright at the graveside, yet within a month she, too, was alone, her husband shot down over the Western Front.

After the war, it was a different world they inherited like everyone else, and Shaw didn't like it. At least he and Lavinia had each other and Shaw Place, although as the years went by and the money grew less, things became increasingly difficult. He was a Conservative member of Parliament for a while and then humiliatingly lost his seat to a Socialist. Like many of his kind, he was violently anti-Semitic, and this, exacerbated by the crushing political blow, led to his involvement with Sir Oswald Mosley and the British Fascist movement.

In all this, he was backed by Lavinia, although her main interest lay in trying to keep their heads above water and hanging on to the estate. Disenchanted with the way society had changed and their own place in it, again like many of their kind, they looked to

Hitler as a role model, admired what he was doing for Germany.

And then at a dinner in London in January 1939 they were introduced to a Major Werner Keitel, a military attaché at the German Embassy. For several months Lavinia enjoyed a passionate affair with him, and he was frequently a visitor at Shaw Place, for he was a Luftwaffe pilot and shared Lavinia's love of flying. She kept a Tiger Moth at the time, housed in an old barn, and used the South Meadow as an airstrip. They frequently flew together in the two-seater biplane, covering large sections of the south coast, and Keitel had been able to indulge in his interest for aerial photography.

Shaw never minded. Lavinia had had relationships before, although he himself had little interest in women. The Keitel thing was different, however, because of what it led to.

"Well, we know where we are with him," Devlin said of Shaw. "He's the kind who used to have children transported to Australia for stealing a loaf of bread."

Schellenberg gave him a cigarette. "Werner Keitel was an Abwehr agent employed at the time to select deep cover agents. Not the usual kind at all. A war was coming, that was obvious, and there was much forward planning for Sea Lion."

"And the old sod's place was perfect," Devlin observed. "The back of beyond and yet only forty-five miles from London, and this South Meadow to land a plane on."

"Yes. Keitel, according to his report, found it amazingly easy to recruit both of them. He supplied them with a radio. The sister already knew Morse code. They were expressly forbidden to engage in any other activities, of course. Keitel, by the way, was killed in the Battle of Britain."

"Did they have a code name?"

Ilse, who had been sitting quietly, produced another sheet from the file. " 'Falcon.' He was to be alerted by the message *Does the Falcon still wait? It is now time to strike.*"

Devlin said, "So there they were. Waiting for the great day, the invasion that never came. And what's the situation now, I wonder?"

"As it happens, there is some further information available," Ilse told him. "We have an article here which appeared in an American magazine." She checked the date. "March nineteen forty-three. 'The British Fascist Movement,' it's called. The journalist got an interview with Shaw and his sister. There's a photo."

Lavinia was sitting on a horse, a scarf around her head, and was far more attractive than Devlin had expected. Shaw stood beside her, a shotgun under his arm.

Schellenberg read the article quickly and passed it to Devlin. "Rather sad. You'll see there that like most of his kind he was detained without trial for a few months under Regulation Eighteen-B in nineteen forty."

"Brixton Prison? That must have been a shock," Devlin said.

"The rest is even more sad. The estate sold off, no servants. Just the two of them hanging on in that decaying old house," Schellenberg said. "It could be perfect, you know. Come and have a look at a map of the Channel." They went to the map table. "Here. Cap de la Hague and Chernay. Used to be a flying club. It's used as a landing strip for emergencies only by the Luftwaffe—refueling, that sort of thing. Only half a dozen men there. It's perfect for our purposes because it's only some thirty miles from the Château de Belle-Île, where the Führer's conference takes place."

"How far to our friends in Romney Marsh?"

"A hundred and fifty miles, most of it over the sea."

"Fine," Devlin said. "Except for one thing. Would the Shaws be willing to be activated?"

"Couldn't Vargas find out?"

"Vargas could drop the lot of us, as I told you. This would be exactly what British intelligence wanted. The chance to pull in everyone they could." Devlin shook his head. "No, the Shaws will have to wait till I get there, just like everything else. If they'll do it, then we're in business."

"But how will you communicate?" Ilse demanded.

"They may still have that radio, and I can handle one of those things. When the Abwehr recruited me to go to Ireland in forty-one, I did the usual radio and Morse code course."

"And if they haven't?"

Devlin laughed. "Then I'll beg, borrow or steal one. Jesus, General, you worry too much."

Shaw saw a rabbit, flung his shotgun up to his shoulder, already too late, and missed. He cursed, took a flask from his pocket and drank. Nell whined, gazing up at him, anxiously. The reeds here were as high as a man, water gurgling in the creeks, running toward the sea. It was a scene of complete desolation, the sky black, swollen with rain. As it started to fall, Lavinia appeared on horseback, galloping along a dike toward him.

She reined in. "Hello, my darling. I heard your shot."

"Can't hit a brick wall these days, old girl." He put the flask to his lips, then gestured dramatically. "Look at it—a dead world, Lavinia, everything bloody dead, including me. If only something would happen—anything." And he raised the flask to his lips again.

Asa Vaughan closed the file and looked up. Schellenberg leaned across the desk and offered him a cigarette. "What do you think?"

"Why me?"

"Because they tell me you're a great pilot who can fly anything."

"Flattery usually gets you everywhere, General, but let's examine this. When I was, shall we say, inducted into the SS, the deal was that I only operated against the Russians. It was made clear to me that I wouldn't have to take part in any act detrimental to my country's cause."

Devlin, sitting by the window, laughed harshly. "What a load of bollocks, son. If you believed that, then you'd believe any old thing. They had you by your short and curlies the minute they got you into that uniform."

"I'm afraid he's right, Captain," Schellenberg said. "You wouldn't get very far with the Reichsführer with that argument."

"I can imagine," Asa said, and an expression of gloom settled on his face.

"What's your problem?" Devlin demanded. "Where would you rather be? Back on the Eastern Front or here? And you've no choice. Say no, and that old sod Himmler will have you in a concentration camp."

"Sounds like no contest, except for one small point," Asa told him. "I end up getting caught in England in this uniform, I'll get the fastest court-martial in American history and a firing squad."

"No you won't, my old son," Devlin said. "They'll hang you. Now the flight. Do you reckon you could make it in?"

"No reason why not. If I am going to do it, I'd need to know the English Channel approach backwards. From what I can see, I'd stay over the water for almost the whole trip. Turn inland for the last few miles."

"Exactly," Schellenberg said.

"This house, Shaw Place. It would mean a night landing. Even with a moon I'd need some sort of guidance." He nodded, thinking about it. "When I was a kid in California, my flying instructor was a guy who had flown with the Lafayette Escadrille in France. I remember him telling me how in those days, things being more primitive, they often used a few cycle lamps arranged in an inverted L-shape with the crossbar at the upwind end."

"Simple enough," Devlin said.

"And the plane. It would have to be small. Something like a Fieseler Stork."

"Yes, well I'm hoping that's taken care of," Schellenberg said. "I've spoken to the officer in command of Enemy Aircraft Flight. They are at Hildorf. It's a couple hours' drive from Berlin, and they're expecting us in the morning. He thinks he's found us a suitable plane."

"Guess that's it." Asa got up. "What happens now?"

"We eat, son," Devlin told him. "The best the black market can offer. Then you come back to Frau Huber's apartment with me, where we'll share the spare room. Don't worry, it's got twin beds."

The chapel at St. Mary's Priory of the Little Sisters of Pity was cold and damp and smelled of candle grease and incense. In the Confession box, Father Frank Martin waited until the sister whose Confession he had heard was gone. He switched off the lights and went out.

He was the pastor of St. Patrick's, two streets away, and with St. Patrick's came the job of father confessor to the priory. He was seventy-six, a small, frail man with very white hair. If it hadn't been for the war, they'd have retired him, but it was like everything else these days, all hands to the pumps.

He went into the sacristy, removed his alb and carefully folded his violet stole. He reached for his raincoat, debating the virtues of an early night, but compassion and Christian charity won the day as usual. Eighteen patients at the moment, seven of them terminal. A last round of the rooms wouldn't come amiss. He hadn't visited since early afternoon, and that wasn't good enough.

He went out of the chapel and saw the mother superior, Sister Maria Palmer, mopping the floor, a menial task designed to remind herself of what she saw as her greatest weakness: the sin of pride.

Father Martin paused and shook his head. "You are too hard on yourself."

"Not hard enough," she said. "I'm glad to see you. There's been a development since you were here earlier. They've given us a German prisoner of war again."

"Really?" They walked out of the chapel into the entrance hall.

"Yes, a Luftwaffe officer, recently wounded, but well on the way to recovery. A Colonel Kurt Steiner. They've put him on the top floor like the other ones we've had."

"What about guards?"

"Half a dozen military police. There's a young second lieutenant called Benson in charge."

At that moment Jack Carter and Dougal Munro came down the main staircase. Sister Maria Palmer said, "Is everything satisfactory, Brigadier?"

"Perfectly," Munro said. "We'll try to inconvenience you as little as possible."

"There is no inconvenience," she said. "This, by the way, is Father Martin, our priest."

"Father," Munro said and turned to Carter. "I'll be off now, Jack. Don't forget to get a doctor in to check him over."

Sister Maria Palmer said, "Perhaps it was not made clear to you that I am a doctor, Brigadier. Whatever Colonel Steiner's requirements are, I'm sure we can take care of them. In fact now that you're finished, I'll visit him to make sure he's settled in properly."

Jack Carter said, "Well actually, Sister, I'm not too sure about that."

"Captain Carter, let me remind you that this priory, of which I am in charge, is not only a house of God, it is a place where we attend to the sick and the dying. I have seen Colonel Steiner's medical record and note that it's only been a matter of weeks since he was gravely wounded. He will need my attention, and as I note from his record that he is also a Roman Catholic by religion, he may also need the ministrations of Father Martin here."

"Quite right, Sister," Munro said. "See to it, Jack, will you?"

He went out, and Carter turned and led the way up the stairs. There was a door at the top, heavily studded and banded with steel. An MP sat at a small table beside it.

"Open up," Carter told him. The MP

knocked on the door, which was opened after a moment by another MP. They passed inside. Carter said, "We're using the other rooms as billets for the men."

"So I see," Sister Maria Palmer said.

The door to the first room stood open. There was a small desk beside a narrow bed, and the young lieutenant, Benson, sat at it. He jumped to his feet. "What can I do for you, sir?"

"Sister and Father Martin have access whenever they require it. Brigadier Munro's orders. We'll talk to the prisoner now."

There was another MP sitting on a chair outside the room at the far end where the passage ran into a blank wall.

"God help us, you're guarding this man well enough," Father Martin said.

Benson unlocked the door, and Steiner, standing by the window, turned to greet them, an impressive figure in the blue-gray Luftwaffe uniform, the Knight's Cross with Oak Leaves at his throat, his other medals making a brave show.

Carter said, "This is the mother superior, Sister Maria Palmer. You didn't get a chance to speak earlier. And Father Martin."

Sister Maria Palmer said, "Tomorrow I'll

have you down to the dispensary for a thorough check, Colonel."

"Is that all right, sir?" Benson asked.

"For goodness sake, bring him down yourself, Lieutenant. Surround him with all your men, but if he's not in the dispensary at ten, we'll have words," she told him.

"No problem," Carter said. "See to it, Benson. Anything else, Sister?"

"No, that will do for tonight."

Father Martin said, "I'd like a word with the colonel, in private, if you wouldn't mind."

Carter nodded and turned to Steiner. "I'll check on you from time to time."

"I'm sure you will."

They all went out except for Father Martin, who closed the door and sat on the bed. "My son, you've had a bad time, I can see it in your face. When were you last at Mass?"

"So long ago I can't remember. The war, Father, tends to get in the way."

"No Confession either? A long time since you were able to ease the burden of your sins."

"I'm afraid so." Steiner smiled, warming to the man. "I know you mean well, Father."

"Good heavens, man, I'm not concerned

161

with you and me. I'm interested only in you and God." Father Martin got up. "I'll pray for you, my son, and I'll visit every day. The moment you feel the need for Confession and Mass, tell me and I'll arrange for you to join us in the chapel."

"I'm afraid Lieutenant Benson would insist on coming too," Steiner said.

"Now wouldn't that do his immortal soul some good too?" The old priest chuckled and went out.

Asa Vaughan sat at the dining table in the living room at Ilse Huber's apartment, Devlin opposite him.

"You really think this thing can work?" the American asked.

"Anything will as long as the engine keeps ticking over, isn't that a fact?"

Asa got up and paced restlessly across the room. "What in the hell am I doing here? Can you understand? Everything kind of overtook me. It just happened. I don't seem to have had a choice. Don't now, when it comes right down to it."

"Of course you do," Devlin said. "You go through with it, fly the plane to England, land and give yourself up."

"And what good would that do? They'd

never believe me, Devlin." There was a kind of horror on his face when he added, "Come to think of it, they never will."

"Then you'd better hope Adolf wins the war," Devlin said.

But the following morning at the air base at Hildorf the American seemed in much better spirits as Major Koenig, the officer commanding the Enemy Aircraft Flight, showed them around. He seemed to have examples of most Allied planes. There was a B-17, a Lancaster bomber, a Hurricane, a Mustang, all bearing Luftwaffe insignia.

"Now this is what I thought might suit your purposes," he said. "Here in the end hangar."

The plane standing there was a high wing-braced monoplane with a single engine and a wing span of more than fifty feet.

"Very nice," Asa said. "What is it?"

"A Westland Lysander. Has a maximum speed of two hundred and thirty at ten thousand feet. Short landing and take-off. Only needs two hundred and forty yards fully loaded."

"That means you could make the flight in just under an hour," Schellenberg said to Asa.

Asa ignored him. "Passengers?"

"How many are you thinking of?" Koenig asked.

"Two."

"Perfect comfort. Can manage three. Even four at a pinch." He turned to Schellenberg. "I thought of it at once when you made your inquiries. We picked this up in France last month. It was RAF. The pilot caught a bullet in the chest when attacked by a Ju night fighter. Managed to land and collapsed before he could destroy it. These planes are used by British intelligence for covert operations. They operate with the French Resistance movement, ferrying agents across from England, taking others out. This is the perfect plane for such work."

"Good—then it's mine," Schellenberg said.

"But, General—" Koenig began.

Schellenberg took the Führer Directive from his pocket. "Read that."

Koenig did and returned it, positively clicking his heels. "At your orders, General."

Schellenberg turned to Asa. "So, what are your requirements?"

"Well, obviously I'll want to try her out.

Get used to the thing, though I don't think that should be a problem."

"Anything else?"

"Yes, I'll want the RAF roundels back in place for the flight into England. But I'd like that to be temporary. Some sort of canvas covers that can be stripped so that I'm Luftwaffe again for the trip back."

"Easily taken care of," Koenig said.

"Excellent," Schellenberg told him. "Hauptsturmführer Vaughan will remain and test-fly the plane now and as much as he wants for the rest of the day. After that you will do whatever work is needed and have the aircraft delivered at the weekend to the destination in France that my secretary will notify you of."

"Certainly, General," Koenig said.

Schellenberg turned to Asa. "Enjoy yourself while you can. I've arranged to borrow a Fieseler Stork from the Luftwaffe. We'll fly down to Chernay and inspect the airstrip tomorrow. I'd also like to have a look at this Château de Belle-Île while we're there."

"And you want me to do the flying?" Asa asked.

"Don't worry, son, we have every confidence in you," Devlin told him as he and Schellenberg went out.

165

In London, Dougal Munro was working at his desk when Jack Carter came in.

"What is it, Jack?"

"I've had a medical report from Sister Maria Palmer, sir, on Steiner."

"What's her opinion?"

"He's still not a hundred percent. Some residual infection. She asked me to help her get hold of some of this new wonder drug penicillin. Apparently it cures just about everything, but it's in short supply."

"Then get it for her, Jack, get it."

"Very well, sir. I'm sure I can."

He hesitated at the door, and Munro said impatiently, "For God's sake, what is it, Jack? I'm up to my ears in work here, not least amongst my worries being a meeting at three of headquarters staff at SHAEF presided over by General Eisenhower himself."

"Well, it's the Steiner thing, sir. I mean, here he is, installed at the priory. What happens now?"

"Liam Devlin, if it is Devlin they choose, is hardly going to parachute into the courtyard at St. Mary's Priory tomorrow night, Jack, and if he did, so what? The only way we could guard Steiner any closer is by having an MP share his bed, and that would never do."

"So we just wait, sir?"

"Of course we do. If they intend to have a go, it'll take weeks to organize, but that doesn't matter. After all, we have Vargas in our pocket. Anything happens, and we'll be the first to know."

"Very well, sir."

As Carter opened the door, Munro added, "We've got all the time in the world, Jack. So has Steiner."

When Steiner went into the chapel that evening, he was escorted by Lieutenant Benson and an MP corporal. The chapel was cold and damp, slightly eerie with the candles down at the altar and the ruby light of the sanctuary lamp. Instinctively he dipped his fingers in the holy water, a kind of regression to childhood, and went and sat on the end of a bench beside two nuns and waited his turn. The mother superior emerged from the confessional box, smiled at him, and passed on. One of the nuns went in. After a while she came out and was replaced by the other.

When it came to Steiner's turn, he went in and kneeled down, finding the darkness surprisingly comforting. He hesitated, and then that ghost from childhood rose again and he said, almost automatically, "Bless me, Father . . ."

Father Martin knew it was him of course, had to. He said, "May the Lord Jesus bless you and help you tell your sins."

"Dammit, Father," Steiner exploded, "I don't even know why I'm here. Maybe I just wanted to get out of that room."

"Oh, I'm sure God will forgive you that, my son." Steiner had an insane desire to laugh. The old man said, "Is there anything you want to say to me? Anything?"

And suddenly Steiner found himself saying, "My father. They butchered my father. Hung him up on a hook like a piece of meat."

"Who did this thing, my son?"

"The Gestapo—the bloody Gestapo." Steiner could hardly breathe, his throat dry, eyes hot. "Hate, that's all I feel and revenge. I want revenge. Now what good is that to a man like you, Father? Am I not guilty of a very great sin?"

Father Martin said quietly, "May our Lord Jesus Christ absolve you, and I, by his authority, absolve you from your sins in the name of the Father, and the Son and the Holy Spirit."

168

"But, Father, you don't understand," Kurt Steiner said. "I can't pray anymore."

"That's all right, my son," Father Martin told him. "I'll pray for you."

7

THE FLIGHT from Berlin to Cap de la Hague took just over three hours, Asa charting a course that took them over parts of occupied Holland, Belgium and then France. They came in to Chernay from the sea. It was a desolate-looking little place. Not even a control tower, just a grass runway, with a wind sock at one end, three old prewar hangars and several huts that looked like Luftwaffe additions. There was also a fuel dump.

Asa raised them on the radio. "Stork as expected from Gatow."

A voice said, "Chernay control. Permission to land granted. Wind southeast, strength three to four and freshening."

"Takes himself seriously," Asa said over his shoulder. "Here we go."

He made a perfect landing and taxied toward the hangars, where half a dozen men waited in Luftwaffe coveralls. As Schellenberg and Devlin got out, a sergeant emerged from the hut with the radio mast and hurried toward them.

He took in Schellenberg's uniform and got his heels together. "General."

"And your name is?"

"Leber, General. Flight sergeant."

"And you are in charge here?"

"Yes, General."

"Read this." Schellenberg handed him the Führer Directive. "You and your men are now under my command. A matter of the utmost importance to the Reich."

Leber got his heels together again, handed the letter back. "At your orders, General."

"Hauptsturmführer Vaughan will be making a hazardous and highly secret flight across the English Channel. The aircraft he will use is an unusual one. You'll see that for yourself when it's delivered."

"And our duties, General?"

"I'll inform you later. Is your radio receiving equipment up to scratch?"

"Oh, yes, General, the best the Luftwaffe can offer. Sometimes aircraft returning across the Channel are in a bad way. We have to be able to talk them in when necessary."

"Good." Schellenberg nodded. "Do you happen to know a place called Château de Belle-Île? According to the map it's about thirty miles from here in the general direction of Carentan."

"I'm afraid not, General."

"Never mind. We'll manage. Now find us a *Kübelwagen*."

"Certainly, General. May I ask if you'll be spending the night?"

Schellenberg glanced around at the desolate landscape. "Well, I'd prefer not to, Sergeant, but one never knows. Have the Stork refueled and made ready for the return trip."

"Jesus," Devlin said as Leber led them toward a jeep parked outside the radio hut. "Would you look at this place? What a lousy posting. I wonder they can put up with it."

"Better than Russia," Asa Vaughan said.

Asa drove, Devlin beside him, Schellenberg in the rear, a map spread across his knees. "Here it is. The road south from Cherbourg goes to Carentan. It's off there somewhere on the coast."

"Wouldn't it make more sense to land at the Luftwaffe base at Cherbourg?" Asa asked.

"As the Führer will when he comes." Schellenberg shook his head. "I prefer to keep our heads down for the moment. We don't need to go through Cherbourg at all.

There's a network of country roads south that cut across to the coast. Thirty miles, thirty-five at the most."

"What's the purpose of this little trip anyway?" Devlin asked him.

"This Belle-Île place intrigues me. I'd like to see what we've got there as long as we're in the neighborhood." He shrugged.

Devlin said, "I was wondering. Does the Reichsführer know we're here?"

"He knows about our flight to Chernay, or he will soon. He likes a regular report."

"Ah, yes, General, that's one thing, but this Belle-Île place would be another."

"You could say that, Mr. Devlin, you could."

"Sweet Mother of God, what a fox you are," Devlin said. "I pity the huntsman when you're around."

Many of the country lanes were so narrow that it would not have been possible for two vehicles to pass each other, but after half an hour they cut into the main road that ran south from Cherbourg to Carentan. It was here that Schellenberg had trouble with his map, and then they had a stroke of luck, a sign at the side of the road outside the village of St.-Aubin that said *12th Parachute Detach-*

ment. There was a spread of farm buildings visible beyond the trees.

"Let's try here," Schellenberg said, and Asa turned off the road.

The men in the farmyard were all *Fallschirm-jäger,* hard young men, old before their time, with cropped hair. Most of them wore camouflaged smocks and jump boots. A number sat on benches against the wall cleaning weapons. A couple worked on the engine of a troop carrier. They glanced up curiously as the *Kübelwagen* arrived, rising to their feet when they saw Schellenberg's uniform.

"That's all right, carry on with what you're doing," he said.

A young captain emerged from the farmhouse. He had the Iron Cross First and Second Class, the cuff titles for Crete and the Afrika Korps. He also had a Winter War ribbon, a tough, hard-faced young man.

"You are in charge here?" Schellenberg asked.

"Yes, General. Hauptmann Erich Kramer. In what way may I help you?"

"We're looking for a place called Château de Belle-Île," Schellenberg told him. "Do you know it?"

"Very well. About ten miles east of here

173

on the coast. Let me show you on my area map."

They followed him into the farmhouse. The living room was fitted out as a command post with radio and large-scale maps on the wall. The back road to Belle-Île was plain enough.

"Excellent," Schellenberg said. "Tell me something. What's your unit's purpose here?"

"Security duties, General. We patrol the area, try to keep the French Resistance in place."

"Do you get much trouble from them?"

"Not really." Kramer laughed. "I only have thirty-five men left in this unit. We were lucky to get out of Stalingrad. This is a rest cure for us."

They went outside, and as they got back into the *Kübelwagen* Devlin said, "Crete and Afrika Korps, I see, and Stalingrad? Did you know Steiner?"

Even the men cleaning their weapons looked up at the mention of the name. Kramer said, "Oberst Kurt Steiner? Who doesn't in our line of work? A legend in the Parachute Regiment."

"You've met him then?"

"Several times. You know him?"

"You could say that."

Kramer said, "We heard a rumor he was dead."

"Ah, well, you mustn't believe everything you hear," Devlin told him.

"Captain." Schellenberg returned his salute as Asa drove away.

"Dear God," Devlin said, "I sometimes wonder why Steiner doesn't make his own way back across the Channel walking on water."

Belle-Île was quite spectacular, a castle crowning a hill beside the sea, a vast estuary stretching beyond it, sand where the tide had just retreated. Asa took the *Kübelwagen* up the single winding road. There was a narrow bridge across a gap that was more ravine than moat. Two great doors stood open in an arched entrance, and they came out into a cobbled courtyard. Asa braked at the foot of broad steps leading up to the front entrance, walls and towers rising above them.

They got out and Schellenberg led the way. The door was of oak, buckled with age and studded with rusting iron bolts and bands of steel. There was a bell hanging from the wall beside it. Schellenberg pulled the chain, and the jangling echoed around the courtyard, bouncing from the walls.

"Jesus," Devlin said. "All we need is Quasimodo."

A moment later the door creaked open and he appeared, or a fair facsimile, a very old man with gray hair down to his shoulders, a black dress coat of velvet that had seen better days, a pair of very baggy corduroy trousers of the type worn by peasants.

His face was wrinkled and he badly needed a shave. *"Oui, monsieurs,"* he said. "What can I do for you?"

"You are the caretaker?" Schellenberg asked.

"Yes, monsieur. Pierre Dissard."

"You live here with your wife?"

"When she is here, monsieur. At present she is with her niece in Cherbourg."

Devlin said to Asa, "Are you getting all this?"

"Not a word. I don't speak French."

"I suppose you spent all your time playing football. The general and I, on the other hand, being men of intellect and learning, can understand everything the old bugger is saying. I'll translate freely when necessary."

Schellenberg said, "I wish to inspect the premises."

He walked past Dissard into a great entrance hall, flagged in granite, a carpet here and there. There was an enormous fireplace to one side and a staircase to the first floor wide enough to take a regiment.

"You are of the SS, monsieur?" Dissard asked.

"I should think that was obvious," Schellenberg told him.

"But the premises have already been inspected, monsieur, the other day. An officer in a similar uniform to your own."

"Do you recall his name?"

"He said he was a major." The old man frowned, trying. "His face was bad on one side."

Schellenberg said calmly, "Berger. Was that his name?"

Dissard nodded eagerly. "That's it, monsieur, Major Berger. His French was very bad."

Asa said, "What's going on?"

"He's telling us someone's been here before us. An SS major named Berger," Devlin said.

"Do you know him?"

"Oh, intimately, particularly his nose, but I'll explain later."

Schellenberg said, "Then you are aware

that these premises are required in the near future. I would appreciate a conducted tour."

"The château has been closed since nineteen forty, monsieur. My master, the Comte de Beaumont, went to England to fight the Boche."

"Really?" Schellenberg said dryly. "So, let's get on with it. We'll go upstairs and work down."

The old man led them up the staircase in front of them. There were innumerable bedrooms, some with four-posters, the furniture draped in sheets, two doors leading to separate wings so long disused that the dust lay thick on the floor.

"Mother of God, is this the way the rich live?" Devlin asked as they went down. "Have you seen how far it is to the bathroom?"

Schellenberg noticed a door at one end of the landing above the entrance. "What's through there?"

"I'll show you, monsieur. Another way into the dining hall."

They found themselves in a long dark gallery above a massive room. The ceiling had arched oaken beams, below was a massive fireplace in a medieval pattern. In front of it was an enormous oak table surrounded by high-backed chairs. Battle standards hung above the fireplace.

They went down the stairs and Schellenberg said, "What are the flags?"

"Souvenirs of war, monsieur. The de Beaumonts have always served France well. See, in the center there, the standard in scarlet and gold. An ancestor of the count carried that at Waterloo."

"Is that a fact?" Devlin commented. "I always thought they lost that one."

Schellenberg looked around the hall, then led the way out through high oak doors back into the entrance hall.

"I have seen enough. What did Major Berger say to you?"

"That he would be back, monsieur." The old man shrugged. "One week, maybe two."

Schellenberg put a hand on his shoulder. "No one must know we have been here, my friend, especially Major Berger."

"Monsieur?" Dissard looked puzzled.

Schellenberg said, "This is a matter of the greatest secrecy and of considerable importance."

"I understand, monsieur."

"If the fact that we had been here came out, the source of the information would be obvious." He patted Dissard's shoulder with his gloved hand. "This would be bad for you."

The old man was thoroughly frightened. "Monsieur—please. Not a word. I swear it."

They went out to the *Kübelwagen* and drove away. Devlin said, "Walter, you can be a cold-blooded bastard when you want to be."

"Only when necessary." Schellenberg turned to Asa. "Can we get back to Berlin tonight?"

The light was already fading, dark clouds dropping toward the sea, and rain drifted in across the wet sands.

"Possible," Asa said. "If we're lucky. We might have to overnight at Chernay. Get off first thing in the morning."

Devlin said, "What a prospect." He pulled up the collar of his overcoat and lit a cigarette. "The glamour of war."

On the following afternoon Devlin was delivered to the UFA film studios for his appointment with the chief makeup artist. Karl Schneider was in his late forties, a tall, broad-shouldered man who looked more like a dock worker than anything else.

He examined a passport-type photo which

Devlin had had taken. "You say this is what they've got on the other side?"

"Something like that."

"It's not much, not for a policeman looking for a face in the crowd. When would you be going?"

Devlin made the decision then for himself, for Schellenberg, for all of them. "Let's say two or three days from now."

"And how long would you be away?"

"Ten days at the most. Can you do anything?"

"Oh, yes." Schneider nodded. "One can change the shape of the face by wearing cheek pads in the mouth and all that sort of thing, but I don't think it's necessary for you. You don't carry a lot of weight, my friend, not much flesh on your bones."

"All down to bad living," Devlin said.

Schneider ignored the joke. "Your hair— dark and wavy and you wear it long. I think the key is what I do to the hair. What role do you intend to play?"

"A priest. Ex-army chaplain. Invalided out."

"Yes, the hair." Schneider draped a sheet around his shoulders and reached for a pair of scissors.

By the time he was finished, Devlin's hair was cropped close to the skull.

"Jesus, is that me?"

"That's only a start. Let's have you over the basin." Schneider washed the hair then rubbed some chemical in. "I've worked with the best actors. Marlene Dietrich before she cleared out. Now she had marvelous hair. Oh, and there was Conrad Veidt. What a wonderful actor. Chased out by these Nazi bastards, and he ends up, so I'm told, playing Nazi bastards in Hollywood."

"A strange old life," Devlin said. He kept his eyes closed and let him get on with it.

He hardly recognized the face that stared out at him. The close-cropped hair was quite gray now, accentuating the cheekbones, putting ten or twelve years on his age.

"That's bloody marvelous."

"One more touch." Schneider rummaged in his makeup case, took out several pairs of spectacles and examined them. "Yes, these, I think. Clear glass, naturally." He placed a pair of steel-rimmed glasses on Devlin's nose and adjusted them. "Yes, excellent. I'm pleased with myself."

"God help me, but I look like Himmler," Devlin said. "Will it last? The hair, I mean."

"A fortnight, and you said you'd be away

ten days at the most." Schneider produced a small plastic bottle. "A rinse with this would keep things going, but not for long."

"No," Devlin told him. "I said ten days and I meant it. It's all one in the end anyway. Any longer and I'll be dead."

"Astonishing!" Schellenberg said.

"I'm glad you think so," Devlin told him. "So let's have the right photos taken. I want to get on with it."

"And what does that mean?"

"I want to go as soon as possible. Tomorrow or the day after."

Schellenberg looked at him gravely. "You're sure about this?"

"There's nothing else to hang about for now that your friend at UFA has given me a new face. We have the setup at Chernay, Asa and the Lysander. That leaves us with three uncertainties. My IRA friend Michael Ryan, the Shaws and the priory."

"True," Schellenberg said. "No matter what the situation at the priory, if your friend Ryan is not available you would be presented with real difficulty. The same with the Shaws."

Devlin said, "Without the Shaws it would

be an impossibility, so the sooner I get there the sooner we know."

"Right," Schellenberg said briskly, and rang for Ilse Huber, who came in. "Papers for Mr. Devlin from the forgery department."

"They'll need photos of the new me," Devlin told her.

"But, Mr. Devlin, the British identity card is what you need. A ration book for certain items of food, clothing coupons, driving license. None of these require a photo."

"That's a pity," Devlin told her. "If you're being checked out by someone, the fact that they can compare you with a photo is so satisfying that you're on your way before you know it."

"Have you decided on your name and circumstances yet?" Schellenberg asked.

"As I've often said, the best kind of lie is the one that sticks closest to the truth," Devlin said. "No sense in trying to sound completely English. Even the great Devlin wouldn't get away with that. So I'm an Ulsterman." He turned to Ilse. "Are you getting this?"

"Every word."

"Conlon. Now there's a name I've always liked. My first girlfriend was a Conlon. And my old uncle, the priest in Belfast I lived with as a boy. He was a Henry, though everyone called him Harry."

"Father Harry Conlon then?" she said.

"Yes, but more than that. Major Harry Conlon, army chaplain, on extended leave after being wounded."

"Where?" Schellenberg asked.

"In my head." Devlin tapped the bullet scar. "Oh, I see what you mean. Geographically speaking."

"How about the Allied invasion of Sicily this year?" Schellenberg suggested.

"Excellent. I got clipped in an air strike on the first day. That way I don't need too much information about the place if anyone asks me."

"I've seen a cross-reference with British army chaplains in the military documentation file," Ilse said. "I remember because it struck me as being unusual. May I go and check on it, General? It would only take a few minutes."

Schellenberg nodded. She went out and he said, "I'll make the arrangements for your flight to Ireland. I've already done some checking with the Luftwaffe. They suggest you take off from the Laville base outside Brest."

"Talk about déjà vu," Devlin said. "That's where I left from before. It wouldn't happen to be a Dornier bomber they suggest, the good old Flying Pencil?"

"Exactly."

"Ah, well, it worked last time, I suppose."

Ilse came in at that moment. "I was right. Look what I found."

The pass was in the name of a Major George Harvey, army chaplain, and there was a photo. It had been issued by the War Office and authorized unrestricted access to both military bases and hospitals.

"Astonishing how powerful the need for spiritual comfort is," Schellenberg said. "Where did this come from?"

"Documents taken from a prisoner of war, General. I'm certain that forging will have no difficulty copying it, and it would give Mr. Devlin the photo he wanted."

"Brilliant," Devlin said. "You're a marvel of a woman."

"You'll need to see the clothing department as well," she said. "Will you want a uniform?"

"It's a thought. I mean, it could come in useful. Otherwise a dark suit, clerical collar, dark hat, raincoat, and they can give me a Military Cross. If I'm a priest, I might as well be a gallant one. Always impressive. And I'll want a travel voucher from Belfast to London. The kind the military use, just in case I do want to play the major."

"I'll get things started."

She went out and Schellenberg said, "What else?"

"Cash. Five thousand quid, I'd say. That's to take care of my having to hand a few bribes out as well as supporting myself. If you find one of those canvas military hold-alls officers carry these days, the money could go in a false bottom of some sort."

"I'm sure there'll be no problem."

"Fivers, Walter, and the real thing. None of the false stuff I happen to know the SS has been printing."

"You have my word on it. You'll need a code name."

"We'll stick with Shaw's. Falcon will do fine. Give me the right details for contacting your radio people at this end and I'll be in touch before you know it."

"Excellent. The Führer's conference at Belle-Île is on the twenty-first. We could be cutting it fine."

"We'll manage." Devlin stood up. "I think I'll try the canteen." He turned at the door. "Oh, just one thing."

"What's that?"

"When I was dropped by parachute into Ireland in forty-one for the Abwehr, I had ten thousand pounds in a suitcase, funds for the IRA. When I opened it I found neat bundles of fivers, each one with a Bank of Berlin band around it. Do you think they could do better this time?"

Schellenberg said, "And they wonder why we're losing the war."

Asa was in the canteen drinking a beer and reading a copy of *Signal*, the magazine for German forces, when Devlin came in. The Irishman got a coffee and joined him.

"I can't believe it," Asa said. "I hardly recognized you."

"The new me, Father Harry Conlon, very much at your service. Also Major Harry Conlon, army chaplain, and I'm on my way tomorrow night."

"Isn't that pushing it?"

"Jesus, son, I want to get on with it."

"Where are you flying from?"

"Laville, near Brest."

"And the plane?"

"Dornier two-fifteen."

"Okay, I'll fly you myself."

"No you won't. You're too valuable. Say

you got me to Ireland and dropped me off, then got shot down by a British night fighter off the French coast on your way back. A right old balls-up that would be."

"Okay," Asa said reluctantly. "But at least I can fly you down to Laville. Nobody can object to that."

"Always nicer to have a friend see you off," Devlin said.

It was just after nine the following night, rain pounding in from the Atlantic, when Asa stood in the control tower at Laville and watched the Dornier take off. He opened a window, listened to it fade into the night. He closed the window and said to the radio man, "Send this message."

Devlin, sitting at the back of the Dornier in a flying suit, his supply bag beside him, was approached by the wireless operator. "A message for you, sir. A bad joke on some-one's part."

"Read it."

"It just says, 'Break a leg.'"

Devlin laughed. "Well, son, you'd have to be an actor to understand that one."

The Dornier made good time, and it was shortly after two in the morning when Devlin jumped at five thousand feet. As on the last occasion, he had chosen County Monaghan, which was an area he knew well and adjacent to the Ulster border.

The necessity of a supply bag to the parachutist is that, dangling twenty feet below him on a cord, it hits the ground first, a useful precaution when landing in the dark. A crescent moon showed occasionally, which helped. Devlin made an excellent landing and within minutes had his suitcase and a trenching shovel out of the supply bag, a dark raincoat and trilby. He found a ditch, scraped a hole, put the supply bag, parachute, and flying suit in it, then tossed the shovel into a nearby pool.

He put on his raincoat and hat, opened the case and found the steel-rimmed spectacles which he carried in there for safety. Underneath the neatly folded uniform was a webbing belt and holster containing a Smith & Wesson .38 revolver, the type frequently issued to British officers. There was a box of fifty cartridges to go with it. Everything seemed in order. He put on the spectacles and stood up.

"Hail Mary full of grace, here am I, a sinner," he said softly. "Do what you can for me." And he crossed himself, picked up his suitcase and moved on.

The Ulster border, to anyone who knew it, was never a problem. He followed a network of country lanes and the occasional field path and by four-fifteen was safe in Ulster and standing on British soil.

And then he had an incredible piece of luck. A farm truck passed him, stopped, and the driver, a man in his sixties, looked out. "Jesus, Father, and where would you be walking to at this time of the morning?"

"Armagh," Devlin said. "To catch the milk train to Belfast."

"Now isn't that the strange thing and me going all the way to Belfast market."

"God bless you, my son," Devlin said and climbed in beside him.

"Nothing to it, Father," the farmer told him as he drove away. "After all, if a priest can't get a helping hand in Ireland where would he get one?"

It was later that morning at ten o'clock when Schellenberg knocked on the Reichsführer's door and went in.

"Yes?" Himmler said. "What is it?"

"I've had confirmation from Laville, Reichsführer, that Devlin jumped into Southern Ireland at approximately two A.M."

191

"Really?" Himmler said. "You've moved fast, Brigadeführer. My congratulations."

"Of course none of this guarantees success, Reichsführer. We have to take even Devlin's safe landing on faith, and the whole business when he gets to London is very open-ended."

"There's been a change in our plans," Himmler said. "The Führer's conference at Belle-Île will now take place on the fifteenth."

"But, Reichsführer, that only gives us a week."

"Yes, well we're in the Führer's hands. It is not for us to query his decisions. Still, I know you'll do your best. Carry on, General."

Schellenberg went out, closing the door, feeling totally bewildered. "For God's sake, what's the bastard playing at?" he said softly and went back to his office.

8

In Belfast, Devlin found it impossible to get a ticket for the crossing to Heysham in Lancashire. There was a waiting list, and the situation was no better on the Glasgow route.

Which left Larne, north of Belfast to Stranraer, the way he had got across the water for Operation Eagle. It was a short run, with a special boat train all the way to London, but this time he wasn't going to take any chances. He caught the local train from Belfast to Larne, went into a public toilet on the docks and locked himself in. When he came out fifteen minutes later, he was in uniform.

It paid off immediately. The boat was full, but not to military personnel. He produced the travel voucher they had given him in Berlin. The booking clerk hardly looked at it, took in the major's uniform, the ribbon for the Military Cross and the clergyman's dog collar and booked him on board immediately.

It was the same at Stranraer, where in spite of the incredible number of people being carried by the train, he was allocated a seat in a first-class carriage. Stranraer to Glasgow, Glasgow down to Birmingham and then to London, arriving at King's Cross at three o'clock the following morning. When he walked from the train, one face among the crowd, the first thing he heard was an air-raid siren.

The beginning of 1944 became known to

Londoners as the Little Blitz as the Luft-waffe, the performance of its planes greatly improved, turned attention to night raids on London again. The siren Devlin heard her-alded the approach of Ju-88 pathfinders from Chartres in France. The heavy bombers came later, but by then he was, like thou-sands of others, far below ground, sitting out a hard night in the comparative safety of a London tube station.

Mary Ryan was a girl that people remarked on, not because she was particularly beauti-ful but because there was a strange, almost ethereal look to her. The truth was her health had never been good, and the pressures of wartime didn't help. Her face was always pale, with dark smudges beneath her eyes, and she had a heavy limp which had been a fact of life for her since birth. She was only nineteen and looked old beyond her years.

Her father, an IRA activist, had died of a heart attack in Mountjoy Prison in Dublin just before the war, her mother of cancer in 1940, leaving her with only one relative, her Uncle Michael, her father's younger brother who had lived in London for years, on his own since the death of his wife in 1938. She had moved from Dublin to London and now kept house for him and worked as an assistant in a large grocery store in Wapping High Street.

No more though, for when she reported for work at eight o'clock that morning, the shop and sizable section of the street was reduced to a pile of smoking rubble. She stayed, watching the ambulances, the firemen dousing things down, the men of the heavy rescue unit sifting through the foundations for those who might still be alive.

After doing what she could to help, she turned and walked away, a strange figure in her black beret and old raincoat, limping rapidly along the pavement. She stopped at a back street shop, purchased milk and a loaf of bread, some cigarettes for her uncle, then went out again. It started to rain as she turned into Cable Wharfe.

There had originally been twenty houses backing onto the river. Fifteen had been demolished by a bomb during the Blitz. Four more were boarded up. She and her uncle lived in the end one. The kitchen door was at the side, opening onto an iron terrace, the waters of the Thames below. She paused at the rail, looking down toward Tower Bridge and the Tower of London in the near distance. She loved the river, never tired of it. The large ships from the London docks passing to and fro, the constant barge traffic. There was a wooden stairway at the end of the terrace dropping down to a small private jetty. Her uncle kept two boats moored there. A rowing skiff and a larger craft, a small motorboat with a cabin. As she looked over, she saw a man smoking a cigarette and sheltering from the rain. He wore a black hat and raincoat, and a suitcase was on the jetty beside him.

"Who are you?" she called sharply. "It's private property down there."

"Good day to you *a colleen*," he called cheerfully and lifted the case and came up the stairs.

"What do you want?" she said.

Devlin smiled. "It's Michael Ryan I'm after. Would you be knowing him? I tried the door, but there was no answer."

"I'm his niece, Mary," she said. "Uncle Michael's not due home just yet. He was on a night shift."

"A night shift?" Devlin asked.

"Yes, on the cabs. Ten till ten. Twelve hours."

"I see." He glanced at his watch. "Another hour and a half then."

She was slightly uncertain, unwilling to

ask him in, he sensed that. Instead she said, "I don't think I've seen you before."

"Not surprising and me only just over from Ireland."

"You know Uncle Michael then?"

"Oh, yes, old friends from way back. Conlon's my name. Father Harry Conlon," he added, opening the top of his dark raincoat so that she could see the dog collar.

She relaxed at once. "Would you like to come in and wait, Father?"

"I don't think so. I'll take a little walk and come back later. Could I leave my suitcase?"

"Of course."

She unlocked the kitchen door, he followed her in and put the case down. "Would you know St. Mary's Priory, by any chance?"

"Oh, yes," she said. "You go along Wapping High Street to Wapping Wall. It's near St. James's Stairs on the river. About a mile."

He stepped back outside. "The grand view you have here. There's a book by Dickens that starts with a girl and her father in a boat on the Thames searching for the bodies of the drowned and what was in their pockets."

"Our Mutual Friend," she told him. "The girl's name was Lizzie."

"By God, girl, and aren't you the well-read one."

She warmed to him for that. "Books are everything."

"And isn't that the fact?" He touched his hat. "I'll be back."

He walked away along the terrace, his footsteps echoing on the boards, and she closed the door.

From Wapping High Street the damage done to the London docks in the Blitz was plain to see, and yet the amazing thing was how busy they were, ships everywhere.

"I wonder what old Adolf would make of this," Devlin said softly. "Give him a nasty surprise, I shouldn't wonder."

He found St. Mary's Priory with no trouble. It stood on the other side of the main road from the river, high walls in gray stone, darkened even more by the filth of the city over the years. The roof of the chapel was clear to see on the other side, a bell tower rising above it. Interestingly enough, the great oak door that was the entrance stood open.

The notice board beside it said, *St. Mary's*

Priory, Little Sisters of Pity, Mother Superior: Sister Maria Palmer. Devlin leaned against the wall and lit a cigarette and watched. After a while a porter in a blue uniform appeared. He stood on the top step looking up and down the road, then went back in.

Below, there was a narrow band of shingle and mud between the river and the retaining wall. Some little distance away were steps down from the wall. Devlin descended casually and strolled along the strip of shingle, remembering the architect's drawings and the old drainage tunnel. The shingle ran out, water lapped in against the wall, and then he saw it, an arched entrance almost completely flooded, a couple of feet of headroom only.

He went back up to the road and on the next corner from the priory found a public house called The Bargee. He went into the saloon bar. There was a young woman in headscarf and slacks mopping the floor. She looked up, surprise on her face.

"Yes, what do you want? We don't open till eleven."

Devlin had unbuttoned his raincoat and she saw the dog collar. "I'm sorry to bother you. Conlon—Father Conlon."

There was a chain around her neck, and

he saw the crucifix. Her attitude changed at once. "What can I do for you, Father?"

"I knew I was going to be in the neighborhood, and a colleague asked me to look up a friend of his. Father Confessor at St. Mary's Priory. Stupid of me, but I've forgotten his name."

"That would be Father Frank." She smiled. "Well, that's what we call him. Father Frank Martin. He's priest in charge at St. Patrick's down the road, and he handles the priory as well. God alone knows how he manages at his age. Has no help at all, but then there's a war on I suppose."

"St. Patrick's you say? God bless you," Devlin told her and went out.

There was nothing very remarkable about the church. It was late Victorian in architecture like most Catholic churches in England, built after changes in English law had legitimized that branch of the Christian religion.

It had the usual smells, candles, incense, religious images, the Stations of the Cross, things which, in spite of his Jesuit education, had never meant very much to Devlin. He sat down in a pew, and after a while Father Martin came out of the sacristy and genuflected at the altar. The old man stayed on his knees praying, and Devlin got up and left quietly.

Michael Ryan was a little over six feet and carried himself well for his sixty years. Sitting at the kitchen table, he wore a black leather jacket and white scarf, a tweed cap beside him. He was drinking tea from a large mug Mary had given him.

"Conlon, you say?" He shook his head. "I never had a friend called Conlon. Come to think of it, I never had a friend who was a priest."

There was a knock at the kitchen door. Mary went and opened it. Devlin stood there in the rain. "God bless all here," he said and stepped inside.

Ryan stared at him, frowning, and then an expression of bewilderment appeared on his face. "Dear God in heaven. It can't be— Liam Devlin. It is you?"

He stood up, and Devlin put his hands on his shoulders. "The years have been kind to you, Michael."

"But you, Liam, what have they done to you?"

"Oh, don't believe everything you see. I needed a change in appearance. A few years added on." He took his hat off and ran his fingers through the gray stubble. "The hair owes more to the chemical industry at the moment than it does to nature."

"Come in, man, come in." Ryan shut the door. "Are you on the run or what?"

"Something like that. It needs explaining."

Ryan said, "This is my niece, Mary. Remember my elder brother, Seamus? He that died in Mountjoy Prison."

"A good man on the worst of days," Devlin said.

"Mary, this is my old friend Liam Devlin."

The effect on the girl was quite extraordinary. It was as if a light had been turned on inside. There was a look on her face that was almost holy. "You are Liam Devlin? Sweet Mother of Jesus, I've heard of you ever since I was a little girl."

"Nothing bad, I hope," Devlin said.

"Sit down, please. Will you have some tea? Have you had your breakfast?"

"Come to think of it, I haven't."

"I've got some eggs and there's a little of Uncle Michael's black market bacon left. You can share it."

While she busied herself at the stove, Devlin took off his coat and sat opposite Ryan. "Have you a telephone here?"

"Yes. In the hall."

"Good. I need to make a call later."

"What is it, Liam? Has the IRA decided to start up again in London?"

"I'm not from the IRA this time," Devlin told him. "Not directly. To be frank, I'm from Berlin."

Ryan said, "I'd heard the organization had had dealings with the Germans, but to what purpose, Liam? Are you telling me you actually approve of that lot?"

"Nazi bastards most of them," Devlin said. "Not all, mind you. Their aim is to win the war, mine is a united Ireland. I've had the odd dealing with them, always for money, money paid into a Swiss account on behalf of the organization."

"And you're here for them now? Why?"

"British intelligence have a man under guard not far from here at St. Mary's Priory. A Colonel Steiner. As it happens, he's a good man and no Nazi. You'll have to take my word for that. It also happens that the Germans want him back. That's why I'm here."

"To break him out?" Ryan shook his head. "There was never anyone else like you. A raving bloody lunatic."

"I'll try not to involve you too much, but I do need a little help. Nothing too strenuous, I promise. I could ask you to do it for old times' sake, but I won't." Devlin picked up the case, put it on the table and opened it. He pushed the clothes out of the way, ran a finger around the bottom and pulled out the lining, revealing the money he had carried in there. He took out a bundle of five-pound notes and laid them on the table. "A thousand pounds, Michael."

Ryan ran his fingers through his hair. "My God, Liam, what can I say?"

The girl put plates of egg and bacon in front of each of them. "You should be ashamed to take a penny piece after the stories you've told me about Mr. Devlin. You should be happy to do it for nothing."

"Oh, what it is to be young." Devlin put an arm around her waist. "If only life were like that, but hang on to your dreams, girl." He turned to Ryan. "Well, Michael?"

"Christ, Liam, you only live once, but to show I'm a weak man, I'll take the thousand quid."

"First things first. Do you happen to have a gun about the place?"

"A Luger pistol from before the war under the floorboards in my bedroom. Must have been there five years, and the ammunition to go with it."

"I'll check it over. Is it convenient for me to stay here? It won't be for long."

"Fine. We've plenty of room."

"Transport. I saw your black cab outside. Is that it?"

"No, I have a Ford van in the shed. I only use it now and then. It's the petrol situation, you see."

"That's fine. I'll use your phone now if I may."

"Help yourself."

Devlin closed the door and stood alone at the telephone. He rang directory inquiries and asked for the telephone number for Shaw Place. There was a delay of two or three minutes only and then the girl gave him the number and he wrote it down. He sat on a chair beside the phone, thinking about it for a while, then picked it up, dialed the operator and gave her the number.

After a while the phone was picked up at the other end and a woman's voice said, "Charbury three-one-four."

"Would Sir Maxwell Shaw be at home?"

"No, he isn't. Who is this?"

Devlin decided to take a chance. Remembering from the file that she had reverted to using her maiden name years ago, he said, "Would that be Miss Lavinia Shaw?"

"Yes it is. Who are you?"

Devlin said, "Does the Falcon still wait? It is now time to strike."

The effect was immediate and dramatic. "Oh, my God!" Lavinia Shaw said, and then there was silence.

Devlin waited for a moment, then said, "Are you there, Miss Shaw?"

"Yes, I'm here."

"I must see you and your brother as soon as possible. It's urgent."

She said, "My brother's in London. He had to see his solicitor. He's staying at the Army and Navy Club. He told me he'd have lunch there and catch the train back this afternoon."

"Excellent. Get in touch with him and tell him to expect me. Let's say two o'clock. Conlon—Major Harry Conlon."

There was a pause. She said, "Is it coming?"

"Is what coming, Miss Shaw?"

"You know—the invasion."

He stifled a strong desire to laugh. "We'll speak again I'm sure after I've seen your brother."

He went back to the kitchen, where Ryan

still sat at the table. The girl, washing dishes at the sink, said, "Is everything all right?"

"Fine," he said. "Every journey needs a first step." He picked up his case. "If you could show me my room. I need to change."

She took him upstairs, led him into a back bedroom overlooking the river. Devlin unpacked his case, laid the uniform out on the bed. The Smith & Wesson he slipped under the mattress with the webbing belt and holster together with an ankle holster in leather which he also took from the case. He found the bathroom at the end of the corridor, had a quick shave and brushed his hair, then returned to the bedroom and changed.

He went downstairs fifteen minutes later resplendent in his uniform. "Jesus, Liam, I never thought I'd see the day," Ryan said.

"You know the old saying, Michael," Devlin told him. "When you're a fox with a pack on your tail you stand a better chance if you look like a hound." He turned to Mary and smiled. "And now, girl dear, another cup of tea would go down just fine."

It was at that moment that the poor girl fell totally in love with him, what the French call a *coup de foudre*, a thunderclap. She felt herself blush and turned to the cooker. "Of course, Mr. Devlin. I'll make some fresh."

To its members, the Army and Navy Club was simply known as the Rag. A great gloomy palazzo of a place in Venetian style and situated on Pall Mall. Its governing committee had been renowned since Victorian times for its leniency toward members disgraced or in trouble, and Sir Maxwell Shaw was a case in point. No one had seen the slightest necessity to blackball him over the business of his detention under Regulation 18B. He was, after all, an officer and a gentleman who had been both wounded and decorated for gallantry in the service of his country.

He sat in a corner of the morning room drinking the Scotch the waiter had brought in and thinking about Lavinia's astonishing telephone call. Quite unbelievable that now, after so long, the summons should come. My God, but he was excited. Hadn't felt such a charge in years.

He called for another Scotch, and at the same moment a porter approached him. "Your guest is here, Sir Maxwell."

"My guest?"

"Major Conlon. Shall I show him in?"

"Yes. Of course. At once, man."

Shaw got to his feet, straightening his tie

208

as the porter returned with Devlin, who held out his hand and said cheerfully, "Harry Conlon. Nice to meet you, Sir Maxwell."

Shaw was dumbfounded, not so much by the uniform, but by the dog collar. He shook hands as the waiter brought his glass of Scotch. "Would you like one of these, Major?"

"No, thanks." The waiter departed and Devlin sat down and lit a cigarette. "You look a little shaken, Sir Maxwell."

"Well goodness, man, of course I am. I mean, what is all this about? Who are you?"

"Does the Falcon still wait?" Devlin asked. "Because it is now time to strike."

"Yes, but—"

"No buts, Sir Maxwell. You made a pledge a long time ago when Werner Keitel recruited you and your sister to, shall we say, the cause? Are you in or are you out? Where do you stand?"

"You mean you've got work for me?"

"There's a job to be done."

"The invasion is finally coming?"

"Not yet," Devlin said smoothly, "but soon. Are you with us?"

He'd been prepared to bring pressure to bear, but in the event, it was unnecessary.

Shaw gulped down the whisky. "Of course I am. What do you require of me?"

"Let's take a little walk," Devlin said. "The park across the road will do fine."

It had started to rain, bouncing from the windows. For a moment, there wasn't a porter in the cloakroom. Shaw found his bowler hat, raincoat and umbrella. Among the jumble of coats there was a military trench coat. Devlin picked it up, followed him outside and put it on.

They went across to St. James's Park and walked along the side of the lake toward Buckingham Palace, Shaw with his umbrella up. After a while they moved into the shelter of some trees and Devlin lit a cigarette.

"You want one of these things?"

"Not at the moment. What is it you want me to do?"

"Before the war your sister used to fly a Tiger Moth. Does she still have it?"

"The RAF took it for training purposes in the winter of thirty-nine."

"She used a barn as a hangar. Is that still there?"

"Yes."

"And the place she used to land and take off. The South Meadow, I think you called it. It's not been plowed up for the war effort or anything?"

"No, all the land around Shaw Place, the land that used to be ours, is used for sheep grazing."

"And South Meadow is still yours?"

"Of course. Is that important?"

"You could say so. A plane from France will be dropping in, and in the not too distant future."

Shaw's face became extremely animated. "Really? What for?"

"To pick up me and another man. The less you know the better, but he's important. Does any of this give you a problem?"

"Good heavens, no. Glad to help, old man." Shaw frowned slightly. "You're not German, I take it?"

"Irish," Devlin told him. "But we're on the same side. You were given a radio by Werner Keitel. Do you still have it?"

"Ah, well there you have me, old man. I'm afraid we don't. You see back in forty-one the government brought in this stupid regulation. I was in prison for a few months."

"I know about that."

"My sister, Lavinia, you know what women are like. She panicked. Thought the

211

police might arrive and turn the house upside down. There's a lot of marsh around our place, some of it bottomless. She threw the radio in, you see." He looked anxious. "Is this a problem, old man?"

"Of a temporary nature only. You're going back home today?"

"That's right."

"Good. I'll be in touch. Tomorrow or the next day." Devlin ground out his cigarette. "Jesus, the rain. That's London for you. Never changes." And he walked away.

When he turned along the terrace at the side of the house at Cable Wharfe, the rain was drifting across the river. There was an awning stretching from the cable of the motorboat over the cockpit. Mary Ryan sat under it, safe from the rain, reading a book.

"Are you enjoying yourself down there?" Devlin called.

"I am. Uncle Michael's in the kitchen. Can I get you anything?"

"No, I'm fine at the moment."

When Devlin went in, Ryan was sitting at the table. He'd covered it with newspaper and was stripping a Luger pistol, oil on his fingers. "God help me, Liam, I've forgotten how to do this."

"Give me a minute to change and I'll handle it," Devlin told him.

He was back in five minutes wearing dark slacks and a black polo-neck sweater. He reached for the Luger parts and got to work oiling them, then put the whole weapon together expertly.

"Did it go well?" Ryan asked.

"If meeting a raving lunatic could ever go well, then yes," Devlin told him. "Michael, I'm dealing with an English aristocrat so totally out of his skull that he's still eagerly awaiting a German invasion, and that's when he's sober."

He told Ryan about Shaw Place, Shaw and his sister. When he was finished, Ryan said, "They sound mad, the both of them."

"Yes, but the trouble is I need a radio and they haven't got one."

"So what are you going to do?"

"I was thinking about the old days when I came over to handle that active service unit. They got weapons and even explosives from underworld sources. Am I right?"

Ryan nodded. "That's true."

"And you, Michael, as I recall, were the man with the contacts."

"That was a long time ago."

"Come off it, Michael. There's a war on,

black market in everything from petrol to cigarettes. Just the same in Berlin. Don't tell me you aren't in it up to your neck, and you a London cabbie."

"All right." Ryan put up a hand defensively. "You want a radio, but the kind you want would have to be army equipment."

"That's right."

"It's no good going to some back-street trader."

There was a silence between them. Devlin broke the Luger down and wiped each piece carefully with a rag. "Then who would I go to?"

Ryan said, "There's a fella called Carver— Jack Carver. Has a brother called Eric."

"What are they, black marketeers?"

"Much more than that. Jack Carver's probably the most powerful gangster in London these days. Anything, but anything, that goes down, Carver gets a piece. Not just black market. Girls, gambling, protection. You name it."

"I used to know a fella in Dublin in the same line of work," Devlin said. "He wasn't so bad."

"Jack Carver's the original bastard, and young Eric's a toad. Every girl on the pavement is terrified of him."

"Do you tell me?" Devlin said. "I'm surprised nobody's stepped in here before now."

"It wasn't New York gangsters who invented cementing dead bodies into new roadways," Ryan said. "Jack Carver patented that idea. He's the one who supplied that active service unit with their guns and explosives back in thirty-six. If he had a grandmother he'd sell her to the Germans if he thought there was money in it."

"I'm frightened to death," Devlin said. "Well, Carver is the kind of man who can lay his hands on anything, so if I want a radio . . ."

"Exactly."

"Fine. Where do I find him?"

"There's a dance hall a couple of miles from here in Limehouse. It's called the Astoria Ballroom. Carver owns it. Has a big apartment upstairs. He likes that. Convenient for his brother to pick up the girls."

"And himself, I suppose?"

"You'd suppose wrong, Liam. Girls don't interest him in the slightest."

Devlin nodded. "I take your drift."

His hands moved suddenly with incredible dexterity, putting the Luger together again. He was finished in seconds and rammed a magazine up the butt.

"Jesus, you look like death himself when you do that," Ryan said.

"It's just a knack, Michael." Devlin wrapped up the oily newspapers and put them in the bin under the sink. "And now I think we'll take a little walk down by the river. I'd like your opinion on something."

He went down the stairway to the boat and found Mary still reading. The rain dripped from the edge of the awning, and there was a slight mist on the river. Devlin was wearing the military trench coat he'd stolen from the Army and Navy Club. He leaned against the rail, hands in his pockets.

"What are you reading?"

She held the book up. *"Our Mutual Friend."*

"I've started something."

She stood up. "We're going to have fog in the next few days. A real pea-souper."

"How can you tell that?"

"I'm not sure, but I'm always right. It's the smell I recognize first."

"And do you like that?"

"Oh, yes. You're alone, enclosed in your own private world."

"And isn't that what we're all looking

216

for?" He took her arm. "Your Uncle Michael and I are taking a little walk in the rain by the river. Why don't you come with us? That's if you've got nothing better to do."

They drove to St. Mary's Priory in Ryan's cab. He parked at the side of the road, and they sat looking at the entrance. There was a Morris saloon car parked outside painted olive green. It said *Military Police* on the side. As they watched, Lieutenant Benson and a corporal came out of the entrance, got in the car and drove off.

"You're not going to get far through the front door," Ryan said.

"More ways of skinning a cat than one," Devlin said. "Let's take that little walk."

The strip of shingle he'd walked along earlier seemed wider, and when he stopped to indicate the archway there was more headroom. "It was almost under the surface this morning," he said.

"The Thames is a tidal river, Liam, and the tide's going out. There'll be times when that thing's under the water entirely. Is it important?"

"Runs close to the foundations of the priory. According to the plans, there's a grille

217

into the crypt under the priory chapel. It could be a way in."

"You'd need to take a look then."

"Naturally, but not now. Later when it's nice and dark."

The rain increased to monsoonlike proportions, and Ryan said, "For Christ's sake, let's get in out of this," and he started back to the steps.

Devlin took Mary's arm. "Would you happen to have yourself a pretty frock tucked away somewhere, because if you do, I'll take you dancing this evening."

She paused, staring at him, and when she started walking again the limp seemed more pronounced. "I don't dance, Mr. Devlin. I can't."

"Oh, yes you can, my love. You can do anything in the whole wide world if you put your mind to it."

9

THE ASTORIA was a typical London dance hall of the period and very crowded. There was a band on each side of the room, one in blue tuxedos, the other in red. Devlin wore his dark clerical suit, but with a soft white shirt and black tie he'd borrowed from Ryan. He waited outside the cloakroom for Mary, who'd gone in to leave her coat. When she came out, he saw that she had on a neat cotton dress and brown stockings. She wore white plastic earrings, fashionable at the moment, and just a hint of lipstick.

"My compliments on the dress," he said. "A vast improvement."

"I don't get a chance to dress up very often," she told him.

"Well let's make the most of it."

He took her hand and pulled her onto the floor before she could protest. One of the bands was playing a slow foxtrot. He started to hum the tune. "You do that well," she said.

"Ah, well, I have a small gift for music. I play the piano badly. You, on the other hand, dance rather well."

"It's better out here in the middle of all these people. Nobody notices."

She was obviously referring to her limp. Devlin said, "Girl dear, nobody notices anyway."

She tightened her grip, putting her cheek against his shoulder, and they moved into the crowd, the glitter-ball revolving on the ceiling, its rays bathing everything with

219

blue lignt. The number came to an end and the other band broke into a fast, upbeat quickstep.

"Oh, no," she protested. "I can't manage this."

"All right," Devlin said. "Coffee it is then."

They went up the stairs to the balcony. "I'm just going to the cloakroom," she said.

"I'll get the coffee and see you back here."

She went around to the other side of the balcony, limping noticeably, passing two young men leaning on the rail. One of them wore a pinstriped double-breasted suit and hand-painted tie. The other was a few years older, in a leather jacket with the flattened nose of a prize fighter and scar tissue around the eyes.

"You fancy that, Mr. Carver?" he asked as they watched Mary go into the cloakroom.

"I certainly do, George," Eric Carver said. "I haven't had a cripple before."

Eric Carver was twenty-two years of age with thin wolfish features and long blond hair swept back from the forehead. A tendency to asthma attacks had kept him out of the army. At least that's what it said on the medical certificate his brother's doctor had provided. His father had been a drunken bully who'd died under the wheels of a cart in the Mile End Road. Jack, already a criminal of some renown and fifteen years his senior, had looked after Eric and their mother until cancer had carried her off just before the war. Her death had brought them even closer. There was nothing Eric couldn't do, no girl he couldn't have, because he was Jack Carver's brother and he never let anyone forget it.

Mary emerged from the cloakroom and limped past them, and Eric said, "I'll see you later, George."

George smiled, turned and walked away and Eric moved around the balcony to where Mary leaned over the rail watching the dancers. He slipped his arm around her waist and then ran one hand up to cup her left breast. "Now then darling and what's your name?"

"Please don't," she said and started to struggle.

"Oh, I like it," he said, his grip tightening.

Devlin arrived, a cup of coffee in each hand. He put them down on a nearby table. "Excuse me," he said.

As Eric turned, slackening his grip, Devlin stood on his right foot, bearing down with all his weight. The young man snarled, trying to pull away, and Devlin picked up one of the cups of coffee and poured it down Eric's shirtfront.

"Jesus, son, I'm sorry," he said.

Eric looked down at his shirt, total amazement on his face. "Why you little creep," he said and swung a punch.

Devlin blocked it easily and kicked him on the shin. "Now why don't you go and play nasty little boys elsewhere?"

There was rage on Eric's face. "You bastard. I'll get you for this. You see if I don't."

He hobbled away, and Devlin sat Mary down and gave her the other cup of coffee. She took a sip and looked up at him. "That was awful."

"A worm, girl dear, nothing to worry about. Will you be all right while I go and see this Carver fella? I shouldn't be long."

She smiled. "I'll be fine, Mr. Devlin." He turned and walked away.

The door at the other end of the balcony said *Manager's Office*, but when he opened it he found himself in a corridor. He went to the far end and opened another door into a carpeted landing. Stairs went down to what was obviously a back entrance, but the sound of

222

music drifted from above, so up he went to the next landing where a door stood open. It was only a small room with a desk and a chair on which the man George sat reading a newspaper while music sounded over the radio.

"Nice that." Devlin leaned on the doorway. "Carroll Gibbons from the Savoy. He plays the grand piano, that man."

George looked him over coldly. "And what do you want?"

"A moment of Jack Carver's valuable time."

"What's it about? Mr. Carver don't see just anybody."

Devlin took out a five-pound note and laid it on the table. "That's what it's about, my old son, that and another one hundred and ninety-nine like it."

George put the newspaper down and picked up the banknote. "All right. Wait here."

He brushed past Devlin and knocked on the other door, then went in. After a while he opened it and looked out. "All right, he'll see you."

Jack Carver sat behind a walnut Regency desk that looked genuine. He was a hard, dangerous-looking man, his face fleshy, the signs of decay setting in early. He wore an excellent suit in navy worsted tailored in Savile Row, a discreet tie. To judge by outward appearances, he could have been a prosperous businessman, but the jagged scar that ran from the corner of the left eye into the dark hairline and the look in the cold eyes belied that.

George stayed by the door, and Devlin glanced around the room, which was furnished in surprisingly good taste. "This is nice."

"All right, so what's it about?" Carver said, holding up the fiver.

"Aren't they beautiful, those things?" Devlin said. "A work of genuine art, the Bank of England five-pound note."

Carver said, "According to George, you said something about another hundred and ninety-nine. That came to a thousand quid when I went to school."

"Ah, you remembered, George," Devlin said.

At that moment, a door opened and Eric entered wearing a clean shirt and fastening his tie. He stopped dead, astonishment on his face that was quickly replaced by anger. "Here, that's him, Jack, the little squirt who spilled coffee down me."

"Oh, an accident surely," Devlin told him.

Eric started toward him, and Jack Carver snapped, "Leave it out, Eric, this is business." Eric stayed by the desk, rage in his eyes, and Carver said, "Now what would I have to do for a thousand quid? Kill somebody?"

"Come off it, Mr. Carver, we both know you'd do that for fun," Devlin said. "No, what I need is an item of military equipment. I hear you're a man who can get anything. At least that's what the IRA seem to think. I wonder what Special Branch at Scotland Yard might make of that tidbit."

Carver smoothed the fiver between his fingers and looked up, his face blank. "You're beginning to sound right out of order."

"Me and my big mouth. I'll never learn," Devlin said. "And all I wanted was to buy a radio."

"A radio?" For the first time Carver looked puzzled.

"Of the transmitting and receiving kind. There's a rather nice one the army uses these days. It's called a twenty-eight set, Mark Four. God knows why. Fits in a wooden box with a carrying handle. Just like a suitcase. Very handy." Devlin took a piece of paper

225

from his pocket and put it on the desk. "I've written the details down."

Carver looked at it. "Sounds a fancy piece of work to me. What would a man want a thing like that for?"

"Now that, Mr. Carver, is between me and my God. Can you handle it?"

"Jack Carver can handle anything. A thousand, you said?"

"But I must have it tomorrow."

Carver nodded. "All right, but I'll take half in advance."

"Fair enough."

Devlin had expected as much, had the money waiting in his pocket. He took it out and dropped it on the table. "There you go."

Carver scooped it up. "And it'll cost you another thousand. Tomorrow night, ten o'clock. Just down the road from here. Black Lion Dock. There's a warehouse with my name over the door. Be on time."

"Sure and you're a hard man to do business with," Devlin said. "But then we have to pay for what we want in this life."

"You can say that again," Carver said. "Now get out of here."

Devlin left, George closing the door behind him. Eric said, "He's mine, Jack. I want him."

"Leave it out, Eric. I've got this." Carver held up the five hundred pounds. "And I want the rest of it. Then he gets squeezed. I didn't like that IRA crack he made at all. Very naughty. Now get out of it. I want to make a phone call."

Mary was sitting quietly watching the dancers when Devlin joined her. "Did it go all right with Carver?" she asked.

"I'd rather shake hands with the devil. That little rat I chastised turned out to be his brother, Eric. Would you like to go now?"

"All right. I'll get my coat and see you in the foyer."

When they went out, it was raining. She took his arm and they walked down the wet pavements toward the main road. There was an alley to the right, and as they approached it, Eric Carver and George stepped out, blocking the way.

"Saw you leaving. Thought we'd say goodnight," Eric said.

"Mother of God!" Devlin put the girl to one side.

"Go on, George, do him up," Eric cried.

"A pleasure." George came in, enjoying himself.

Devlin simply stepped to the left and

kicked sideways at his kneecap. George screamed in agony, doubled over, and Devlin raised a knee into his face. "Didn't they teach you that one, George?"

Eric backed away in terror. Devlin took Mary's arm and walked past him. "Now where were we?"

Jack Carver said, "I told you to leave it out, Eric. You never learn."

"The bastard's half crippled George. Dislodged his kneecap. I had to take him to Dr. Aziz round the corner."

"Never mind George. I phoned Morrie Green. He knows more about surplus military equipment than any man in London."

"Does he have this radio the little bastard wanted?"

"No, but he can get one. No trouble. He'll drop it in tomorrow. The interesting thing is what he said about it. It's no ordinary radio. Sort of thing the army would use operating behind enemy lines."

Eric looked bewildered. "But what's it mean, Jack?"

"That there's a lot more to that little sod than meets the eye. I'm going to have some fun with him tomorrow night." Carver laughed harshly. "Now pour me a Scotch."

Devlin and Mary took the turning down to Harrow Street. "Shall I try and get a cab?" he asked.

"Oh, no, it's not much more than a mile and a half, and I like walking in the rain." She kept her hand lightly on his arm. "You're very quick, Mr. Devlin, you don't hesitate. Back there, I mean."

"Yes, well I never could see the point."

They walked in companionable silence for a while alongside the river toward Wapping. There was a heavy mist on the Thames, and a large cargo boat slipped past them, green and red navigation lights plain in spite of the blackout.

"I'd love to be like that boat," she said. "Going to sea, to faraway distant places, something different every day."

"Jesus, girl, you're only nineteen. It's all waiting for you out there, and this bloody war can't last forever."

They paused in the shelter of a wall while he lit a cigarette. She said, "I wish we had time to walk all the way down to the Embankment."

"Too far surely."

"I saw this film once. I think it was Fred Astaire. He walked along the Embankment with a girl and his chauffeur followed along behind in a Rolls-Royce."

"And you liked that?"

"It was very romantic."

"Ah, there's a woman for you."

They turned along Cable Wharfe and paused on the little terrace before going into the house.

"I've had a lovely time."

He laughed out loud. "You must be joking, girl."

"No, really. I like being with you."

She still held his arm and leaned against him. He put his other arm around her and they stayed there for a moment, rain glistening as it fell through the shaded light above the door. He felt a sudden dreadful sadness for everything there had never been in his life, remembering a girl in Norfolk just like Mary Ryan, a girl he had hurt very badly indeed.

He sighed and Mary looked up. "What is it?"

"Oh, nothing, I was just wondering where it had all gone. It's a touch of that three o'clock in the morning feeling when you feel past everything there ever was."

"Not you, surely. You've got years ahead of you."

"Mary, my love. You are nineteen and I am an old thirty-five who's seen it all and doesn't believe in much anymore. In a few days I'll be on my way, and a good thing." He gave her one small hug. "So let's get inside before I lose what few wits I have entirely."

Ryan, sitting on the other side of the table, said, "Jack Carver's bad news, Liam, always was. How can you be certain he'll play straight?"

"He couldn't if he wanted to," Devlin said, "but there's more to this. Much more. The radio I need, the twenty-eight set. It's an unusual piece of equipment, and the more Carver realizes that, the more he's going to want to know what's going on."

"So what are you going to do?"

"I'll think of something, but that can wait. What can't is an inspection of that drainage tunnel under the priory."

"I'll come with you," Ryan said. "We'll go in the motorboat. Only take fifteen minutes to get there."

"Would that be likely to cause attention?"

"No problem." Ryan shook his head. "The Thames is the busiest highway in London these days. Lots of craft work the river at night. Barges. Freighters."

Mary turned from the sink. "Can I come?"

Before Devlin could protest, Ryan said, "A good idea. You can mind the boat."

"But you stay on board," Devlin told her. "No funny business."

"Right, I'll go and change." She rushed out.

"Oh, to be young," Devlin said.

Ryan nodded. "She likes you, Liam."

"And I like her, Michael old friend, and that's where it will end. Now, what do we need?"

"The tide is low, but it's still going to be wet. I'll dig out some overalls and boots," Ryan told him and went out.

The small motorboat moved in toward the strand, its engine a muted throbbing. The prow carved its way into mud and sand, and Ryan cut the engine. "Right, Mary. Keep an eye on things. We shouldn't be long."

He and Devlin in their dark overalls and boots went over the side and faded into the darkness. Ryan carried a bag of tools and Devlin a large torch of the type used by workmen. There was three feet of water in the tunnel.

Ryan said, "So we'll have to wade."

As they moved into the water, the smell was pungent. Devlin said, "Christ, you can tell it's a sewer."

"So try not to fall down, and if you do, keep your mouth closed," Ryan said. "The terrible place for diseases, sewers."

Devlin led the way, the tunnel stretching ahead of them in the rays of the lamp. The brickwork was obviously very old, corroded and rotting. There was a sudden splash and two rats leapt from a ledge and swam away.

"Filthy creatures," Ryan said in disgust.

"It can't be far," Devlin said. "A hundred yards. Not much more surely."

Suddenly there it was, an iron grille perhaps four feet by three, just above the surface of the water. They looked through into the crypt, and Devlin played the light across the interior. There were a couple of tombs almost completely covered with water and stone steps in the far corner going up to a door.

"One thing's for sure," Ryan said. "The grille's done nothing to help their drainage system."

"It was put in nearly forty years ago," Devlin said. "Maybe it worked then."

Ryan got a crowbar from his bag of tools. Devlin held the bag for him while the other man pushed into the mortar in the brickwork beside the grille. He jumped back in alarm as the wall buckled and five or six bricks tumbled into the water. "The whole place is ready to come down. We can have this grille out in a fast ten minutes, Liam."

"No, not now. I need to know what the situation is upstairs. We've found out all we need for the moment, which is that the grille can be pulled out anytime we want. Now let's get out of here."

At the same moment in Romney Marsh, the wind from the sea rattled the French windows of the drawing room as Shaw closed the curtains. The furniture was no longer what it had been, the carpets were faded, but there was a log fire burning in the hearth, Nell lying in front of it. The door opened and Lavinia came in. She was wearing slacks and carried a tray. "I've made coffee, darling."

"Coffee!" he roared. "To hell with the coffee. I found a bottle of champagne in the cellar. Bollinger. That's what we need to-night."

He took it from a bucket on the table, opened it with a flourish and poured some into two glasses.

"This man Conlon," she said. "What did you say he was like?"

"I've told you about five times, old girl."

"Oh, Max, isn't it exciting? To you, my darling."

"And to you, old girl," he said and toasted her back.

In Berlin, it was very quiet in Schellenberg's office as he sat working through some papers in the light of a desk lamp. The door opened and Ilse looked in. "Coffee, General?"

"Are you still here? I thought you'd gone home."

"I'm going to spend the night in the emergency accommodation. Asa's stayed on too. He's in the canteen."

"We might as well join him." Schellenberg stood up and buttoned his tunic.

"Are you worried, General, about Devlin?"

"My dear Ilse. Liam Devlin is a man of infinite resource and guile. Given those attributes, you could say I've nothing to worry about." He opened the door and smiled. "Which is why I'm frightened to death instead."

From Steiner's window he could see across to the river. He peered through a chink in his blackout curtain and closed it again. "A large ship going downriver. Amazing how active things are out there even at night."

Father Martin, sitting by the small table, nodded. "As the song says, Old Father Thames just goes rolling along."

"During the day I sometimes sit at the window and watch for a couple of hours at a time."

"I understand, my son. It must be difficult for you." The priest sighed and got to his feet. "I must go. I have a Midnight Mass."

"Good heavens, Father, do you ever stop?"

"There's a war on, my son." Father Martin knocked on the door.

The MP on duty unlocked it and the old priest went along the corridor to the outer door. Lieutenant Benson was sitting at the desk in his room and glanced up. "Everything all right, Father?"

"As right as it will ever be," Martin said and passed through.

As he went down the stairway to the foyer, Sister Maria Palmer came out of her office. "Still here, Father? Don't you ever go home?"

"So much to do, Sister."

"You look tired."

"It's been a long war." He smiled. "Goodnight and God bless you."

The night porter came out of his cubbyhole, helped him on with his raincoat and gave him his umbrella, then unbolted the door. The old man paused, looking out at the rain, then put up his umbrella and walked away wearily.

Munro was still in his office, standing at a map table, charts of the English Channel and the Normandy approaches spread before him, when Carter limped in.

"The invasion, sir?"

"Yes, Jack. Normandy. They've made their decision. Let's hope the Führer still believes it will be the Pas de Calais."

"I understand his personal astrologer's convinced him of it," Carter said.

Munro laughed. "The ancient Egyptians

would only appoint generals who'd been born under the sign of Leo."

"I never knew that, sir."

"Yes, well you learn something new every day. No going home tonight, Jack. Eisenhower wants a blanket report on the strength of the French Resistance units in this general area and he wants it in the morning. We'll have to snatch a few hours here."

"Very well, sir."

"Was there anything else?"

"Vargas gave me a call."

"What did he want?"

"Another message from his cousin in Berlin. Could he send as much information as possible about St. Mary's Priory."

"All right, Jack, cook something up in the next couple of days, staying as close to the truth as possible, and pass it on to Vargas. We've got more important things to take care of at the moment."

"Fine, sir. I'll organize some tea and sandwiches."

"Do that, Jack. It's going to be a long night."

Carter went out and Munro returned to his maps.

10

THE FOLLOWING morning Father Martin knelt at the altar rail and prayed, eyes closed. He was tired, that was the trouble, had felt so tired for such a long time, and he prayed for strength to the God he had loved unfalteringly all his life and the ability to stand upright.

"I will bless the Lord who gives me counsel, who even at night directs my heart. I keep the Lord ever in my sight."

He had spoken the words aloud and faltered, unable to think of the rest. A strong voice said, *"Since He is at my right hand I shall stand firm."* Father Martin half turned and found Devlin standing there in uniform, the trench coat over one arm. "Major?" The old man tried to get off his knees, and Devlin put a hand under his elbow.

"Or Father. The uniform is only for the duration. Conlon—Harry Conlon."

"And I'm Frank Martin, pastor. Is there something I can do for you?"

"Nothing special. I'm on extended leave. I was wounded in Sicily," Devlin told him. "Spending a few days with friends not too far from here. I saw St. Pat's and thought I'd look in."

"Well then, let me offer you a cup of tea," the old man said.

Devlin sat in the small crowded sacristy while Martin boiled water in an electric kettle and made the tea.

"So you've been in it from the beginning?"

Devlin nodded. "Yes, November thirty-nine I got my call."

"I see they gave you an MC."

"The Sicilian landings, that was," Devlin told him.

"Was it bad?" Father Martin poured the tea and offered an open tin of condensed milk.

"Bad enough." The old man sipped his tea and Devlin lit a cigarette. "Just as bad for you, though. The Blitz, I mean. You're rather close to the London docks."

"Yes, it was hard." Martin nodded. "And it doesn't get any easier. I'm on my own here these days."

He suddenly looked very frail, and Devlin felt a pang of conscience, and yet he had to take this as far as it would go, he knew that. "I called in at the local pub, The Bargee I think it was called, for some cigarettes. I was talking to a girl there who mentioned you warmly."

"Ah, that would be Maggie Brown."

"Told me you were father confessor at the hospice near here. St. Mary's Priory?"

"That's right."

"Must give you a lot of extra work, Father."

"It does indeed, but it must be done. We all have to do our bit." The old man looked at his watch. "In fact, I'll have to be off there in a few minutes. Rounds to do."

"Do you have many patients there?"

"It varies. Fifteen, sometimes twenty. Many are terminal. Some are special problems. Servicemen who've had breakdowns. Pilots occasionally. You know how it is."

"I do indeed," Devlin said. "I was interested when I walked by earlier to see a couple of military policemen going in. It struck me as odd. I mean, military police in a hospice."

"Ah, well there's a reason for that. Occasionally they keep the odd German prisoner of war on the top floor. I don't know the background, but they're usually special cases."

"Oh, I see the reason for the MPs then. There's someone there now?"

"Yes, a Luftwaffe colonel. A nice man.

I've even managed to persuade him to come to Mass for the first time in years."

"Interesting."

"Well, I must make a move." The old man reached for his raincoat, and Devlin helped him on with it. As they went out into the church, he said, "I've been thinking, Father. Here's me with time on my hands and you carrying all this burden alone. Maybe I could give you a hand? Hear a few Confessions for you at least."

"Why, that's extraordinarily kind of you," Father Martin said.

Liam Devlin had seldom felt lower in his life, but he went on. "And I'd love to see something of your work at the priory."

"Then so you shall," the old man said and led the way down the steps.

The priory chapel was as cold as could be. They moved down to the altar and Devlin said, "It seems very damp. Is there a problem?"

"Yes, the crypt has been flooded for years. Sometimes quite badly. No money available to put it right."

Devlin could see the stout oak door banded with iron in the shadows in the far corner. "Is that the way in then?"

"Yes, but no one goes down there anymore."

"I once saw a church in France with the same trouble. Could I take a look?"

"If you like."

The door was bolted. He eased it back and ventured halfway down the steps. When he flicked on his lighter, he saw the dark water around the tombs and lapping at the grille. He retraced his steps and closed the door.

"Dear, yes, there's not much to be done for it," he called.

"Yes. Well, make sure you bolt it again," the old man called back. "We don't want anyone going down there. They could do themselves an injury."

Devlin rammed the bolt home, the solid sound echoing through the chapel, then quietly eased it back. Shrouded in shadows, the door was in the corner; it would be remarkable if anyone noticed. He rejoined Father Martin, and they moved up the aisle to the outer door. As they opened it, Sister Maria Palmer came out of her office.

"Ah, there you are," Father Martin said. "I looked in when we arrived, but you weren't there. I've been showing Father Conlon—" He laughed, correcting himself. "I'll start again. I've been showing Major

Conlon the chapel. He's going to accompany me on my rounds."

"Father suits me just fine." Devlin shook her hand. "A pleasure, Sister."

"Major Conlon was wounded in Sicily."

"I see. Have they given you a London posting?" she asked.

"No, I'm still on sick leave. In the neighborhood for a few days. Just passing through. I met Father Martin at his church."

"He's been kind enough to offer to help me out at the church. Hear a few Confessions and so on," Father Martin said.

"Good, you need a rest. We'll do the rounds together." As they started up the stairs, she said, "By the way, Lieutenant Benson's gone on a three-day pass. That young sergeant's in charge. What's his name? Morgan, isn't it?"

"The Welsh boy?" Father Martin said. "I called in on Steiner last night. Did you?"

"No, we had an emergency admission after you'd gone, Father. I didn't have time. I'll see him now though. I'm hoping the penicillin's finally cleared the last traces of his chest infection."

She went up the stairs in front of them briskly, skirts swirling, and Devlin and Father Martin followed.

They worked their way from room to room, staying to talk here and there to various patients, and it was half an hour before they reached the top floor. The MP on duty at the table outside the outer door jumped up and saluted automatically when he saw Devlin. The door was opened by another MP and they passed through.

The young sergeant sitting in Benson's room stood up and came out. "Sister—Father Martin."

"Good morning, Sergeant Morgan," Sister Maria Palmer said. "We'd like to see Colonel Steiner."

Morgan took in Devlin's uniform and the dog collar. "I see," he said uncertainly.

"Major Conlon's having a look round with us," she informed him.

Devlin took out his wallet and produced the fake War Office pass Schellenberg's people had provided, the one that guaranteed unlimited access. He passed it across.

"I think you'll find that takes care of it, Sergeant."

Morgan examined it. "I'll just get the details for the admittance sheet, sir." He did so and handed it back. "If you'd follow me."

He led the way along to the end of the corridor, nodded, and the MP on duty unlocked the door. Sister Maria Palmer led the way in followed by Father Martin, Devlin bringing up the rear. The door closed behind them.

Steiner, sitting by the window, stood up, and Sister Maria Palmer said, "And how are you today, Colonel?"

"Fine, Sister."

"I'm sorry I couldn't see you last night. I had an emergency, but Father Martin tells me he called in."

"As usual." Steiner nodded.

The old priest said, "This is Major Conlon, by the way. As you can see, an army chaplain. He's on sick leave. Like yourself, recently wounded."

Devlin smiled amiably and put out his hand. "A great pleasure, Colonel."

Kurt Steiner, making one of the most supreme efforts of his life, managed to keep his face straight. "Major Conlon." Devlin gripped the German's hand hard, and Steiner said, "Anywhere interesting? Where you picked up your wound, I mean."

"Sicily," Devlin said.

"A hard campaign."

"Ah, well, I wouldn't really know. I got mine the first day there." He walked to the window and looked out down to the road beside the Thames. "A fine view you've got here. You can see right down to those steps and that little beach, the boats passing. Something to look at."

"It helps pass the time."

"So, we must go now," Sister Maria Palmer said and knocked at the door.

Father Martin put a hand on Steiner's shoulder. "Don't forget I'll be in the chapel tonight at eight to hear Confessions. All sinners welcome."

Devlin said, "Now then, Father, didn't you say I'd take some of the load off your shoulders? It's me who'll be sitting in the box tonight." He turned to Steiner. "But you're still welcome, Colonel."

"Are you sure you don't mind?" Father Martin said.

As the door opened, Sister Maria Palmer cut in. "An excellent idea."

They moved along the corridor and Morgan opened the outer door for them. Father Martin said, "Just one thing. I usually start at seven. The MPs bring Steiner down at eight because everyone's gone by then. They prefer it that way."

"So you see him last?"

"That's right."

"No problem," Devlin said.

They reached the foyer and the porter handed them their raincoats. Sister Maria Palmer said, "We'll see you tonight then, Major."

"I'll look forward to it," Devlin said and went down the steps with the old priest.

"God save us, talk about Daniel in the lion's den," Ryan said. "You've the cheek of Old Nick himself."

"Yes, well it worked," Devlin said. "But I wouldn't like to hang about there too much. Asking for trouble that."

"But you will go back this evening?"

"I have to. My one chance of speaking properly to Steiner."

Mary, sitting at one end of the table hugging herself, said, "But Mr. Devlin, to sit there in the box and hear people's Confessions, and some of them nuns. That's a mortal sin."

"I've no choice, Mary. It must be done. It doesn't sit well with me to make a fool of that fine old man, but there it is."

"Well, I still think it's a terrible thing to be doing." She left the room, came back a moment later in her raincoat and went outside.

"The temper on her sometimes," Ryan said.

"Never mind that now, we've things to discuss. My meeting tonight with Carver. Black Lion Dock. Could we get there in your boat?"

"I know it well. Take about thirty minutes. Ten o'clock you said."

"I'd like to be there earlier. To review the situation, if you follow me."

"Leave at nine then. You'll be back from the priory before, surely."

"I would think so." Devlin lit a cigarette. "I can't go down to Shaw Place in your taxi, Michael. A London cab would definitely look out of place in Romney Marsh. This Ford van of yours. Is it in running order?"

"Yes. As I said, I use it now and then."

"One very important point," Devlin said. "When I get Steiner out, we move and move fast. Two hours to Shaw Place, the plane waiting and out of it before the authorities know what's hit them. I'll need the van that night and it would be a one-way trip. It wouldn't be a good idea for you to try and get it back."

Ryan smiled. "I took it as payment for a bad debt from a dealer in Brixton two years ago. The logbook's so crooked it's a joke and so is the numberplate. No way could it be traced back to me, and it's in good order. You know me and engines. They're my hobby."

"Ah, well, a bob or two extra for you for that," Devlin said and got up. "I'll go and make my peace with your niece now."

She was sitting under the awning in the boat reading again as he went down the steps.

"What is it this time?" he said.

"*The Midnight Court,*" she told him reluctantly.

"In English or Irish?"

"I don't have the Irish."

"The great pity. I used to be able to recite the whole of it in Irish. My uncle gave me a Bible for doing that. He was a priest."

"I wonder what he'd say about what you're doing this evening," she said.

"Oh, I know very well," Devlin told her. "He'd forgive me." And he went back up the steps.

Devlin sat in the box in uniform, just a violet stole about his neck, and listened patiently to four nuns and two male patients as they confessed their sins. It was nothing very dreadful that he heard. Sins of omission in the main, or matters so petty they were hardly worth a thought, and yet they were to those anonymous people talking to him on the other side of the grille. He honestly did the best he could, tried to say the right thing, but it was an effort. His last client departed. He sat there in the silence, and then the chapel door opened and he heard the ring of army boots on the stone floor.

The confessional box door opened and closed. From the darkness Steiner said, "Bless me, Father, for I have sinned."

"Not as much as I have, Colonel." Devlin switched on his light and smiled through the grille at him.

"Mr. Devlin," Steiner said. "What have they done to you?"

"A few changes, just to put the hounds off." Devlin ran his hands through his gray hair. "How have you been?"

"Never mind that. The British were hoping you would turn up. I was interviewed by a Brigadier Munro of Special Operations Executive. He told me they'd made sure my presence in London was known in Berlin by passing the information through a man at the Spanish Embassy called Vargas. He works for them."

"I knew it," Devlin said. "The bastard."

"They told me two things. That General Walter Schellenberg was in charge of organizing my escape and that they expected him to use you. They're waiting for you, hoping you'll show up."

"Yes, but I allowed for British intelligence handling it the way they have. Vargas is still getting messages asking for more information. They will be thinking I'm still in Berlin."

"Good God!" Steiner said.

"How many MPs escort you down here?"

"Two. Usually Benson the lieutenant, but he's on leave."

"Right. I'm going to have you out of here in the next two or three days. We'll exit through the crypt. It's pretty well organized. There'll be a boat waiting on the river. After that a two-hour drive to a place where we'll be picked up by plane from France."

"I see. Everything organized down to the last detail, just like Operation Eagle, and remember how that turned out."

"Ah, yes, but I'm in charge this time." Devlin smiled. "The evening we go you'll come down to Confession just like tonight. Usual time."

"How will I know?"

"A fine view from your window and the

steps down to the little beach by the Thames. Remember?"

"Ah, yes."

"The day we decide to go, there'll be a young girl standing by the wall at the top of those steps. She'll be wearing a black beret and an old raincoat. She'll be there at noon exactly, so watch at noon each day, and she has a strong limp, Colonel, very pronounced. You can't miss her."

"So, I see her, then we go that evening?" Steiner hesitated. "The MPs?"

"A detail only." Devlin smiled. "Trust me. Now three Hail Marys and two Our Fathers and be off with you."

He switched off the light. The door banged, there was a murmur of voices, the sound of boots again and the outer door opening and closing.

Devlin came out and moved toward the altar. "God forgive me," he murmured.

He checked that the bolt of the crypt door was still pulled back, then went into the sacristy, got his trench coat and left.

Ryan stood at the door as Devlin changed quickly from the uniform into dark slacks and sweater. He pulled up his right trouser leg and strapped the ankle holster to it, tucking his sock up around the end. He slipped the Smith & Wesson .38 into it and pulled down his trouser.

"Just in case." He picked up the old leather jacket Ryan had loaned him and put it on. Then he opened his suitcase, took out a wad of fivers and put them in his inside pocket.

They went downstairs and found Mary sitting at the table reading again. "Is there any tea in the pot?" Devlin asked.

"A mouthful, I think. Are we going now?" She poured the tea into a cup.

He opened the kitchen table drawer, took out the Luger, checked it and slipped it inside his jacket. "You're not going anywhere, girl dear, not this time," he told her and swallowed his tea.

She started to protest, but her uncle shook his head. "He's right, girl, it could get nasty. Best stay out of it."

She watched, disconsolate, as they went down the steps to the boat and cast off. As Ryan started the engine, Devlin moved into the little wheelhouse beside him and lit a cigarette in cupped hands.

"And the same applies to you, Michael," he said. "Stay out of it. My affair, not yours."

Jack and Eric Carver arrived at the Black Lion Dock at nine forty-five in a Humber limousine, George driving. The dock was almost completely dark except for the light over the main warehouse doors, shaded as required by the blackout regulations. The sign on the warehouse said, *Carver Brothers—Export and Import,* and Jack Carver looked up at it with satisfaction as he got out of the car.

"Very nice that. The sign writer did a good job."

It was very quiet, the only sounds those of shipping on the river. Eric followed him, and George limped around to the back of the car, opened the boot and took out the radio set in its wooden case painted olive green.

"I'll carry that, it's worth money." Carver turned to his brother. "All right, Eric, let's get on with it."

Eric unlocked the Judas gate in the main door, stepped inside and found the light switch. His brother and George followed him. The warehouse was stacked with packing cases of every kind. There was a table in the center and a couple of chairs, obviously used by a shipping clerk.

"Right, put it on the table." George did

as he was told, and Carver added, "You've got the shooter?"

George took a Walther PPK from one pocket, a silencer from the other and screwed it into place.

Carver lit a cigar. "Look at that, Eric, bloody marvelous. Just sounds like a cork popping."

"I can't wait for that little bastard to get here," Eric said.

But Devlin had actually been there for some time, hidden in the shadows at the rear of the building, having gained access through an upstairs window. He watched George position himself behind a stack of packing cases, the Carver brothers sitting down at the table, then he turned and slipped out the way he had come.

A couple of minutes later he approached the main door, whistling cheerfully, opened the Judas gate and went in. "God save all here," he called and approached the table. "You got it then, Mr. Carver?"

"I told you. I can get anything. You didn't mention your name last night, by the way."

"Churchill," Devlin said. "Winston."

"Very funny."

Devlin opened the case. The radio fitted inside, headphones, Morse tapper, aerials, everything. It looked brand-new. He closed the lid again.

"Satisfied?" Carver asked.

"Oh, yes."

"Then cash on the table."

Devlin took the thousand pounds from his pocket and passed it over. "The hard man, eh, Mr. Carver?"

"Hard enough." Carver dropped the money back on the table. "Of course, we now come to the other matter."

"And what matter would that be?"

"Your insulting treatment of my brother and your threats to me. IRA and Special Branch. I can't have that. I've got a reputation to think of. You need chastising, my son." He blew cigar smoke in Devlin's face. "George."

George moved fast, considering his damaged knee, had the Walther at the back of Devlin's neck in a second. Eric reached inside the Irishman's jacket and relieved him of the Luger. "Look at that, Jack. Cunning bastard."

Devlin spread his arms. "All right, Mr. Carver, so you've got me. What happens now?"

He walked across to a packing case, sat

down and took out a cigarette. Carver said, "You're a cool bastard, I'll give you that."

"I'll tell you what happens now," Eric said, taking a cut-throat razor from his pocket and opening it. "I'm going to slice your ears off, that's what I'm going to do."

"While George holds the gun on me?" Devlin asked.

"That's the general idea," Eric told him.

"Only one problem with that," Devlin said. "That gun is a Walther PPK and you have to pull the slider back to put yourself in business and I don't think George has done that."

George pulled at the slider desperately, Devlin hitched up his trouser, yanked the Smith & Wesson from the ankle holster and fired, all in one smooth motion, drilling him through the upper arm so that he cried out and dropped the Walther.

Devlin picked it up. "Nice," he said. "Thanks very much." He pushed it into his waistband.

Carver sat there, a look of total disbelief on his face. Eric looked frightened to death as Devlin put first the money and then the Luger inside his leather jacket. He picked up the case containing the radio and walked away.

As he reached the door, he turned. "Jesus, Eric, I was forgetting. You said something about slicing my ears off."

His arm swung up, he fired, and Eric screamed as the lower half of his right ear disintegrated. He grabbed at it, blood spurting.

Devlin said, "A good job you don't wear earrings."

He stepped out and the Judas gate banged behind him.

Schellenberg was in his office when the door burst open and Ilse appeared. Asa Vaughan was at her shoulder, excitement on his face.

"What on earth is it?" Schellenberg demanded.

"You must come to the radio room now. It's Devlin." She could hardly get the words out. "It's Devlin, General, calling from London."

The radio was open on the kitchen table, the aerials looped all the way around the walls. Ryan and Mary sat watching in fascination as Devlin tapped away in Morse code.

"Jesus," he said, frowning. There was a little more action and then he stopped. "That's it. Get the aerials down."

259

Mary moved around the kitchen coiling up the wires. Ryan said, "Is everything all right, Liam?"

"All wrong, old son. We were supposed to try and be back in France for the twenty-first. Now they say the great occasion is on the fifteenth, and as tonight is the twelfth, that doesn't give us much time."

"Is it possible, Liam?"

Devlin said, "First thing in the morning we'll take a run down to Romney Marsh. See what the situation is at Shaw Place." He turned to Mary. "Would you like a day out in the country?"

"It sounds just fine to me."

"Good, then I'll give the Shaws a call and warn them to expect me."

Back in his office, Schellenberg sat at his desk studying the message in front of him, Asa Vaughan and Ilse watching.

"So, what do we know?" Schellenberg said. "He's there at his IRA friend's house, he's made contact with Shaw and now with Steiner."

"Everything fits," Asa said.

"Perhaps, but he can't make the fifteenth, it would be impossible, even for Devlin."

"I'm beginning to wonder if anything is impossible to that guy," Asa said.

"'Stand by tomorrow,'" Schellenberg commented. "That was his final instruction. Well, we shall see." He stood up. "I doubt whether the canteen can run to champagne, but whatever they can manage is on me."

11

SOUTH OF the Thames, they took the road to Maidstone, Ryan driving, Devlin squeezed in beside him. He wasn't in uniform, but wore his trench coat over the clerical suit and dog collar, the black trilby slanted over one ear. Ryan had told him the truth. The Ford's engine was in apple pie order in spite of the vehicle's rattletrap appearance.

"You were right, Michael," Devlin said. "She's a runner, this old van of yours."

"Sure and I could race her at Brooklands if they were still racing at Brooklands." Ryan grinned.

Mary was sitting in the back of the van reading a book as usual. "Are you all right back there?" Devlin asked her.

"I'm fine."

"We'll stop for a cup of tea in a while."

In Maidstone, Ryan drove around the center of the town until he found a cycle shop. Devlin went in and bought half a dozen standard bicycle lamps with fresh batteries.

"I've cleaned him out," he said when he returned. "Told him I wanted them for my church scout troop. There's no doubt about it this collar comes in useful on occasion."

"And why would you want those?" Mary asked.

"An airplane coming in through the darkness at night is like a lost bird, girl dear. It needs a welcome. A little light on the situation, you might say."

On the other side of Ashford they pulled in at the side of the road and Mary opened a Thermos flask and they had tea. There was a track leading to a little copse. It had stopped raining but was still very damp. The sky was dark and threatening all the way to Romney Marsh and the sea in the distance. Mary and Devlin strolled along the track and stood under a tree, taking it all in.

He nodded at her book. "What this time?"

"Poetry," she said. "Robert Browning. Do you like poetry?"

"I had some published once. What's called

in the trade a slim volume." He laughed. "I could make the stuff up at the drop of a hat, and then I realized one day just how bad it was."

"I don't believe you. Make something up about me."

He stuck a cigarette in his mouth. "All right." He thought for a moment then said, "Mystery girl, who are you? Hurrying nowhere in your tight skirt and frizzled hair, legs heavy with promise."

There was a look of mischief on his face, and she struck him lightly with her clenched fist. "That's terrible."

"I warned you." He lit his cigarette. "Good poetry says it all for you in a few lines."

"All right, what would sum me up?"

"Easy. 'Now, Voyager, sail thou forth to seek and find.'"

"That's marvelous," she said. "Did you write that?"

"Not exactly. A Yankee fella called Walt Whitman thought of it first." It started to rain, and he put a hand on her elbow. "But I wish I'd written it for you. Let's get moving." And they hurried back to the van.

At the apartment over the Astoria, Jack

Carver was sitting at the table by the window having a late breakfast when Eric came in. His ear was heavily bandaged, tape running diagonally up across his forehead holding the dressing in place. He looked terrible.

"How do you feel?" Carver asked.

"Shocking, Jack, the pain's bloody awful. Aziz gave me some pills, but they don't seem to have much effect."

"He tells me George is in a bad way. That bullet splintered the bone. He could be left with a permanently stiff arm, as well as the leg."

Eric poured coffee, his hand shaking. "That little sod, Jack. We've got to get our hands on him. We've got to."

"We will, son," Jack said. "And then it'll be our turn. I've put his description out all over London. He'll turn up. Now drink your coffee and have something to eat."

Using the road map, Ryan found Charbury easily enough and an inquiry at the little village store led them to Shaw Place. The great rusting iron gates at the end of the drive stood open; the drive, stretching toward the old house, had grass growing through the gravel.

"This place has seen better days," Ryan commented.

Devlin stepped out, opened the van doors and got the radio and the bag of cycle lamps out. "You can leave me here," he said. "I'll walk up to the house."

"What time shall we call back?" Ryan asked.

"Give me four hours, and if I'm not here, just wait. Go and have a look at Rye or one of those places."

"Fine," Ryan said. "Take care, Liam." And he drove away.

Devlin picked up the case and started up the long drive. The house showed every evidence of lack of money. The long shutters at the windows badly needed a coat of paint, as did the front door. There was a bell pull. He gave it a heave and waited, but there was no response. After a while he picked up the case and went around to the rear of the house, where there was a cobbled courtyard. One of the stable doors stood open and there were sounds of activity. He put the case down and looked in.

Lavinia Shaw wore riding breeches and boots, her hair bound in a scarf as she curried a large black stallion. Devlin put a cigarette in his mouth and snapped open his lighter.

The sound startled her and she looked around.

"Miss Lavinia Shaw?" he inquired.

"Yes."

"Harry Conlon. I phoned your brother last night. He's expecting me."

"Major Conlon." There was a sudden eagerness about her. She put down the brush and comb she was using and ran her hands over her breeches. "Of course. How wonderful to have you here."

The well-bred upper-class voice, her whole attitude, was quite incredible to Devlin, but he took the hand she offered and smiled. "A pleasure, Miss Shaw."

"Maxwell is out on the marsh somewhere with his gun. Goes every day. You know how it is. Food shortages. Anything's good for the pot." She didn't seem to be able to stop talking. "We'll go into the kitchen, shall we?"

It was very large, the floor flagged with red tiles, an enormous pine table in the center with chairs around it. There were unwashed dishes in the sink, and the whole place was cluttered and untidy, the lack of servants very evident.

"Tea?" she said. "Or would you like something stronger?"

"No, tea would be fine."

He put the case carefully on the table with the bag of cycle lamps, and she boiled water and made the tea quickly, so excited and nervous that she poured it before it had brewed properly.

"Oh, dear, I've ruined it."

"Not at all. It's wet isn't it and hot?" Devlin said.

He poured a little milk in, and she sat on the other side of the table, arms folded under her full breasts, eyes glittering now, never leaving him. "I can't tell you how absolutely thrilling all this is. I haven't been so excited for years."

She was like a character in a bad play, the duke's daughter coming in through the French windows in her riding breeches and gushing at everyone in sight.

"You've been in Germany recently?" she asked.

"Oh, yes," he told her. "I was in Berlin only the other day."

"How marvelous to be part of all that. People here are so complacent. They don't understand what the Führer's done for Germany."

"For all of Europe you might say," Devlin told her.

"Exactly. Strength, a sense of purpose, discipline. Whereas here—" She laughed contemptuously. "That drunken fool Churchill has no idea what he's doing. Just lurches from one mistake to another."

"Ah, yes, but he would, wouldn't he?" Devlin said dryly. "Do you think we could have a look round? The old barn you used for your Tiger Moth and the South Meadow."

"Of course." She jumped up so eagerly that she knocked over the chair. As she picked it up, she said, "I'll just get a coat."

The meadow was larger than he had expected and stretched to a line of trees in the distance. "How long?" Devlin asked. "Two-fifty or three hundred yards?"

"Oh, no," she said. "Getting on for three-fifty. The grass is so short because we leased it to a local farmer to graze sheep, but they've gone to market now."

"You used to take off and land here a lot in the old days?"

"All the time. That's when I had my little Puss Moth. Great fun."

"And you used the barn over there as a hangar?"

"That's right. I'll show you."

The place was quite huge, but like everything else the massive doors had seen better days, dry rot very evident, planks missing. Devlin helped her open one of the doors slightly so they could go inside. There was a rusting tractor in one corner, some moldering hay at the back. Otherwise it was empty, rain dripping through holes in the roof.

"You'd want to put a plane in here?" she asked.

"Only for a short while, to be out of sight. A Lysander. Not too large. It would fit in here and no trouble."

"When exactly?"

"Tomorrow night."

"My goodness, you are pushing things along."

"Yes, well time's important."

They went out and he closed the door. Somewhere in the far distance a shotgun was fired. "My brother," she said. "Let's go and find him, shall we?"

As they walked across the meadow, she said, "We had a German friend who used to come here in the old days, Werner Keitel. We used to fly all over the place together. Do you happen to know him?"

"He was killed in the Battle of Britain."

She paused for a moment only, then carried on. "Yes, I thought it would be something like that."

"I'm sorry," Devlin told her.

She shrugged. "A long time ago, Major." And she started to walk faster.

They followed a dike through the small reeds, and it was Nell who appeared first, splashing through water, gamboling around them before running away again. There was another shot, and then Shaw emerged from the reeds in the distance and came toward them.

"Look at this, old girl." He held up a couple of rabbits.

"See who's here," she called.

He paused and came forward again. "Conlon, my dear chap. Nice to see you. Won't shake hands. Blood on them." He might have been welcoming Devlin to a weekend in the country. "Better get home and find you a drink."

They started back along the dike. Devlin looked out across the expanse of reeds intersected by creeks. "Desolate country this."

"Dead, old man. Everything about the damn place is dead. Rain, mist and the ghosts of things past. Of course it was different in my grandfather's day. Twenty-five servants in the house alone. God knows how many on the estate." He didn't stop talking for a moment as they walked along. "People don't want to work these days, that's the trouble. Damn Bolshies all over the place. That's what I admire about the Führer. Gives people some order in their lives."

"Makes them do as they're told, you mean," Devlin said.

Shaw nodded enthusiastically. "Exactly, old man, exactly."

Devlin set up the radio in a small study behind the old library. Shaw had gone to have a bath, and it was Lavinia who helped festoon the aerials around the room and watched intently as the Irishman explained the set to her.

"Is it much different from the one you had before?" he asked.

"A bit more sophisticated, that's all."

"And your Morse code. Can you still remember it?"

"Good heavens, Major Conlon, you never forget something like that. I was a Girl Guide when I first learned it."

"Right," Devlin said. "Let's see what you can do then."

In the radio room at Prinz Albrechtstrasse,

Schellenberg studied Devlin's first message, then turned to Ilse and Asa Vaughan. "Incredible. He intends to pull Steiner out tomorrow evening. He wants you at Shaw Place in time to leave no later than midnight."

"Then we'll have to get moving," Asa told him.

"Yes, well the Lysander was delivered to Chernay yesterday," Schellenberg said. "It's only a matter of getting ourselves down there." He said to the radio operator, "Take this message to Falcon. *Will meet your requirements. Departure time will be confirmed to you tomorrow night.*"

He started to walk out, and the operator called, "I have a reply, General."

Schellenberg turned. "What is it?"

"A pleasure to do business with you."

Schellenberg smiled and kept going, Asa and Ilse Huber following him.

In the study, Lavinia turned from the radio set. "Did I do all right?"

Her brother was sitting by the empty fireplace, a tumbler of whisky in his hand. "Seemed fine to me."

"You were excellent," Devlin said. "Now this set is different from the one you threw away in one respect. It has a direct voice capacity for short ranges only. Say twenty-five miles. That was why I gave them the frequency reading. I've adjusted it, and all you do is switch on and you're in business. That means you can talk to the pilot when he's close."

"Marvelous. Anything else?"

"Sometime after seven they'll contact you from the French base to confirm departure time, so stand by. Afterwards, you place the cycle lamps in the meadow as I described to you."

"I will. You may depend on it." She turned to Shaw. "Isn't it marvelous, darling?"

"Terrific, old girl," he said, eyes already glazed, and poured another drink.

But by then Devlin had had enough and he got up. "I'll be on my way. See you tomorrow night."

Shaw mumbled something, and Lavinia took Devlin back to the kitchen where he got his coat and hat.

"Will he be all right?" Devlin asked as she took him to the front door.

"Who, Max? Oh, yes. No need to worry there, Major."

"I'll see you then."

It started to rain as he went down the drive, and there was no sign of the van. He stood there, hands in pockets, and it was thirty minutes before it turned up.

"Did it go well?" Ryan asked

Mary cut in. "We've had a lovely time. Rye was a fine place."

"Well, I'm happy for you," Devlin said sourly. "Those two didn't even offer me a bite to eat."

Asa was just finishing a late lunch in the canteen when Schellenberg hurried in. "A slight change in plan. I've had a message saying the Reichsführer wants to see me. The interesting thing is I'm to bring you."

"What in the hell for?"

"It seems you've been awarded the Iron Cross First Class, and the Reichsführer likes to pin them on SS officers himself."

Asa said, "I wonder what my old man would say. I went to West Point, for Christ's sakes."

"The other complication is that he's at Wewelsburg. You've heard of the place, of course?"

"Every good SS man's idea of heaven. What does this do to our schedule?"

"No problem. Wewelsburg has a Luftwaffe feeder base only ten miles away. We'll fly there in the Stork and carry on to Chernay afterwards." Schellenberg glanced at his watch. "The appointment's for seven, and he takes punctuality for granted."

At six-thirty it was totally dark on the Thames as Ryan nudged the motorboat in toward the shingle strand. He said to Mary, "Just sit tight. It shouldn't take long."

Devlin picked up the bag of tools and the torch. "Right, let's get moving." And he went over the side.

The water in the tunnel was deeper than it had been before, at one point chest high, but they pressed on and reached the grille in a few minutes.

"Are you sure about this?" Ryan asked.

"Michael, you said you thought it would come away easy. Now wouldn't I look the original fool if I turned up to grab Steiner tomorrow night and found the damn grille wouldn't budge?"

"All right, let's get on with it," Ryan said.

"And no banging. I don't want someone on their knees up there in the chapel wondering what's happening down here."

Which is what made the whole thing rather more difficult than it had at first appeared. The slow, careful probing between the brickwork took time. On occasion, several bricks fell out of place at once, but others proved more difficult. It took half an hour to clear one side.

Fifteen minutes into working on the other, Ryan said, "You were right, dammit, the thing's a sod."

He pulled at the grille angrily and it fell forward. Devlin grabbed at his arm, pulling him out of the way and got a hand to the side of the grille at the same time, easing it down.

He took the lamp and peered inside, then handed it to Ryan. "You hold the light while I go and take a look."

"Watch your step now."

Devlin went through the hole and waded inside. In there, the water was now up to his armpits, covering the tops of the tombs. He made it to the steps and started up. A rat scurried past him and dived into the water. He paused on the top step, then very gently tried the handle.

There was the faintest of creaks and the door eased open. He could see the altar, the Virgin on the other side floating in candlelight. He peered around the door cautiously. The chapel was quite deserted, and then the outer door opened and a nun came in. Very quietly Devlin closed the door and retreated down the steps.

"Perfect," he said to Ryan as he clambered through the hole. "Now let's get out of here."

At the Luftwaffe base, Schellenberg gave orders for the Stork to be refueled, commandeered the station commander's Mercedes and driver and set out for Wewelsburg with Asa. It started to snow, and as they approached, Wewelsburg was plain to see, light at the windows and over the main gate in total disregard of any blackout regulations.

Asa looked up at the castle and its towers in the falling snow. "My God!" he said in awe. "It's incredible."

"I know." Schellenberg reached forward and closed the glass partition so that the Luftwaffe driver couldn't hear what they were saying. "Looks like a film set. Actually it's a personal retreat for the Reichsführer, a center for racial research and a home-from-home to the elite of the SS."

"But what do they do there?"

"The Reichsführer is obsessed with King Arthur and the Knights of the Round Table. So he has his twelve most trusted lieutenants sit at a round table. His knights, you see."

"And you're not one of them, I take it."

"Very definitely not. No, you have to be a lunatic to indulge in those games. They have a memorial hall with a swastika in the ceiling, a pit in which the remains of these special ones will be burnt on death. There are twelve pedestals and urns waiting for the ashes."

"You've got to be kidding!" Asa said.

"No, quite true. I'll show you if we get a chance." Schellenberg laughed and shook his head. "And people like these are handling the destinies of millions."

They booked in at the entrance hall and left their greatcoats and caps with the sergeant of the guard, who checked his register.

"Yes, General Schellenberg, the Reichsführer is expecting you for seven o'clock in his private sitting room in the south wing. I'll take you up, sir."

"No need. I know the way."

As Asa followed Schellenberg across the hall and they turned along a corridor, he said, "You're right. This place puts Louis B. Mayer to shame."

Schellenberg checked his watch. "We've got fifteen minutes. Come on, I'll show you that memorial hall I told you about. It's just along here. There's a little gallery, as I remember. Yes, here we are."

There were perhaps a dozen steps up to an oak door. It opened easily, and he could immediately hear voices. He paused, frowning, then turned to Asa and put a finger to his lips. Then he opened the door cautiously and they went in.

The circular room was a place of shadows, only dimly lit. Asa was aware of the pedestals and urns Schellenberg had described, the pit beneath the ceiling swastika, but it was the people present who were most interesting. Rossman, Himmler's aide, stood to one side waiting. The Reichsführer stood in the pit itself, face to face with Sturmbannführer Horst Berger. They all wore black dress uniforms.

"I have brought you here, Berger, to this holy place before you depart on what I can only describe as your sacred mission."

"An honor, Reichsführer."

"Now let's go over the details. You will meet the Führer's plane, which will land at the Luftwaffe base at Cherbourg at six tomorrow night. I shall be with him. You will escort us to this Château de Belle-Île, where we will spend the night. At seven o'clock the following morning the Führer will have breakfast with Rommel and Admiral Canaris. They will arrive by road."

"And when do I take action, Reichsführer?"

Himmler shrugged. "It doesn't really matter. I suppose the end of the meal might be appropriate. How many men will you have in the guard?"

"Thirty."

"Good. That should be enough."

"Hand-picked, Reichsführer."

"Good—the fewer the better. We are a special brotherhood, those of us involved in this, for there are some who would not agree with what we intend."

"As you say, Reichsführer."

"General Schellenberg, for instance, but he's cleverer than the proverbial fox. That's why I wanted him elsewhere these past three weeks. So I gave him this ridiculous mission to occupy him. To bring Steiner out of England. An impossibility. I happen to know from our intelligence people that the agent working for us in London, Vargas, also works for the British. We didn't tell Schellenberg that, did we Rossman?"

"No, Reichsführer."

"So we may deduce that the Irishman Devlin will not last too long over there."

"I couldn't be more pleased, Reichsführer," Berger said.

"We could have won this war at Dunkirk, Berger, if the Führer had allowed the Panzers to roll onto the beaches. Instead he ordered them to halt. Russia, one disaster after another. Stalingrad, the most catastrophic defeat the German army has ever suffered." Himmler shuffled away and turned. "Blunder after blunder and he still won't listen."

"I see, Reichsführer," Berger said. "All men of sense would."

"And so inexorably Germany, our beloved country, sinks deeper into the pit of defeat, and that is why the Führer must die, Berger, and to accomplish that is your sacred task. Rommel, Canaris, the Führer. A dastardly attack on their part leading to the Führer's unfortunate death, followed by their own deaths at the hands of loyal SS men."

"And afterwards?" Berger said.

"We of the SS will naturally assume all governmental powers. The war may then be continued as it should be. No weakness, no shirking by anyone." He put a hand on Berger's shoulder. "We belong to the same sacred brotherhood, Major. I envy you this opportunity."

281

Schellenberg nodded to Asa, edged him out and closed the door.

"Jesus!" Asa said. "Now what happens?"

"We keep the appointment. If he finds out we overheard that lot, we'll never get out of here alive." As they hurried along the corridor, Schellenberg said, "Whatever he wants, follow my lead and not a mention that Devlin's got things to the stage they are."

He led the way up a back stair, along a corridor, and reached the door to Himmler's sitting room in the south wing very quickly.

Schellenberg sat in the chair behind Rossman's desk. "Now we wait. They'll probably come up by the back entrance to his room."

A moment later the door opened and Rossman looked out. "Ah, there you are."

"Right on time." Schellenberg led the way in.

Himmler, behind his desk, looked up. "So, General, and this is Hauptsturmführer Vaughan, the pilot you recruited for the Steiner affair?"

"Yes, Reichsführer."

"Any news of your Mr. Devlin?"

Schellenberg said, "I'm afraid not, Reichsführer."

"Ah, well, it was always a problematical mission to say the least. The Führer flies to Cherbourg, arrives at Belle-Île tomorrow night. Canaris and Rommel are to have breakfast the following morning at seven. I'll be there, of course. The idiots are junketing around Normandy at the moment. They have a crazy idea the invasion will come there and hope to persuade the Führer to agree with them."

"I see, Reichsführer."

"However, to the reason for your visit and why I asked you to bring the officer with you." He turned. "Rossman."

As he stood up, Rossman opened a medal case. Himmler took the Iron Cross it contained, came around the table and pinned it to Asa Vaughan's tunic.

"To you, Hauptsturmführer Asa Vaughan of the George Washington Legion, in acknowledgement of supreme valor in aerial combat over Poland."

"Reichsführer," said Asa, keeping his face straight with a supreme effort.

"And now you may go. I have work to do."

Schellenberg and Asa hurried down the stairs, retrieved their greatcoats and caps and went out to the waiting Mercedes.

"Back to the base," Schellenberg said to the driver, and he and Asa got in.

As they drove away, Asa closed the glass partition and said, "What do you make of it?"

"I know one thing," Schellenberg said. "Killing Hitler is the worst thing that could happen. At least with the Führer making one foul-up after another, there's a prospect of a reasonably early end to the war, but Himmler would be another story. Can you imagine that animal in total control, the SS in charge of government, the army? The war could go on for years."

"So what are you going to do? Warn Rommel and Canaris?"

"First of all, I don't know exactly where they are, and second, it's a question of belief, Asa. Why should anyone believe me? My word against that of the Reichsführer of the SS."

"Come off it, General. According to Liam Devlin, you're a very smart guy. Surely you can come up with something."

"I'll put my heart and soul into it," Schellenberg promised him. "But for the moment, let's concentrate on getting back to the airfield and the Stork. We fly out at once. The sooner we're at Chernay, the happier I'll be."

12

THE DUTY MP usually brought Steiner a cup of tea at eleven each morning. He was five minutes late and found the German by the window reading.

"There you go, General."

"Thank you, Corporal."

"I suppose you'd prefer coffee, sir," the corporal said, lingering, for he rather liked Steiner.

"But I was raised on tea, Corporal," Steiner told him "I went to school right here in London. St. Paul's."

"Is that a fact, sir?"

He turned to the door and Steiner said, "Is Lieutenant Benson back yet?"

"His leave is up at midnight, sir, but if I know him, he'll look in this evening. You know what these young officers are like. Dead keen. Looking for that second pip on his shoulders."

He left, the bolt rammed home and Steiner went back to his seat by the window, waiting for noon as he had on the previous day, drinking his tea and trying to compose himself to patience.

It was raining again and there was fog in the city, so heavy already that he could barely see the other side of the river. A very large cargo boat eased down from the London docks followed by a line of barges. He watched for a while, wondering where it was going, and then he saw the girl, just as Devlin had described—black beret and shabby raincoat.

Mary limped along the pavement, collar up, hands thrust deep into her pockets. She stopped at the entrance leading down to the strand and leaned on the wall, watching the boats on the river. She didn't look up at the priory at all. Devlin had been most explicit about that. She just stayed there watching for ten minutes, then turned and walked away.

Steiner was aware of intense excitement and gripped the bars at his window to steady himself. The door opened behind him and the corporal reappeared.

"If you're finished, Colonel, I'll take your tray."

"Yes, I am, thank you." The MP picked up the tray and turned to the door. "Oh, I don't know who's on duty this evening, but I'll be going down to Confession," Steiner said.

"Right, sir. I'll make a note of it. Eight o'clock as usual."

He went out and locked the door. Steiner listened to the sound of his boots receding along the corridor, then turned, gripping the bars again.

"Now we pray, Mr. Devlin," he said softly. "Now we pray."

When Devlin went into St. Patrick's, he was in his military trench coat and uniform. He wasn't really sure why he had come. Conscience again, he supposed, or perhaps just tying up loose ends. He only knew he couldn't leave without a word with the old priest. He'd used him, he knew that, and it didn't sit well. What was worse was the fact that they would meet again and for the last time in the chapel at St. Mary's that evening. No avoiding that or the distress it would cause.

The church was quiet, only Frank Martin down at the altar arranging a few flowers. He turned at the sound of Devlin's approach, and there was genuine pleasure on his face. "Hello, Father."

Devlin managed a smile. "I just dropped in to tell you I'm on my way. I got my orders this morning."

"That's unexpected, isn't it?"

"Yes, well, they're easing me back in." Devlin lied in his teeth. "I'm to report to a military hospital in Portsmouth."

"Ah, well, as they say, there's a war on."

Devlin nodded. "The war, the war, the bloody war, Father. It's gone on too long, and we all of us have to do things we normally would never do. Every soldier, whichever side he's on. Things to shame us."

The old man said gently, "You're troubled, my son. Can I help in any way?"

"No, Father, not this time. Some things we have to live with ourselves." Devlin put out his hand and the old priest took it. "It's been a genuine pleasure, Father."

"And for me," Frank Martin said.

Devlin turned and walked away, the door banged. The old priest stood there for a moment, puzzlement on his face, and then he turned and went back to his flowers.

There was the merest hint of fog at Chernay too at four o'clock when Schellenberg went in search of Asa. He found him in the hangar with the Lysander and Flight Sergeant Leber.

"How is it?" Schellenberg asked.

"Perfection, General," Leber told him.

"Couldn't be better." He smiled. "Naturally, the Hauptsturmführer has just been checking everything out for the fifth time, but that's understandable."

The Lysander had RAF roundels in place on canvas strips as Asa had requested, and the swastika on the tailplane had been blocked out with black canvas.

"Of course there's no absolute guarantee that they won't come off in flight," Asa said. "We'll just have to keep our fingers crossed."

"And the weather?" Schellenberg asked.

Leber said, "It's uncertain. Visibility could be restricted. There are a couple of conflicting fronts moving in. I've checked with our base at Cherbourg, and the truth is it's one of those times when they don't really know."

"But the plane is ready?"

"Oh, yes," Asa told him. "One good thing about this beauty is that she's fitted with an emergency fuel tank. I suppose the RAF had that done because of the kind of operation it was employed on. I'm allowing an hour and a half for the flight, and thanks to Luftwaffe intelligence at Cherbourg, I can tune my radio to the RAF frequency as I approach the English coast."

"Good. Let's go for a walk. I feel like the air."

It was raining only slightly as they walked along the airfield and Schellenberg smoked a cigarette, not speaking for a while. They reached the end and leaned on a fence, looking out to sea.

Schellenberg said, "You feel all right about this?"

"The trip?" Asa shrugged. "The flight itself doesn't worry me. It's the situation at the other end that's problematical."

"Yes, we are all in Mr. Devlin's hands there."

Asa said, "Assuming everything goes well and I put down here with our friends sometime early tomorrow morning, what happens then? What about the Belle-Île situation? Have you any ideas?"

"Only one and it would be a desperate venture. On the other hand simple, and I like simplicity. It pleases me."

"I'm all ears."

"Well, the Führer will be having breakfast with Rommel, the admiral and the Reichsführer. Berger will strike at the end of the meal."

"Yes, I know that. I was there, remember?"

"What if you and I and Mr. Devlin arrived to join them for breakfast and exposed the plot."

"But we'd go down the hole too, that's obvious," Asa said. "Even if you said your piece to the Führer, Berger and his chums would just get on with it."

"Oh, yes, and it would suit the Reichsführer to have me out of the war." Schellenberg smiled. "There is a wild card I haven't mentioned. Remember when we were driving to Belle-Île? The Twelfth Parachute Detachment outside St.-Aubin? Hauptmann Erich Kramer and thirty-five paratroopers?"

"Sure I do."

"What do you think would happen if Colonel Kurt Steiner, the living legend of the Parachute Regiment, appeared and told them he needed their services because there was an SS plot ten miles up the road to kill the Führer?"

"Jesus!" Asa said. "Those guys would follow Steiner anywhere."

"Exactly. And the *Fallschirmjäger* have always been notorious for their dislike of the SS."

"It could work," Asa said.

"If everything else did."

"Let me get this straight. We'd go in first? Steiner would follow on?"

"Yes, let's say fifteen minutes later."

Asa said, "That could be one hell of a breakfast."

"Yes, well, I prefer not to think of it right now," Schellenberg said. "I've got other things on my mind. Let's go and have a cup of coffee."

In Ryan's kitchen, Devlin had various items laid out on the table. "Let's see what I've got here," he said. "Those MPs carry handcuffs, but I'll take a little extra twine for emergencies, just in case."

"I've made up three gags," Ryan said. "Bandages and sticking plaster. You've the priest too, remember."

"I'd prefer to forget him, but there you are," Devlin said.

"And a weapon?"

"I'll take the Smith and Wesson in the ankle holster for emergencies and that Walther with the silencer I got from Carver."

"Would you anticipate any killing?" Ryan asked and looked troubled.

"The last thing I want. Have you got that sap of yours?"

"God, I was forgetting."

292

Ryan opened the kitchen table drawer and produced the leather sap. It was loaded with lead and there was a loop for the wrist. It was a thing carried by many London taxi drivers for self-protection. Devlin weighed it in his hand and put it down beside the Walther.

"That's everything then," Ryan said.

Devlin smiled lightly. "All we need is Steiner now."

The door opened and Mary came in. Her uncle said, "God, I'm starving, girl. Bacon and eggs all round if you can manage it."

"No problem," she said, "but we're out of bread and tea. I'll just run along to the High Street before the shop closes. I shan't be long." And she took her beret and raincoat down from behind the door and went out.

The old lady at the shop managed her a tin of black market salmon and some cigarettes as well as the bread and tea, and Mary was carrying them in a carrier bag when she left. The fog was rolling in, the traffic slow, and she stopped cautiously on the next corner before crossing the road.

Eric Carver, at the wheel of his brother's Humber limousine, had stopped at the traffic lights. She was only a yard or two away as she passed, but he saw her clearly. She crossed the road and turned into a side street. As the lights changed, he went after her, pulled the Humber in at the curb, got out and followed cautiously.

Mary turned into Cable Wharfe, walking as quickly as she could, and crossed to the house. As she went around the corner, Eric hurried across and peered around cautiously. She had just reached the kitchen door.

It opened, and he heard Devlin say, "Ah, there you are, girl. Will you come in out of that?"

The door closed. Eric said softly, "Right, you bastard. I've got you." And he turned and hurried away.

Jack Carver was in his bedroom when Eric burst in. Carver said, "How often have I told you, Eric? I don't like anyone coming in here when I'm dressing, and that includes you."

"But I've found him, Jack. I've found where that rotten little bastard's shacked up. I saw the girl. I followed her home and he was there."

"You're sure?"

"Of course I bloody am."

"Where was this?"

"A place called Cable Wharfe. It's in Wapping."

"Right." Carver nodded in satisfaction, put on his jacket and went through to the sitting room, Eric following.

"So, what are we going to do?" Eric demanded as his brother sat behind his desk.

"Do? We're going to sort him," Carver said.

"When?"

Carver checked his watch. "I've got a big game on tonight, you know that. Probably finish around ten. We'll pay him a call after that, when he thinks he's nicely tucked up for the night." Carver smiled, opened a drawer and took out a Browning. "Just you and me and our friend here."

There was an unholy look on Eric's face. "Christ, Jack, I can't wait," he said.

Lieutenant Benson arrived at the priory just before seven. He said hello to the porter who admitted him and went straight upstairs. Strictly speaking, as the MP had told Steiner that morning, Benson's leave wasn't up until midnight, but the only available train to London from his parents' home in Norwich had been an early one. When he was admitted to the corridor in the upper floor, he found a corporal sitting in his office who jumped to his feet at once.

"You're back, sir."

"I should have thought that was obvious, Smith. Where's Sergeant Morgan?"

"Went off about an hour ago, sir."

"Everything calm while I've been away?"

"I think so, sir."

"Let's have a look at the log." Smith handed it over and Benson leafed through it. "What's this entry here on the admittance sheet? Major Conlon?"

"Oh, yes, sir, the padre. He did a tour of the place with the sister and Father Martin."

"Who gave him permission?"

"He had a War Office pass, sir. You know, those unrestricted access things. I think you'll find Sergeant Morgan put the details down."

"I can see that. The point is, what was Conlon doing here?"

"Search me, sir. Nice-looking man. Gray hair, glasses. Looked like he'd had a hard time. Oh, and he had an MC, sir."

"Yes, well, that could mean anything," Benson said sourly. "I'm going down to see Sister."

She was in her office when he knocked

and went in; she glanced up and smiled. "You're back. Did you have a good leave?"

"Yes, not bad. Is Father Martin around?"

"Just went into the chapel to hear Confessions. Anything I can do?"

"There was a Major Conlon here when I was away."

"Ah, yes, the army chaplain. A nice man. On sick leave. I understand he was wounded in Sicily last year."

"Yes, but what was he doing here?"

"Nothing. We just showed him round and he took over for Father Martin one evening. He's not been well, you know."

"Has he been back?"

"No. I understand from Father Martin that he's been posted. A military hospital in Portsmouth, I believe." She looked slightly bewildered. "Is anything wrong?"

"Oh, no, it's just that when unexpected guests turn up with War Office passes one likes to know who they are."

"You worry too much," she said.

"Probably. Goodnight, Sister."

But it wouldn't go away, the nagging doubt, and when he got back upstairs to his office he phoned Dougal Munro.

Jack Carter had gone to York for the day.

His train wasn't due into London until ten, so Munro was working alone in his office when he took the call. He listened patiently to what Benson had to say.

"You were right to call me," he said. "I don't much like the idea of officers with War Office passes sticking their noses into our business, but there it is. One of the problems with using a place like the priory, Benson. These religious types don't behave like other people."

"I've got Conlon's details here on the admission sheet, sir. Do you want them?"

"Tell you what. I'm packing up here quite soon and going home," Munro said. "I'll call in and see you. About an hour and a half."

"I'll expect you, sir."

Benson put down the phone, and Corporal Smith, standing at the door, said, "You'll see Colonel Steiner's booked for chapel, sir."

"What in the hell has he got to confess cooped up in here?" Benson demanded.

"Eight o'clock as usual, sir. Shall I do it with Corporal Ross?"

"No," Benson said. "We'll do it together. I'm expecting Brigadier Munro, but he won't be here until half past eight. Now get me a cup of tea."

At Chernay, the elements were very definitely against them, fog rolling in from the sea and rain with it. Schellenberg and Asa Vaughan stood in the radio room waiting while Flight Sergeant Leber checked the situation with Cherbourg.

After a while he turned to them. "The Führer's plane got in all right, General. Landed at six just before this lot started."

"So, what's the verdict?" Asa demanded.

"Parts of the Channel you'll find winds gusting up to force eight."

"Hell, I can handle wind," Asa said. "What else do they say?"

"Fog over southern England, from London down to the Channel coast. Another thing. They say it will get worse here during the night." He looked worried. "To be frank, sir, it stinks."

"Don't worry, Sergeant, I'll find a way."

Asa and Schellenberg went out into the wind and rain and hurried across to the hut they were using. Schellenberg sat on one of the beds and poured schnapps into an enamel cup. "Do you want some?"

"Better not." Asa lit a cigarette instead.

There was silence, then Schellenberg said, "Look, if you think it's not on, if you don't want to go . . ."

"Don't be silly," Asa told him. "Of course I'm going. Devlin's depending on me. I can't leave him in the lurch. Wind doesn't bother me. I flew for the Finns in their Winter War, remember, when we had blizzards every day. Let me tell you about fog. Taking off in it's nothing, but landing is something else and it worries me that I might not be able to land when I get there."

"Then you'll have to come back."

"Fine, except for the fact that, as Leber has just informed us, it's not going to get any better here."

"So what do you want to do?"

"Leave it as late as possible. Devlin wanted me there for a midnight departure. Let's cut it really close. I won't leave until ten o'clock. That will give the weather a chance to clear."

"And if it doesn't?"

"I go anyway."

"Fine." Schellenberg got up. "I'll send a signal to that effect to Shaw Place now."

Lavinia Shaw, seated at the radio in the study in her headphones, took the message. She tapped out a quick reply: *Message received and understood.* She took off her headphones and turned. Her brother sat by the fire cleaning his shotgun, Nell at his feet, a tumbler of Scotch beside him.

"They won't be leaving until ten o'clock, darling. It's this damn weather."

She went to the French windows, pulled back the curtains and opened the windows, looking out at the fog.

Shaw moved to her side. "I should have thought this bloody stuff was all to the good for this kind of secret landing."

Lavinia said, "Don't be silly, Max, the worst thing in the world for any pilot. Don't you remember when I couldn't land at Helmsley back in thirty-six? Stooged around until I ran out of fuel and crashed into that field wall. I was nearly killed."

"Sorry, old girl, I was forgetting." Rain started to spot the terrace in front of them in the light from the window. "There you are," Shaw said. "That should help clear it. Now close the window and let's have another drink."

"You've got everything?" Michael Ryan asked as the motorboat coasted in to the little strand.

Devlin wore loose blue overalls and boots. He tapped at his pockets, checklisting each item. "Everything in perfect working order."

Ryan said, "I wish you'd let me come with you."

"My affair, this one, Michael, and if there's the slightest hint of trouble you and Mary get the hell out of it. This bloody fog is a blessing in a way." He turned and smiled at Mary through the darkness. "You were right about that."

She reached up and kissed him on the cheek. "God bless you, Mr. Devlin. I've prayed for you."

"Then everything will be all right." And he went over the side.

The water was not quite as deep, which was something, and he moved on, the light from his lamp splaying against the tunnel until he reached the hole in the wall. He checked his watch. It was a couple of minutes past eight. He climbed in and waded through the water then started up the steps.

Dougal Munro had finished a little earlier than he had intended, so he called a staff car and told the driver to take him to St. Mary's Priory. It was a difficult journey, crawling along at fifteen miles an hour in the fog, and it was just after eight o'clock when they arrived.

"I shan't be long," the brigadier said as he got out.

"I'll get off the road, sir, while I'm waiting," his driver replied. "Otherwise someone will be shunting me up the rear. I'll just turn up the side, sir. There's a yard there."

"I'll find you." Munro went up the steps and rang the bell at the door.

The night porter opened it to him. "Good evening, Brigadier," he said.

"Sister Maria about?" Munro asked.

"No, she was called to the Cromwell Road Hospital."

"All right. I'll go on upstairs. I want to see Lieutenant Benson."

"I saw him go into the chapel a few minutes ago, sir, with one of the corporals and that German officer."

"Really?" Munro hesitated, then crossed to the chapel door.

Devlin eased open the door at the top of the steps and got the shock of his life. Corporal Smith was standing with his back to him no more than six feet away. He was examining a religious figure. Benson was up by the door. Devlin didn't hesitate. He pulled out the sap and lashed Smith across the back of the neck and moved back into the shelter of the door as the corporal went down with a clatter.

Benson called, "Smith, what's going on?"

He ran along the aisle and paused, staring down at the body. It was then, sensing too late that something was very wrong indeed, that he reached for the Webley revolver in his holster.

Devlin stepped out, the silenced Walther in his left hand, the sap in his right. "I wouldn't do that, son. This thing makes no more noise than you or me coughing. Now turn round."

Benson did as he was told, and Devlin gave him the same as Smith. The young lieutenant groaned, sank to his knees and fell across the corporal. Quickly Devlin searched them for handcuffs, but only Smith appeared to be carrying them.

"Are you there, Colonel?" he called.

Steiner stepped out of the confessional box, and Father Martin joined him. The old priest looked shocked and bewildered. "Major Conlon? What's happening here?"

"I'm truly sorry, Father." Devlin turned him around and handcuffed his wrists behind him.

He sat the old man down in a pew and

took out one of his makeshift gags. Martin said, "You're not a priest, I take it."

"My uncle was, Father."

"I forgive you, my son," Frank Martin said and submitted himself to the gag.

At that moment, the door opened and Dougal Munro walked in. Before he could say a word, Kurt Steiner had him around, an arm like steel across his throat.

"And who might this be?" Devlin demanded.

"Brigadier Dougal Munro," Steiner told him. "Of SOE."

"Is that a fact?" Devlin held the Walther in his right hand now. "This thing is silenced, as I'm sure you will know, Brigadier, so be sensible."

Steiner released him and Munro said bitterly, "My God, Devlin—Liam Devlin."

"As ever was, Brigadier."

"What happens now?" Steiner asked.

Devlin was excited, a little cocky. "A short trip down river, a gentle drive through the country and you'll be away while this lot are still running round in circles looking for us."

"Which must mean you intend to fly," Munro said. "Very interesting."

"Me and my big mouth," groaned Devlin.

He tapped Munro under the chin with the gun. "If I leave you, you'll have the RAF on the job before we know where we are. I could kill you, but I'm in a very generous mood."

"Which leaves what alternative?"

"We'll have to take you with us." He nodded to Steiner. "Watch him." And he eased open the door.

At that moment the night porter emerged from his cubbyhole with a tray containing a pot of tea, two cups and a milk jug. He went up the stairs whistling.

Devlin said, "Wonderful. No need for you lads to get your feet wet. We're going straight out of the front door and across the road. It's thick fog, so no one will notice a thing." He opened the door and urged Munro across the hall, the Walther at his back. "Don't forget, Brigadier, a wrong word and I blow your spine out."

It was Steiner who opened the door and led the way down to the pavement. The fog was thick and brown as only a London pea-souper could be and tasted sour at the back of the throat. Devlin pushed Munro across the road, Steiner followed. They didn't see a soul, and alone in their private world they went down the steps to the strand. At the bottom, Devlin paused and passed the gun to Steiner.

"I've got friends I don't want this old bugger to see or he'll be hanging them at Wadsworth Prison for treason."

"Only if they deserve it," Munro told him.

"A matter of opinion."

Devlin quickly tied the brigadier's hands with some of the twine he'd brought. Munro was wearing a silk scarf against the cold. The Irishman took that and bound it around his eyes.

"Right, let's go."

He started along the strand, a hand at Munro's elbow, and the motorboat loomed out of the darkness.

"Is that you, Liam?" Ryan called softly.

"As ever was. Now let's get the hell out of here," Devlin replied.

In the bedroom, Devlin changed quickly into the clerical suit and a dark polo-neck sweater. He collected what few belongings he needed, put them in a holdall together with the Luger and the Walther. He checked the Smith & Wesson in the ankle holster, picked up the bag and went out. When he went into the kitchen, Steiner was sitting at the table drinking tea with Ryan, Mary watching him in awe.

"Are you fit, Colonel?" Devlin demanded.

"Never better, Mr. Devlin."

Devlin tossed him the military trench coat he'd stolen from the Army and Navy Club the day he'd met Shaw. "That should do to cover the uniform. I'm sure Mary can find you a scarf."

"I can indeed." She ran out and returned with a white silk scarf which she gave to Steiner.

"That's kind of you," he said.

"Right, let's move it." Devlin opened the cupboard under the stairs to reveal Munro sitting in the corner with his hands tied and still wearing the scarf around his eyes. "Let's be having you, Brigadier."

He pulled Munro up and out and walked him to the front door. Ryan had already got the van from the garage, and it stood at the curb. They put Munro in the back, and Devlin checked his watch.

"Nine o'clock. A long hour, Michael, me old son. We'll be off now."

They shook hands. When he turned to Mary, she was in tears. Devlin put his bag in the van and opened his arms. She rushed into them and he embraced her.

"The wonderful life you'll have ahead of you and the wonderful girl you are."

"I'll never forget you." She was really crying now. "I'll pray for you every night."

He was too full to speak himself, got in beside Steiner and drove away. The German said, "A nice girl."

"Yes," Devlin said. "I shouldn't have involved them or that old priest, but there was nothing else I could do."

"The nature of the game we're in, Mr. Devlin," Munro said from the rear. "Tell me something, just to assuage my idle curiosity. Vargas."

"Oh, I smelt a rat there from the beginning," Devlin said. "It always seemed likely you were inviting us in, so to speak. I knew the only way to fool you was to fool Vargas as well. That's why he's still getting messages from Berlin."

"And your own contacts? Nobody recently active, am I right?"

"That's about it."

"You're a clever bastard, I'll say that for you. Mind you, as that fine old English saying has it: *There's many a slip between the cup and the lip.*"

"And what's that supposed to mean?"

"Fog, Mr. Devlin, fog," Dougal Munro said.

13

JACK CARVER'S big game in the back room at the Astoria Ballroom had not gone his way at all, and if there was one thing guaranteed to put him in a bad mood it was losing money. He broke off the game angrily at eight-thirty, lit a cigar and went down to the ballroom. He leaned on the balcony rail watching the crowd; and Eric, dancing down there with a young girl, saw him at once.

"Sorry, sweetness, another time," he said and went up the stairs to join his brother. "You've finished early, Jack."

"Yes, well I got bored, didn't I?"

Eric, who knew the signs, didn't pursue the matter. Instead he said, "I was thinking, Jack. You're sure you don't want to take some of the boys along when we pay that call?"

Carver was furiously angry. "What are you trying to say? That I can't take care of that little squirt on my own? That I need to go in team-handed?"

310

"I didn't mean anything, Jack, I was just thinking—"

"You think too bloody much, my son," his brother told him. "Come on, I'll show you. We'll go and see that little Irish bastard now."

The Humber, Eric at the wheel, turned into Cable Wharfe no more than ten minutes after the van had left.

"That's the house at the far end," Eric said.

"Right, we'll leave the motor here and walk. Don't want to alert them." Carver took the Browning from his pocket and pulled the slider. "Got yours?"

"Sure I have, Jack." Eric produced a Webley .38 revolver.

"Good boy. Let's go and give him some stick."

Mary was sitting at the table reading and Ryan was poking the fire when the kitchen door burst open and the Carvers entered. Mary screamed and Ryan turned, poker in hand.

"No you don't." Carver extended his arm, the Browning rigid in his hand. "You make one wrong move and I'll blow your head off. See to the bird, Eric."

311

"A pleasure, Jack." Eric slipped his revolver into his pocket, went and stood behind Mary and put his hands on her shoulders. "Now you be a good girl."

He kissed her neck and she squirmed in disgust. "Stop it!"

Ryan took a step forward. "Leave her alone."

Carver tapped him with the barrel of the Browning. "I give the orders here, so shut your face. Where is he?"

"Where's who?" Ryan demanded.

"The other Mick. The one who came dancing at the Astoria with the kid here. The clever little bastard who shot half my brother's ear off."

It was Mary who answered defiantly, "You're too late, they've gone."

"Is that a fact?" Carver said to Eric, "Leave her. Check upstairs and make sure you have your shooter in your hand."

Eric went out and Carver gestured at the other chair. "Sit," he ordered Ryan. The Irishman did as he was told, and Carver lit a cigarette. "She didn't say we'd missed him, she said we'd missed them."

"So what?" Ryan said.

"So who was that pal of yours and who's

he mixed up with? I want to know and you're going to tell me."

"Don't say a word, Uncle Michael," Mary cried.

"Not me, girl."

Carver hit him across the side of the face with the Browning, and Ryan went over backwards in the chair. As Mary screamed again, Carver said, "You should have stayed back home in the bogs where you belong, you and your mate."

Eric came back at that moment. "Here, what have I missed?"

"Just teaching him his manners. Anything?"

"Not a sausage. There was a major's uniform in one of the bedrooms."

"Is that a fact?" Carver turned back to Ryan, who was wiping blood from his face. "All right, I haven't got all night."

"Go stuff yourself."

"A hard man, eh? Watch the girl, Eric."

Eric moved behind her, pulled her up from the chair, his arms about her waist. "You like that, don't you? They all do."

She moaned, trying to get away, and Carver picked up the poker from the hearth and put it into the fire. "All right, hard man, we'll see how you like this. Either you tell me what I want to know or I put this, once it's nice and hot, to your niece's face. Not that she's much in the looks department, but this would really finish her off."

Mary tried to move, but Eric held her, laughing. Ryan said, "You bastard."

"It's been said before," Carver told him. "But it ain't true. Slur on my old lady, that."

He took the poker out. It was white hot. He put it to the tabletop and the dry wood burst into flame. Then he moved toward Mary, and the girl screamed in terror.

It was the scream which did it and Ryan cried out, "All right, I'll tell you."

"Okay," Carver said. "His name."

"Devlin—Liam Devlin."

"IRA? Am I right?"

"In a way."

"Who was with him?" Ryan hesitated and Carver turned and touched the girl's woolen cardigan so that it smoldered. "I ain't kidding, friend."

"He was doing a job for the Germans. Breaking out a prisoner they had here in London."

"And where is he now?"

"Driven off to a place near Romney. He's going to be picked up by a plane."

"In this fog? He'll be bleeding lucky.

What's this place they're going to?" Ryan hesitated, and Carver touched the poker to the girl's hair. The stench of burning was terrible and she screamed again.

Ryan broke completely. He was a good man, but it was impossible to accept what was happening. "Like I said, a place near Romney."

"Don't, Uncle Michael," Mary cried.

"A village called Charbury. Shaw Place is the house."

"Marvelous." Carver put the poker down on the hearth. "That wasn't too bad, was it?" He turned to Eric. "Fancy a little drive down to the country?"

"I don't mind, Jack." Eric kissed Mary on the neck again. "As long as I can have ten minutes upstairs with this little madam before we go."

She cried out in terror and revulsion, reached back and clawed his face. Eric released her with a howl of pain, then, as he turned, slapped her. She backed away as he advanced on her slowly, reached behind her and managed to get the kitchen door open. He grabbed at her, she kicked out at him, then staggered back across the terrace against the wall. There was an ugly snapping

315

sound as it gave way and she disappeared into darkness.

Ryan gave a cry and started forward, and Carver had him by the collar, the barrel of the Browning at his ear. "Go and check on her," he called to Eric.

Ryan stopped struggling and waited in silence. After a while Eric appeared, his face pale. "She's croaked, Jack. Fell on a jetty down there. Must have broken her neck or something."

Ryan kicked back against Carver's shin, shoving him away. He picked up the poker from the hearth, turned with it raised above his head, and Carver shot him in the heart.

There was silence. Eric wiped blood from his face. "What now, Jack?"

"We get out of here, that's what."

He led the way and Eric followed, closing the kitchen door. They turned along the wharf and got in the Humber. Carver lit a cigarette. "Where's that RAC map book?" Eric found it in the glove compartment, and Carver flipped through it. "Here we are, Romney Marsh and there's Charbury. Don't you remember? Before the war I used to take you and Mum down there to Rye for a day out by the sea."

Eric nodded. "Mum liked Rye."

"Let's get going then."

"To Charbury?" Eric said.

"Why not? We don't have anything better to do, and there's one aspect to all this that doesn't seem to have occurred to you, my old son. We catch up with Devlin and this German and take care of them, we'll be bleeding heroes." He tossed his cigarette out and replaced it with a cigar. "Move it, Eric," he said and leaned back in his seat.

At Chernay, visibility was no more than a hundred yards. Schellenberg and Asa stood in the radio room and waited while Leber checked the weather. The American wore a leather helmet, fur-lined flying jacket and boots. He smoked a cigarette nervously.

"Well?" he demanded.

"They've listened to RAF weather reports for the south of England. It's one of those situations, Captain—thick fog, but every so often the wind blows a hole in it."

"Okay," Asa said. "Let's stop monkeying around."

He went out, Schellenberg following, and walked to the plane. Schellenberg said, "Asa, what can I say?"

Asa laughed and pulled on his gloves. "General, I've been on borrowed time ever since I crash-landed in that blizzard in Finland. Take care of yourself."

He clambered into the cockpit and pulled down the cupola. Schellenberg stepped back out of the way. The Lysander started to move. It turned at the end of the field and came back into the wind. Asa boosted power and gave it everything, rushing headlong into that wall of fog, darkness and rain. He pulled back the column and started to climb, turning out to sea.

Schellenberg watched him go in awe. "Dear God," he murmured, "where do we find such men?"

He turned and walked back to the radio room.

In the study at Shaw Place Lavinia turned from the radio and removed her headphones. She hurried out and found Shaw in the kitchen cooking bacon and eggs.

"Felt a bit peckish, old girl." There was the usual tumbler of whisky close to hand, and for once she felt impatient.

"Good God, Max, the plane's on its way, and all you can think of is your wretched stomach. I'm going down to South Meadow."

She got her shooting jacket, one of her

brother's old tweed hats, found the bag of cycle lamps and set off, Nell following her. There was electricity in the barn, so she switched on the lights when she got there. It was obvious that, considering the weather, breaking the blackout regulations wouldn't matter, and there wasn't another house for two miles. She put the cycle lamps by the door and stood outside checking the wind direction. The fog was as thick as ever, showed no sign of lifting at all. Suddenly it was like a curtain parting and she could see a chink of light from her house three hundred yards away.

"How marvelous, Nell." She leaned down to fondle the dog's ears, and the fog dropped back into place as the wind died.

Getting out of London itself was the worst part, as Devlin discovered, crawling along in a line of traffic at fifteen to twenty miles an hour.

"A sod this," he said to Steiner.

"It will make us late for the rendezvous, I presume," Steiner said.

"A midnight departure was the aim. We're not done yet."

Munro said from the back, "Put a bit of a spoke in your wheel this lot, Mr. Devlin."

Devlin ignored him and kept on going. Once they were through Greenwich, there was much less traffic and he was able to make better time. He lit a cigarette with one hand. "We're on our way now."

Munro said, "I wouldn't count your chickens."

Devlin said, "You're a great man for the sayings, Brigadier. What about one from the Bible? 'The laughter of fools is as the crackling of thorns under a pot.'" And he increased speed.

The Carver brothers in the Humber had exactly the same problem getting out of London, and Eric managed to take the wrong turning in Greenwich town center, going three miles in the other direction. It was Jack who sorted him, getting out the RAC handbook and checking their route.

"It's bleeding simple. Greenwich to Maidstone, Maidstone to Ashford. From there you take the road to Rye and we turn off halfway for Charbury."

"But there's hardly any road signs these days, you know that, Jack," Eric said.

"Yes, well there's a war on, isn't there, so just get on with it."

Jack Carver leaned back, closed his eyes and had a nap.

There was a school of thought in both the Luftwaffe and RAF that recommended approaching an enemy coastline below the radar screen all the way on important missions. Asa remembered trying that with his old squadron during the Russo-Finnish war, coming in low off the sea to catch the Reds by surprise, all nice copy-book stuff, only nobody had counted on the presence of the Russian navy. Five planes that one had cost.

So he charted a course for Dungeness that took him along the Channel in a dead straight line. There were strong crosswinds, and that slowed him down, but it was good monotonous flying, and all he had to do was check for drift every so often. He stayed at eight thousand for most of the way, well above the fog, keeping a weather eye cocked for other planes.

When it came, it took even an old hand like him by surprise, the Spitfire that lifted out of the fog, banked and took up station to starboard. Up there, visibility was good with a half-moon, and Asa could see the pilot of the Spitfire clearly in the cockpit in helmet and goggles. The American raised a hand and waved.

A cheerful voice crackled over his radio. "Hello, Lysander, what are you up to?"

"Sorry," Asa replied. "Special Duties Squadron, operating out of Tempsford."

"A Yank, are you?"

"In the RAF," Asa told him.

"Saw the movie, old man. Terrible. Take care." The Spitfire banked away to the east very fast and disappeared into the distance.

Asa said softly, "That's what comes of living right, old buddy."

He went down into the fog until his altimeter showed a thousand feet, then turned in toward Dungeness and Romney Marsh.

Shaw had his meal and a considerable amount of whisky after it. He was slumped in his chair beside the sitting-room fire, his shotgun on the floor, when Lavinia came in.

"Oh, Max," she said. "What am I going to do with you?"

He stirred when she put a hand on his shoulder and looked up. "Hello, old girl. Everything all right?"

She went to the French windows and opened the curtains. The fog was as thick as ever. She closed the curtains and went back to him. "I'm going to go down to the barn, Max. It must be close now, the plane, I mean."

"All right, old girl."

He folded his arms and turned his head, closing his eyes again, and she gave up. She went into the study and hurriedly took down the radio's aerial, and then she packed everything into the carrying case. When she opened the front door, Nell slipped out beside her and they went down to the South Meadow together.

She stood outside the barn listening. There was no sound, the fog embracing everything. She went in and switched on the light. There was a workbench by the door. She set the radio up there, running the aerial wires along the wall, looping them over rusting old nails. She put on the headphones and switched to the voice frequency as Devlin had shown her and heard Asa Vaughan's voice instantly.

"Falcon, are you receiving me? I say again, are you receiving me?"

It was eleven forty-five, and the Lysander was only five miles away. Lavinia stood in the entrance to the barn looking up, holding the headphones in one hand against her left ear. Of the plane, there was no sound.

"Am receiving you, Lysander. Am receiving you."

"What are conditions in your nest?" Asa's voice crackled.

"Thick fog. Visibility down to fifty yards. Wind gusting occasionally. I estimate strength four to five. It only clears things intermittently."

"Have you placed your markers?" he asked.

She'd totally forgotten. "Oh, God, no, give me a few minutes."

She put down the headphones, got the bag of cycle lamps and ran out into the meadow. She arranged three of them in an inverted L shape, the cross bar at the upwind end, and switched them on so that their beams shone straight up into the sky. Then she ran to a point two hundred yards along the meadow, Nell chasing after her, and spaced out three more lamps.

She was panting for breath when she returned to the barn and reached for the headphones and mike. "Falcon here. Markers in place."

She stood in the doorway of the barn looking up. She could hear the Lysander clearly. It seemed to pass at a few hundred feet and moved away.

"Falcon here," she called. "I heard you. You were directly overhead."

"Can't see a thing," Asa replied. "It's bad."

At that moment Sir Maxwell Shaw appeared from the darkness. He was not wearing a raincoat or hat and was very drunk, his speech slurred and halting. "Ah, there you are, old girl, everything all right?"

"No it isn't," she told him.

Asa said, "I'll keep circling, just in case things change."

"Right, I'll stand by."

There was a crash of some sort just outside Ashford, a large produce truck and a private car, potatoes all over the road. Devlin, gripping the wheel impatiently, sat there in a queue of traffic for fifteen minutes before pulling out and turning the van.

"Already midnight," he said to Steiner. "We can't afford to hang about here. We'll find another way."

"Oh, dear," Munro said. "Having trouble are we, Mr. Devlin?"

"No, you old sod, but you will be if you don't shut up," Devlin told him and took the next road on the left.

It was at about the same time that Asa Vaughan took the Lysander down for the fourth attempt. The undercarriage was of the nonretractable type, and there were landing spotlights fitted in the wheel spats. He had them on, but all they showed him was the fog.

"Falcon, it's impossible. I'm not getting anywhere."

Strangely enough it was Maxwell Shaw who came up with the solution. "Needs more light," he said. "Lots more light. I mean, he'd see the bloody house if it was on fire, wouldn't he?"

"My God!" Lavinia said and reached for the mike. "Falcon here. Now listen carefully. I'm a pilot so I know what I'm talking about."

"Let's hear it," Asa said.

"My house is three hundred yards south of the meadow and down wind. I'm going to go up there now and put on every light in the place."

"Isn't that what they call advertising?" Asa said.

"Not in this fog, and there isn't another house for two miles. I'm going now. Good luck." She put down her headphones and

326

mike. "You stay here, Max, I shan't be long."

"All right, old girl."

She ran all the way to the house, got the front door open, gasping for breath, and started. She climbed the stairs first, going into every room, even the bathrooms, switched on the lights and yanked back the blackout curtains. Then she went down to the ground floor and did the same thing. She left quickly, and when she stopped after some fifty yards to look back, the house was ablaze with lights.

Maxwell Shaw was drinking from a hip flask when she returned. "Bloody place looks like a Christmas tree," he told her.

She ignored him and reached for the mike. "Right, I've done it. Is that any better?"

"We'll take a look," Asa said.

He took the Lysander down to five hundred feet, suddenly filled with a strange fatalism. "What the hell, Asa," he said softly. "If you survive this damn war, they'll only give you fifty years in Leavenworth, so what have you got to lose?"

He went in hard, and now the fog was suffused with a kind of glow, and a second later Shaw Place, every window alight, came into view. He had always been a fine pilot, but for a moment greatness took over as he pulled back the column and lifted over the house with feet to spare. And there on the other side were the lights of the meadow, the open barn door.

The Lysander landed perfectly, turned and taxied toward the barn. Lavinia got the doors fully open, her brother watching, and gestured Asa inside. He switched off the engine, took off his flying helmet and got out.

"I say, that was a bit hairy," she said and stuck out her hand. "I'm Lavinia Shaw and this is my brother Maxwell."

"Asa Vaughan. I really owe you one."

"Not at all. I'm a pilot myself. Used to fly a Tiger Moth from here."

"Good heavens, the fellow sounds like a damn Yank," Maxwell Shaw said.

"Well you could say I grew up there." Asa turned to Lavinia. "Where are the others?"

"No sign of Major Conlon, I'm afraid. Fog all the way from London to the coast. I expect they've got held up."

Asa nodded. "Okay, let's get a message out to Chernay right now telling them I'm down in one piece."

At Chernay in the radio room Schellenberg was in despair, for the RAF weather reports

Cherbourg had been monitoring indicated just how impossible the situation was. And then Leber, sitting by the radio in headphones, was convulsed into action.

"It's Falcon, General." He listened, writing furiously on his pad at the same time, tore off the sheet and passed it to Schellenberg. "He's made it, General, he managed to set that lovely bitch down."

"Yes," Schellenberg said. "He certainly did, but his passengers weren't waiting for him."

"He said delayed by the fog, General."

"Yes, well let's hope so. Tell him we'll be standing by."

Leber tapped out the message quickly and pulled the headphones down to his neck. "Why don't you go and put your feet up for an hour, General? I'm all right here."

"What I will do is go and have a shower and freshen myself up," Schellenberg told him. "Then we'll have some coffee together, Flight Sergeant."

He walked to the door, and Leber said, "After all, there's no rush. He'd never be able to get the Lysander in here until this weather improves."

"Yes, well let's not think about that for now," Schellenberg said and went out.

At Shaw Place, Asa helped Lavinia put out all the lights, going from room to room. Shaw was slumped in his chair by the fire, eyes glazed, very far gone indeed.

"Is he often like that?" Asa asked.

She left the French windows open but drew the curtains. "My brother isn't a happy man. Sorry, I didn't ask you your rank."

"Captain," he said.

"Well, Captain, let's say the drink helps. Come into the kitchen. I'll make some tea or coffee if you'd like it."

"Coffee would be great."

He sat on the edge of the table smoking a cigarette while she made the coffee, very handsome in the SS uniform, and she was acutely aware of him. He took off his flying jacket, and she saw the cuff title on his sleeve.

"Good heavens, the George Washington Legion. I didn't know there was such a thing. My brother was right. You are an American."

"I hope you won't hold it against me," he said.

"We won't, you beautiful Yankee bastard." As Asa turned, Liam Devlin came through the door and threw his arms around him. "How in the hell did you manage to land in that stuff, son? It took us all our time to make it from London by road."

"Genius, I suppose," Asa said modestly.

Munro appeared behind Devlin, still with his wrists bound and the scarf around his eyes. Steiner was at his shoulder. "Colonel Kurt Steiner, the object of the exercise, plus a little excess baggage we acquired along the way," Devlin said.

"Colonel, a pleasure." Asa shook Steiner's hand.

Lavinia said, "Why don't we all go into the living room and have a cup of coffee? It's just made."

"What a charming idea," Munro said.

"What you like and what you get are two different things, Brigadier," Devlin told him. "Still, if it's made, there's no harm. Five minutes and we're away."

"I wouldn't count on that. I'll have to check the situation at Chernay," Asa said to him as they moved through. "The weather was just as bad there when I left."

Devlin said, "That's all we need." In the living room he pushed Munro down into the other chair by the fire and looked at Maxwell Shaw in disgust. "Christ, if you struck a match he'd catch fire."

"He's really tied one on," Asa said.

Shaw woke up and opened his eyes. "What's that, eh?" He focused on Devlin. "Conlon, that you?"

"As ever was," Devlin answered.

Shaw sat up and looked across at Munro. "Who in the hell is that? What's he got that stupid thing round his eyes for?" He reached across and pulled off the scarf before anyone could stop him. Munro shook his head, blinking in the light. Shaw said, "I know you, don't I?"

"You should, Sir Maxwell," Dougal Munro told him. "We've been fellow members of the Army and Navy Club for years."

"Of course." Shaw nodded foolishly. "Thought I knew you."

"That's torn it, Brigadier," Devlin told him. "I'd intended to dump you somewhere in the marsh before we left to find your own way home, but now you know who these people are."

"Which means you have two choices. Shoot me or take me with you."

It was Steiner who said, "Is there room, Captain?"

"Oh, sure, we could manage," Asa said.

Steiner turned to the Irishman. "It's up to you, Mr. Devlin."

Munro said, "Never mind, my friend. I'm sure your Nazi masters will pay well for me."

Asa said, "I haven't had the chance to fill you in on what the score is over there yet. You'd better know now, because you'll be up to your necks in it if we get back over there in one piece."

"You'd better tell us then," Steiner said.

So Asa did.

The fog was as bad as ever as they all stood around the radio in the barn, Lavinia scribbling on the pad in front of her. She handed the message to Asa, who read it and passed it to Devlin. "They suggest we delay take-off for another hour. There's a slight chance conditions at Chernay might have improved by then."

Devlin glanced at Steiner. "We don't seem to have much choice."

"Well, I can't say I'm sorry for you." Munro turned to Lavinia with a smile of devastating charm. "I was wondering, my dear. Do you think when we get back to the house I might have tea this time."

Shaw was sprawled in his chair by the fire fast asleep. Munro sat opposite, wrists still bound. Asa was in the kitchen helping Lavinia.

Devlin said to Steiner, "I was thinking, Colonel, you might need a sidearm." He picked up his holdall, put it on the table and opened it. The silenced Walther was lying inside on top of a couple of shirts.

"A thought," Steiner said.

There was a gust of wind, a creaking at the French windows, and then the curtains were pulled back and Jack and Eric Carver stepped into the room, guns in their hands.

14

DEVLIN SAID, "Look what the wind's blown in."

Steiner said calmly, "Who are these men?"

"Well, the big ugly one is Jack Carver. He runs most of London's East End. Makes an honest bob out of protection, gambling, prostitution."

"Very funny," Carver said.

"The other one, the one who looks as if he's just crawled out of his hole, is his brother, Eric."

"I'll teach you." Eric advanced on him,

his face pinched and angry. "We'll give you what we gave that pal of yours and his niece."

Devlin went cold inside, his face on the instant turned deathly pale. "What are you telling me?"

"No funny stuff this time," Carver said. "Check to see if he has that bleeding gun up his trouser leg."

Eric dropped to one knee and relieved Devlin of the Smith & Wesson. "It won't work twice, you cunning sod."

"My friends?" Devlin said calmly. "What happened to them?"

Carver was enjoying himself. He took a cigar from his pocket, bit off the end and stuck it in his mouth. "I put the word out on you, my son. Didn't get anywhere, and then we had a stroke of luck. Eric saw the bird in Wapping High Street last evening. Followed her home."

"And?"

"We paid them a visit not long after you left. A little persuasion was all it took and here we are."

"And he talked, my friend, as easily as that?" Devlin asked. "I find that hard to believe." He turned to Steiner. "Don't you, Colonel?"

"I do indeed," Steiner said.

"Oh, I wouldn't think too badly of him." Carver flicked his lighter and put the flame to his cigar. "I mean, it was his niece he was concerned about. He had to do the decent thing there."

"Not that it did either of them much good." Eric smiled sadistically. "Want to know what happened to her? She made a run for it, went over the rail down to that jetty by the house. Broke her neck."

"And Michael?" Devlin asked Carver, barely managing to keep from choking.

"I shot him, didn't I? Isn't that what you do with dogs?"

Devlin took a step toward him, and the look on his face was terrible to see. "You're dead, the both of you."

Carver stopped smiling. "Not us, you little sod—you. What's more, I'm going to give you it in the belly so it takes time."

It was at that moment that Shaw came back to life. He opened his eyes, stretched and looked around him. "Now then, what's all this?"

At the same moment, the double doors were flung open and Lavinia appeared holding a tray, Asa beside her. "Tea everyone," she said, then froze.

"Just hold it right there, the both of you," Carver told them.

She looked absolutely terrified but didn't say a word.

It was Dougal Munro who tried to help her. "Steady, my dear. Just keep calm."

Shaw, on his feet, swayed drunkenly, eyes bloodshot, speech slurred. "You bloody swine. Who do you think you are coming into my house waving guns about?"

"Another step, you old fool, and I'll blow you away," Carver told him.

Lavinia shouted, "Do as he says, Max." She dropped the tray with a crash and took a step forward.

Carver turned and shot her, more as a reflex action than anything else. Maxwell Shaw, with a cry of rage, jumped at him, and Carver fired again, shooting him twice at close quarters.

Asa was on his knees beside Lavinia. He looked up. "She's dead."

"I warned you, didn't I?" Carver said, his face contorted.

"You certainly did, Mr. Carver," Kurt Steiner told him.

His hand went into Devlin's open holdall on the table, found the butt of the silenced Walther, brought it out in one smooth motion and fired once. The bullet caught Carver in the center of the forehead and he went back over the chair.

"Jack!" Eric screamed. And as he took a step forward, Devlin grabbed for his wrist, twisting it until Eric dropped the revolver.

Eric backed away and Devlin said, "You killed that girl, is that what you're telling me?"

He leaned down and picked up Maxwell Shaw's shotgun from the floor beside the chair.

Eric was terrified. "It was an accident. She was running away. Went over the rail." The curtains billowed in the wind from the open French windows, and he backed out onto the terrace.

"But what made her run? That's the thing," Devlin said, thumbing back the hammers.

"No!" Eric cried, and Devlin gave him both barrels, lifting him over the balustrade.

At Chernay it was almost two o'clock. Schellenberg was dozing in the chair in the corner of the radio room when Leber called to him.

"Falcon coming in, General."

Schellenberg hurried to his side. "What is it?"

"Another check on the weather. I've told him how bad things are here."

"And?"

"Just a moment, General, he's coming in again." He listened intently and looked up. "He says he's not prepared to wait any longer. He's leaving now."

Schellenberg nodded. "Just say good luck."

He went to the door, opened it and went out. The fog rolled in from the sea remorselessly, and he turned up the collar of his greatcoat to walk aimlessly along the side of the airstrip.

At roughly the same time, Horst Berger was sitting by the window in the room they had allocated to him at Belle-Île. He had found himself unable to sleep, the prospect of the morning was too momentous, so he sat there in the darkness, the window open, listening to the rain falling through the fog. There was a knock at the door, it opened, light falling into the room.

One of the SS duty sentries stood there. "Sturmbannführer," he called softly.

"I'm here. What is it?"

"The Reichsführer wants you. He's waiting now at his apartment."

"Five minutes," Berger told him, and the man went out.

In the sitting room of his apartment, Himmler was standing by the fire in full uniform when Berger knocked and entered. The Reichsführer turned. "Ah, there you are."

"Reichsführer."

"The Führer obviously can't sleep. He's sent for me. Asked particularly that I bring you."

"Does the Reichsführer think this is of any significance?"

"Not at all," Himmler said. "The Führer's health has been something of a problem for quite some time. His inability to sleep is only one of many symptoms. He has come to rely on the ministrations of his personal physician, Professor Morell, to an inordinate degree. Unfortunately, from the Führer's point of view at the moment, Morell is in Berlin and the Führer is here."

"Morell is of such vital importance then?" Berger asked.

"There are those who would consider him a quack," Himmler said. "On the other hand, the Führer can't be considered an easy patient."

"I see, Reichsführer. But why am I commanded?"

"Who knows? Some whim or other." Himmler consulted his watch. "We are due at his suite in fifteen minutes. With the Führer, Berger, time is everything. Not one minute more, not one minute less. There's fresh coffee on the table there. Time for you to have a cup before we go."

In the barn at Shaw Place, everyone waited while Devlin tapped out his message on the radio. He put down the headphones, switched off and turned to Steiner and Asa, who stood there, Dougal Munro, his hands still bound, between them.

"That's it," Devlin said. "I've told Schellenberg we're leaving."

"Then let's get the plane out," Asa said.

Munro stood against the wall while the three of them manhandled the Lysander out into the fog. They rolled it some distance away from the barn. Asa got the cupola up and reached for his helmet.

"What about our friend in the barn?" Steiner asked.

"He stays," Devlin said.

Steiner turned to him. "You're sure?"

"Colonel," Devlin said, "you're a nice

man, and due to the vagaries of war, I happen to be on your side at the moment, but this is a personal thing. I haven't the slightest intention of handing over the head of Section D at SOE to German intelligence. Now you two get in and start up. I'll be with you in a minute."

When he went in the barn, Munro was half sitting on the table by the radio, struggling with the twine around his wrists. He paused as Devlin entered. The Irishman took a small pocketknife from his pocket and opened the blade.

"Here, let me, Brigadier."

He sliced through the twine, freeing him, and Munro rubbed at his wrists. "What's this?"

"Sure and you didn't really think I was going to hand you over to those Nazi bastards, now did you? There was a small problem for a while, Shaw exposing you to things, as it were, but there's no one left. My good friend Michael Ryan and Mary, his niece, at Cable Wharfe, the Shaws here. All gone. No one you could hurt."

"God help me, Devlin, I'll never understand you."

"And why should you, Brigadier, when I don't understand myself most of the time?"

The engine of the Lysander started up, and Devlin stuck a cigarette in his mouth. "We'll be going now. You could alert the RAF, but they'd need the luck of the devil to find us in this fog."

"True," Munro agreed.

Devlin flicked his lighter. "On the other hand, it's just possible you might think Walter Schellenberg has the right idea."

"Strange," Munro said. "There have been moments in this war when I'd have jumped for joy at the idea of someone killing Hitler."

"A great man once said that as the times change, sensible men change with them." Devlin moved to the door. "Goodbye, Brigadier, I don't expect we'll be seeing each other again."

"I wish I could count on that," Munro said.

The Irishman hurried across to the Lysander, where Steiner was stripping the canvas with the RAF roundels from the wings, revealing the Luftwaffe insignia. Devlin ran to the tailplane, did the same there, then scrambled inside after Steiner. The Lysander taxied to the end of the meadow and turned into the wind. A moment later, it roared down the runway and took off. Munro stood there listening to the sound of it disappear into the night. There was a sudden whimper, and Nell slipped out of the darkness and sat there looking up at him. When he turned and started back to the house, she followed him.

Jack Carter, in the outer office at SOE headquarters, heard the red phone's distinctive sound and rushed in at once to answer it.

"Jack?" Munro said.

"Thank God, sir, I've been worried as hell. I got in from York and walked straight into a minefield. All hell broken loose at St. Mary's Priory, and the porter said you were there, sir. I mean, what the hell happened?"

"It's quite simple, Jack. A rather clever gentleman called Liam Devlin made fools of the lot of us and is at this very moment flying back to France with Colonel Kurt Steiner."

"Shall I alert the RAF?" Carter asked.

"I'll take care of it. More important things to do. Number one, there's a house on Cable Wharfe in Wapping owned by a man called Ryan. You'll find him and his niece there dead. I want a disposal team as soon as possible. Use that crematorium in North London."

"Right, sir."

"I also want a disposal team here, Jack.

That's Shaw Place outside the village of Charbury in Romney Marsh. Come yourself. I'll wait for you."

He put the phone down. No question of phoning the RAF of course. Schellenberg was right and that was that. He left the study and went to the front door. When he opened it, the fog was as thick as ever. Nell whined and sat on her haunches, staring up at him.

Munro bent down and fondled her ears. "Poor old girl," he said. "And poor old Devlin. I wish him luck."

When Himmler and Berger were admitted to the Führer's apartment, Adolf Hitler was sitting beside an enormous stone fireplace in which a log fire burned brightly. He had a file open on his knees which he continued to read as they stood there waiting. After a while he looked up, a slightly vacant look in his eyes.

"Reichsführer?"

"You wished to see me and Sturmbannführer Berger."

"Ah, yes." Hitler closed the file and put it on a small table. "The young man who has so brilliantly organized my security here. I'm impressed, Reichsführer." He stood and put a hand on Berger's shoulder. "You've done well."

Berger held himself stiff as a ramrod. "My honor to serve, my Führer."

Hitler touched Berger's Iron Cross First Class with one finger. "A brave soldier too, I see." He turned to Himmler. "Obersturmbannführer would be more appropriate here, I think."

"I'll take care of it, my Führer," Himmler told him.

"Good." Hitler turned back to Berger and smiled indulgently. "Now off you go. The Reichsführer and I have things to discuss."

Berger clicked his heels and raised his right arm. "Heil Hitler," he said, turned on his heel and went out.

Hitler returned to his chair and indicated the one opposite. "Join me, Reichsführer."

"A privilege."

Himmler sat down and Hitler said, "Insomnia can be a blessing in disguise. It gives one extra time to ponder the really important things. This file, for example." He picked it up. "A joint report from Rommel and Canaris in which they try to persuade me that the Allies will attempt an invasion by way of Normandy. Nonsense, of course. Even Eisenhower couldn't be so foolish."

"I agree, my Führer."

"No, it's obvious that the Pas de Calais will be the target, any idiot can see that."

Himmler said carefully, "And yet you still intend to confirm Rommel as Commander of Army Group B with full responsibility for the Atlantic Wall defenses?"

"Why not?" Hitler said. "A brilliant soldier, we all know that. He'll have to accept my decision in this matter with good grace and follow orders, as will Canaris."

"But will they, my Führer?"

"Do you doubt their loyalty?" Hitler asked. "Is that what you are implying?"

"What can I say, my Führer. The admiral has not always been as enthusiastic toward the cause of National Socialism as I would like. As for Rommel"—Himmler shrugged—"the people's hero. Such popularity easily leads to arrogance."

"Rommel will do as he is told," Hitler said serenely. "I am well aware, as are you, of the existence of those extremists in the army who would destroy me if they could. I am also aware that it is a distinct possibility that Rommel is in sympathy with such aims. At the right moment there will be a noose waiting for all such traitors."

"And richly deserved, my Führer."

Hitler got up and stood with his back to the fire. "One must learn how to handle these people, Reichsführer. That's why I insisted they join me for breakfast at seven. As you know, they're staying in Rennes overnight. This means they must rise at a rather early hour to get here in time. I like to keep people like this slightly unbalanced. I find it pays."

"Brilliant, my Führer."

"And before you go, remember one thing." Hitler's face was very calm, and Himmler stood up. "Since I took power, how many attempts on my life? How many plots?"

Himmler for once was caught. "I'm not sure."

"At least sixteen," Hitler said. "And this argues divine intervention. The only logical explanation."

Himmler swallowed hard. "Of course, my Führer."

Hitler smiled benignly. "Now be off with you. Try and get a little sleep and I'll see you at breakfast." He turned to look down at the fire, and Himmler left quickly.

The English Channel was fogged in for most of the way to Cap de la Hague, and Asa took advantage of it, using the cover, making good time, finally turning in toward the French coast just after three.

He called Chernay over the radio. "Chernay, Falcon here. What's the situation?"

In the radio room, Schellenberg sprang from his chair and crossed to Leber. The flight sergeant said, "We've had some clearance with wind but not enough.

Ceiling zero one minute, then it clears to maybe a hundred feet, then back again."

"Is there anywhere else to go?" Asa demanded.

"Not round here. Cherbourg's totally closed in."

Schellenberg took the mike. "Asa, it's me. Are you all there?"

"We sure as hell are. Your Colonel Steiner, Devlin and me, only we don't seem to have any place to go."

"What's your fuel position?"

"I figure I'm good for about forty-five minutes. What I'll do is stooge around for a while. Keep on the line and let me know the second there's any kind of improvement."

Leber said, "I'll have the men light runway flares, General, it might help."

"I'll take care of that," Schellenberg told him. "You stay on the radio." And he hurried out.

After twenty minutes, Asa said, "This is no good. Sit tight and I'll give it a shot."

He took the Lysander down, his wheel spots on, and the fog enveloped him, just as it had done at Shaw Place. At six hundred feet he pulled the column back into his stomach and went up, coming out of the mist and fog at around a thousand.

The stars still glistened palely, and what was left of the moon was low, dawn streaking the horizon. Asa called, "It's hopeless. Suicide to try and land. I'd rather put her down in the sea."

"The tide's out, Captain," Leber answered.

"Is that a fact? How much beach do you get down there?"

"It runs for miles."

"Then that's it. It's some sort of a chance anyway."

Schellenberg's voice sounded. "Are you sure, Asa?"

"The only thing I'm sure of, General, is that we don't have any choice. We'll see you or we won't. Over and out."

Schellenberg dropped the mike and turned to Leber. "Can we get down there?"

"Oh, yes, General, there's a road leading to an old slipway."

"Good. Then let's get moving."

"If I have to land in the sea, this thing's not going to float for very long," Asa said over his shoulder to Steiner and Devlin. "There's a dinghy pack there behind you. The yellow thing. Get it out fast, pull the red tag and it inflates itself."

Steiner smiled. "You swim, of course, Mr. Devlin."

Devlin smiled back. "Some of the time."

Asa started down, easing the column forward, sweat on his face, all the way to five hundred and his altimeter kept on going. The Lysander bucked in a heavy gust of wind, and they passed three hundred.

Devlin cried, "I saw something."

The fog seemed to open before them, as if a curtain was being pulled to each side and there were great waves surging in from the Atlantic, half a mile of wet sand stretching toward the cliffs of Cap de la Hague. Asa heaved the column back, the Lysander leveled out no more than fifty feet above the whitecaps that pounded into surf on the shore.

Asa slammed the instrument panel with

one hand. "You beautiful, beautiful bitch. I love you," he cried and turned into the wind to land.

The truck containing Schellenberg, Leber and several Luftwaffe mechanics had reached the slipway at the very moment the Lysander burst into view.

"He made it, General," Leber cried. "What a pilot!" He ran forward waving, followed by his men.

Schellenberg felt totally drained. He lit a cigarette and waited as the Lysander taxied toward the end of the slipway. It came to a halt, and Leber and his men cheered as Asa switched off the engine. Devlin and Steiner got out first and Asa followed, taking off his flying helmet and tossing it into the cockpit.

Leber said, "Quite a job, Captain."

Asa said, "Treat her with care, Flight Sergeant. Only the best. She's earned it. Will she be safe here?"

"Oh, yes, the tide is on the turn, but it doesn't come up this far."

"Fine. Do an engine check, and you'll have to refuel by hand."

"As you say, Captain."

Schellenberg stood waiting as Steiner and Devlin came toward him. He held out his hand to Steiner. "Colonel, a pleasure to see you here."

"General," Steiner said.

Schellenberg turned to Devlin. "As for you, my mad Irish friend, I still can't believe you're here."

"Well, you know what I always say, Walter, me old son, all you have to do is live right." Devlin grinned. "Would you think there might be a bit of breakfast somewhere? I'm starved."

They sat around the table in the little canteen drinking coffee. Schellenberg said, "So, the Führer arrived safely last night."

"And Rommel and the admiral?" Devlin asked.

"I've no idea where they've been staying, but they will be joining him very soon now. Must be on their way."

Steiner said, "This plan of yours makes a wild kind of sense, but there is a considerable uncertainty."

"You don't think the men of this parachute detachment will follow you?"

"Oh, no, I mean what happens to the three of you in the château before we arrive."

"Yes, well, we've no choice," Schellenberg said. "There's no other way."

"Yes, I see that."

There was a moment's silence, and Schellenberg said, "Are you with me in this, Colonel, or not? There isn't much time."

Steiner got up and moved to the window. It had started to rain heavily, and he stared out for a moment and turned. "I have little reason to like the Führer and not just because of what happened to my father. I could say he's bad for everybody, a disaster for the human race, but for me, the most important thing is that he's bad for Germany. Having said that, Himmler as head of state would be infinitely worse. At least with the Führer in charge, one has the prospect of an end to this bloody war."

"So you will join with me in this?"

"I don't think any of us have a choice."

Asa shrugged. "What the hell, you can count me in."

Devlin stood up and stretched. "Right, well, let's get on with it." And he opened the door and went out.

When Schellenberg went into the hut he and Asa had been using, Devlin had a foot on the bed, his trouser leg rolled up as he adjusted the Smith & Wesson in the ankle holster.

"Your ace in the hole, my friend?"

"And this." Devlin took the silenced Walther from his holdall and put it into his waistband at the rear. Then he took out the Luger. "This is the one for the pocket. I doubt those SS guards will let us through the door armed, so best to have something to give them."

"Do you think it will work?" Schellenberg asked.

"Uncertainty—and from you at this stage, General?"

"Not really. You see the Allies have made one thing very clear. No negotiated peace. Total surrender. The last thing Himmler could afford."

"Yes, there's a rope waiting for him all right one of these days."

"And me also, perhaps. I am, after all, a general of the SS," Schellenberg said.

"Don't worry, Walter." Devlin smiled. "If you end up in a prison cell, I'll break you out and for free. Now let's get moving."

Field Marshal Erwin Rommel and Admiral Canaris had left Rennes at five o'clock in a Mercedes limousine driven, for reasons of security, by Rommel's aide, a Major Carl Ritter. Two military police motorcyclists were their only escort and led the way as they twisted and turned through the narrow French lanes in the early morning gloom.

"Of course, the only reason we've had to turn out at such a ridiculous time is because he wants us at a disadvantage," Canaris said.

"The Führer likes all of us at a disadvantage, Admiral," Rommel said. "I'd have thought you'd have learned that long ago."

"I wonder what he's up to," Canaris said. "We know he's going to confirm your appointment as Commander of Army Group B, but he could have made you fly to Berlin for that."

"Exactly," Rommel said. "And there are such things as telephones. No, I think it's the Normandy business."

"But surely we can make him see sense there," Canaris said. "The report we've put together is really quite conclusive."

"Yes, but unfortunately the Führer favors the Pas de Calais, and so does his astrologer."

"And Uncle Heini?" Canaris suggested.

"Himmler always agrees with the Führer, you know that as well as I do."

Beyond, through a break in the rain, they saw Belle-Île. "Impressive," Rommel said.

"Yes, very Wagnerian," Canaris said dryly. "The castle at the end of the world.

The Führer must like that. He and Himmler must be enjoying themselves."

"Have you ever wondered how it came to happen, Admiral? How we came to allow such monsters to control the destinies of millions of people?" Erwin Rommel asked.

"Every day of my life," Canaris replied.

The Mercedes turned off the road and started up to the château, the motorcyclists leading the way.

15

It was just after six, and Hauptmann Erich Kramer, commanding the 12th Parachute Detachment at St.-Aubin, was having coffee in his office when he heard a vehicle drive into the farmyard. He went to the window and saw a *Kübelwagen*, its canvas hood up against the rain. Asa got out first, followed by Schellenberg and Devlin.

Kramer recognized them instantly from the last visit and frowned. "Now what in the hell do they want?" he said softly.

And then Kurt Steiner emerged. Having no cap, he had borrowed a Luftwaffe sidecap from Flight Sergeant Leber, what was commonly referred to as a *Schiff*. It was, as it happened, an affectation of many old-timers in the Parachute Regiment. He stood there in the rain in his blue-gray flying blouse with the yellow collar patches, jump trousers and boots. Kramer took in the Knight's Cross with Oak Leaves, the silver and gold eagle of the paratrooper's badge, the Kreta and Afrika Korps cuff titles. He recognized him, of course, a legend to everyone in the Parachute Regiment.

"Oh, my God," he murmured as he reached for his cap and opened the door, buttoning his blouse. "Colonel Steiner— sir." He got his heels together and saluted, ignoring the others. "I can't tell you what an honor this is."

"A pleasure. Captain Kramer, isn't it?" Steiner took in Kramer's cuff titles, the ribbon for the Winter War. "So, we are old comrades, it would seem."

"Yes, Colonel."

Several paratroopers had emerged from their canteen, curious about the arrivals. At the sight of Steiner they all jumped to attention. "At ease, lads," he called and said to Kramer, "What strength have you here?"

"Thirty-five only, Colonel."

"Good," Steiner told him. "I'm going to

need everyone, including you, of course, so let's get in out of this rain and I'll explain."

The thirty-five men of the 12th Parachute Detachment stood in four ranks in the rain in the farmyard. They wore the steel helmets peculiar to the Parachute Regiment, baggy jump smocks, and most of them had Schmeisser machine pistols slung across their chests. They stood there, rigid at attention, as Steiner addressed them, Schellenberg, Devlin and Asa Vaughan behind him, Kramer at one side.

Steiner hadn't bothered with niceties, only the facts. "So there it is. The Führer is to meet his death very shortly at the hands of traitorous elements of the SS. Our job is to stop them. Any questions?"

There wasn't a word, only the heavy rain drumming down, and Steiner turned to Kramer. "Get them ready, Captain."

"Zu befehl, Herr Oberst." Kramer saluted.

Steiner turned to the others. "Will fifteen minutes be enough for you?"

"Then you arrive like a Panzer column," Schellenberg told him. "Very fast indeed."

He and Asa got in the *Kübelwagen*. Devlin, the black hat slanted over one ear, his trench coat already soaked, said to Steiner, "In a way, we've been here before."

"I know, and the same old question. Are we playing the game or is the game playing us?"

"Let's hope we have better luck than we did last time, Colonel." Devlin smiled and got in the back of the *Kübelwagen*, and Asa drove away.

At the Château de Belle-Île, Rommel, Canaris and Major Ritter went up the steps to the main entrance. One of the two SS guards opened the door and they went inside. There seemed to be guards everywhere.

Rommel said to Canaris as he unbuttoned his coat, "It looks rather like some weekend SS convention, the kind they used to have in Bavaria in the old days."

Berger came down the stairs and advanced to meet them. "Herr Admiral, Herr Field Marshal, a great pleasure. Sturmbannführer Berger in charge of security."

"Major." Rommel nodded.

"The Führer is waiting in the dining hall. He has requested that no one bears arms in his presence."

Rommel and Ritter took their pistols from

their holsters. "I trust we're not late," the field marshal said.

"Actually, you are early by two minutes." Berger gave him the good-humored smile of one soldier to another. "May I show you the way?"

He opened the great oak door and they followed him in. The long dining table was laid for four people only. The Führer was standing by the stone fireplace looking down into the burning logs. He turned and faced them. "Ah, there you are."

Rommel said, "I trust you are well, my Führer."

Hitler nodded to Canaris. "Herr Admiral." His eyes flickered to Ritter, who stood rigidly at attention clutching a briefcase. "And who have we here?"

"My personal aide, Major Carl Ritter, my Führer. He has further details on the Normandy situation that we have already discussed," Rommel said.

"More reports?" Hitler shrugged. "If you must, I suppose." He turned to Berger. "Have another place laid at the table and see what's keeping the Reichsführer."

As Berger moved to the door, it opened and Himmler entered. He wore the black dress uniform and his face was pale, a faint

edge of excitement to him that he found difficult to conceal. "I apologize, my Führer, a
phone call from Berlin as I was about to leave
my room." He nodded. "Herr Admiral,
Field Marshal."

"And the field marshal's aide, Major Ritter." Hitler rubbed his hands together. "I
really feel extraordinarily hungry. You know,
gentlemen, perhaps one should do this more
often. The early breakfast, I mean. It leaves
so much of the day for matters of importance. But come. Sit."

He himself took the head of the table.
Rommel and Canaris on his right, Himmler
and Ritter on the left. "So," he said. "Let's
begin. Food before business."

He picked up the small silver bell at his
right hand and rang it.

It was no more than ten minutes later that
the *Kübelwagen* arrived at the main gate.
Schellenberg leaned out. The sergeant who
came forward took in his uniform and saluted.

"The Führer is expecting us," Schellenberg told him.

The sergeant looked uncertain. "I've orders to admit no one, General."

"Don't be stupid, man," Schellenberg

said. "That hardly applies to me." He nodded to Asa. "Drive on, Hauptsturmführer."

They drove into the inner courtyard and stopped. Devlin said, "You know what the Spaniards call the instant when the bullfighter goes in for the kill and doesn't know whether he'll live or die? The moment of truth."

"Not now, Mr. Devlin," Schellenberg said. "Let's just keep going." And he marched up the wide steps and reached for the handle of the front door.

Hitler was enjoying himself, working his way through a plate of toast and fruit. "One thing about the French, they really do make rather excellent bread," he said and reached for another slice.

The door opened and an SS sergeant major entered. It was Himmler who spoke to him. "I thought I made it clear we were not to be disturbed for any reason."

"Yes, Reichsführer, but General Schellenberg is here with a Hauptsturinführer and some civilian. Says it is imperative he sees the Führer."

Himmler said, "Nonsense, you have your orders!"

Hitler cut in at once. "Schellenberg? Now

I wonder what that can be about. Bring them in, Sergeant Major."

Schellenberg, Devlin and Asa waited in the hall by the door. The sergeant major returned. "The Führer will see you, General, but all weapons must be left here. I have my orders. It applies to everyone."

"Of course." Schellenberg took his pistol from its holster, slapping it down on the table.

Asa did the same, and Devlin took the Luger from his coat pocket. "All contributions graciously given."

The sergeant major said, "If you would follow me, gentlemen." He turned and led the way across the hall.

When they went in, Hitler was still eating. Rommel and Canaris looked up curiously. Himmler was deathly pale.

Hitler said, "Now then, Schellenberg, what brings you here?"

"I regret the intrusion, my Führer, but a matter of the gravest urgency has come to my attention."

"And how urgent would that be?" Hitler demanded.

"A question of your very life, my Führer, or should I say an attempt on your life."

"Impossible," Himmler said.

Hitler waved him to silence and glanced at Devlin and Asa Vaughan. "And who have we here?"

"If I may explain. The Reichsführer recently gave me the task of planning the safe return to the Reich of a certain Colonel Kurt Steiner, who was held prisoner in the Tower of London for a while. Herr Devlin here and Hauptsturmführer Vaughan succeeded triumphantly in this matter, delivered Steiner to me at the small Luftwaffe base nearby a short time ago."

Hitler said to Himmler, "I knew nothing of this."

Himmler looked quite wretched. "It was to be a surprise, my Führer."

Hitler turned again to Schellenberg. "This Colonel Steiner, where is he?"

"He'll be here soon. The thing is, I received an anonymous telephone call only a couple of hours ago. I regret to have to say this in the presence of the Reichsführer, but whoever it was spoke of treachery, even within the ranks of the SS."

Himmler was almost choking. "Impossible."

"An officer named Berger was referred to."

Hitler said, "But Sturmbannführer Berger is in charge of my security here. I've just had him promoted."

"Nevertheless, my Führer, that is what I was told."

"Which just goes to show you can't trust anyone," Horst Berger called, and moved out of the shadows at the end of the dining hall, an SS man on either side of him holding a machine pistol.

Steiner and Captain Kramer led the way up the hill to the château in a *Kübelwagen*, the top down in spite of the rain. The paratroopers followed packed into two troop carriers. Steiner had a stick grenade tucked into the top of one of his jump boots and a Schmeisser ready in his lap.

"When we go, we go hard, no stopping, remember that," he said.

"We're with you all the way, Colonel," Kramer told him.

He slowed at the outer gate, and the SS sergeant came forward. "What's all this?"

Steiner raised the Schmeisser, lifted him back with a quick burst, was on his feet and swinging to cut down the other guard as Kramer took the *Kübelwagen* forward with a surge of power.

As they reached the bottom of the steps leading to the front door, more SS appeared from the guardhouse on the right. Steiner pulled the stick grenade from his boot and tossed it into the center of them, then he leapt from the *Kübelwagen* and started up the steps. Behind him the paratroopers jumped from the troop carriers and stormed after him, firing across the courtyard at the SS.

"You dare to approach me like this, a gun in your hand?" Hitler said to Berger, his eyes blazing.

"I regret to have to say it, my Führer, but your moment has come—you, Field Marshal Rommel here, the admiral." Berger shook his head. "We can no longer afford any of you."

Hitler said, "You can't kill me, you young fool, it's an impossibility."

"Really?" Berger said. "And why would that be?"

"Because it is not my destiny to die here," Hitler told him calmly. "Because God is on my side."

Somewhere in the distance was the sound of shooting. Berger half turned to glance at the door, and Major Ritter leapt to his feet, threw his briefcase at him and ran for the door. "Guards!" he shouted.

One of the SS men fired his Schmeisser, shooting him in the back several times.

Schellenberg said, "Mr. Devlin."

Devlin's hand found the butt of the silenced Walther in his waistband against the small of his back. His first bullet caught the man who had just machine-gunned Ritter in the temple, the second took the other SS man in the heart. Berger swung to face him, his mouth open in a terrible cry of rage, and Devlin's third bullet hit him between the eyes.

Devlin walked across and looked down at him, the Walther slack in his hand. "You wouldn't be told, son, would you? I said you needed a different class of work."

Behind him the doors burst open and Kurt Steiner rushed in at the head of his men.

When Schellenberg knocked and entered Himmler's room, he found the Reichsführer standing at the window. It was instantly evident that he intended to brazen it out.

"Ah, there you are, General. A most unfortunate business. It reflects so terribly on all of us of the SS. Thank goodness the Führer sees Berger's abominable treachery as an individual lapse."

"Fortunate for all of us, Reichsführer."

Himmler sat down. "The anonymous phone call you mentioned. You've absolutely no idea who it was?"

"I'm afraid not."

"A pity. Still . . ." Himmler looked at his watch. "The Führer intends to leave at noon, and I shall fly back to Berlin with him. Canaris goes with us. Rommel has already left."

"I see," Schellenberg said.

"Before he leaves, the Führer wants to see you and the other three. I believe he thinks decorations are in order."

"Decorations?" Schellenberg said.

"The Führer is never without them, General, carries a supply in his personal case wherever he goes. He believes in rewarding loyal service, and so do I."

"Reichsführer."

Schellenberg turned to the door, and Himmler said, "Better for all of us if this shocking affair never happened. You follow me, General? Rommel and Canaris will keep their mouths shut, and easy enough to handle those paratroopers. A posting back to the Russian Front will take care of them."

"I see, Reichsführer," Schellenberg said carefully.

"Which, of course, leaves us with Steiner, Hauptsturmführer Vaughan and the man Devlin. I feel they could all prove a serious embarrassment, as I'm sure you will agree."

"Is the Reichsführer suggesting . . ." Schellenberg began.

"Nothing," Himmler told him. "I'm suggesting nothing. I simply leave it to your own good sense."

It was just before noon in the library, as Schellenberg, Steiner, Asa and Devlin waited, that the door opened and the Führer entered followed by Canaris and Himmler, who carried a small leather briefcase.

"Gentlemen," Hitler said.

The three officers jumped to attention, and Devlin, sitting on the window seat, got up awkwardly. Hitler nodded to Himmler, who opened the case which was full of decorations.

"To you, General Schellenberg, the German Cross in Gold, and also to you, Hauptsturmführer Vaughan." He pinned on the decorations, then turned to Steiner. "You, Colonel Steiner, already have the Knight's

Cross with Oak Leaves. I now award you the Swords."

"Thank you, my Führer," Kurt Steiner replied with considerable irony.

"And to you, Mr. Devlin," the Führer said, turning to the Irishman, "the Iron Cross First Class."

Devlin couldn't think of a thing to say, stifled an insane desire to laugh as the cross was pinned to his jacket.

"You have my gratitude, gentlemen, and the gratitude of all the German people," Hitler told them. He turned and went out, Himmler trailing behind.

Canaris lingered for a moment at the door. "A most instructive morning, but I'd take care if I were you from now on, Walter."

The door closed. Devlin said, "What happens now?"

"The Führer returns to Berlin at once," Schellenberg said. "Canaris and Himmler go with him."

"What about us?" Asa Vaughan asked.

"There's a slight problem there. The Reichsführer has made it plain he doesn't want you three back in Berlin. In fact, he doesn't want you around at all."

"I see," Steiner said. "And you're supposed to take care of us?"

"Something like that."

"The old sod," Devlin said.

"Of course there is the Lysander waiting on the beach at Chernay," Schellenberg said. "Leber will have had it checked out by now and refueled."

"But where in the hell do we go?" Asa Vaughan demanded "We just got out of England by the skin of our teeth, and Germany's certainly too hot for us."

Schellenberg glanced inquiringly at Devlin, and the Irishman started to laugh. "Have you ever been to Ireland?" he asked Vaughan.

It was cold on the beach, the tide much higher than it had been that morning, but there was still ample space to take off.

"I've checked everything," Flight Sergeant Leber said to Asa. "You shouldn't have any problems, Hauptsturmführer."

Schellenberg said, "You go back to the airfield now, Flight Sergeant. I'll join you later."

Leber saluted and walked away. Schellenberg shook hands with Steiner and Asa. "Gentlemen, good luck." They got into the Lysander, and he turned to Devlin. "You are a truly remarkable man."

Devlin said, "Come with us, Walter, nothing for you back there."

"Too late, my friend. As I've said before, far too late to get off the merry-go-round now."

"And what will Himmler say when he hears that you let us go?"

"Oh, I've thought of that. An excellent marksman like you should have no difficulty in shooting me in the shoulder. Let's make it the left one. A flesh wound, naturally."

"Jesus, it's the cunning old fox you are."

Schellenberg walked away, then turned. Devlin's hand came out of his pocket holding the Walther. It coughed once and Schellenberg staggered, clutching at his shoulder. There was blood between his fingers, and he smiled. "Goodbye, Mr. Devlin."

The Irishman scrambled in and pulled down the cupola. Asa turned into the wind, the Lysander roared along the beach and lifted off. Schellenberg watched as it sped out to sea. After a while he turned and, still clutching his shoulder, walked back toward the slipway.

Lough Conn, in the County of Mayo and not too far from Killala Bay on the west coast of Ireland, is better than ten miles long. On that evening in the failing light as darkness swept down from the mountains, its surface was like black glass.

Michael Murphy farmed close to the southern end of the lough, but that day he had been fishing and drinking poteen until, in the words of his old grannie, he didn't know whether he was here or there. It started to rain with a sudden rush, and he reached for his oars, singing softly to himself.

There was a roaring in his ears, a rush of air and what he could only describe afterwards as a great black bird that passed over his head and vanished into the shadows at the other end of the lough.

Asa made a masterly landing on the calm surface several hundred yards from the shore, dropping his tail at the last moment. They skidded to a halt and rested there and then water started to come in. He got the cupola up and heaved the dinghy package out. It inflated at once.

"How deep is it here?" he asked Devlin.

"Two hundred feet."

"That should take care of her then. Poor lovely bitch. Let's get moving."

He was into the dinghy in a moment, followed by Steiner and Devlin. They paddled away and then paused to look back. The Lysander's nose went under. For a moment there was only the tailplane showing with the Luftwaffe swastika, and then that too disappeared below the surface.

"That's it, I guess," Asa said.

They started to paddle toward the darkening shore. Steiner said, "What now, Mr. Devlin?"

"A long walk before us, but the whole night to do it in. My great aunt Eileen O'Brien has an old farmhouse above Killala Bay. Nothing but friends there."

"And then what?" Asa demanded.

"God knows, my old son. We'll have to see," Liam Devlin told him.

The dinghy drifted in to a small beach. Devlin went first, knee deep, and pulled them in to shore.

"*Cead mile failte*," he said, putting out a hand to Kurt Steiner.

"And what's that?" the German demanded.

"Irish." Liam Devlin smiled. "The language of kings. It means a hundred thousand welcomes."

BELFAST
1975

16

IT WAS almost four in the morning. Devlin stood up and opened the sacristy door. The city was quiet now, but there was the acrid smell of smoke. It started to rain, and he shivered and lit a cigarette.

"Nothing quite like a bad night in Belfast."

I said, "Tell me something. Did you ever have dealings with Dougal Munro again?"

"Oh, yes." He nodded. "Several times over the years. He liked his fishing did old Dougal."

As usual I found it difficult to take him seriously and tried again. "All right, what happened afterwards? How did Dougal Munro manage to keep it all under wraps?"

"Well, you must remember that only Munro and Carter knew who Steiner really was. To poor old Lieutenant Benson, Sister Maria Palmer and Father Martin he was just a prisoner of war. A Luftwaffe officer."

"But Michael Ryan and his niece? The Shaws?"

"The Luftwaffe had started on London again at the beginning of that year. The Little Blitz it was called, and that was very convenient for British intelligence."

"Why?"

"Because people died in the bombing raids, people like Sir Maxwell Shaw and his sister, Lavinia, killed in London during a Luftwaffe raid in January nineteen forty-four. Look up *The Times* for that month. You'll find an obituary."

"And Michael Ryan and Mary? Jack and Eric Carver?"

"They didn't rate *The Times*, but they ended up in the same place, a crematorium in North London. Five pounds of gray ash and no need for an autopsy. All listed as victims of the bombing."

"Nothing changes," I said. "And the others?"

"Canaris didn't last much longer. Fell out of favor later that year, then the attempt to kill Hitler in July failed. Canaris was arrested amongst others. They killed him in the last week of the war. Whether Rommel was involved or not has always been a matter of speculation, but the Führer thought he was.

Couldn't bear to have the people's hero re-vealed as a traitor to the Nazi cause, so Rom-mel was allowed to commit suicide with the promise that his family would be spared."

"What bastards they all were," I said.

"We all know what happened to the Füh-rer holed up in his bunker at the end. Himm-ler tried to make a run for it. Shaved off his mustache, even wore an eye patch. Didn't do him any good. Took cyanide when they caught him."

"And Schellenberg?"

"Now there was a man, old Walter. He fooled Himmler when he got back. Said we'd overpowered him. The wound helped, of course. He became head of the Combined Secret Services before the end of the war. Outlasted the lot of them. When it came to the war crimes trials, the only thing they could get him for was being a member of an illegal organization, the SS. All sorts of witnesses came forward to speak for him at the trial, Jews amongst them. He only served a couple of years in jail, and they let him out. He died in Italy in fifty-one—cancer."

"So that's it," I said.

He nodded. "We saved Hitler's life. Did we do right?" He shrugged. "It seemed like a good idea at the time, but I can imagine why they put a hundred-year hold on that file."

He opened the door again and looked out. I said, "What happened afterwards? To you and Steiner and Asa Vaughan! I know you were a professor at some American college in the years after the war, but what happened in between?"

"Ah, Jesus, son, and haven't I talked enough? I've given you enough for another book. The rest will have to wait until next time. You should be getting back to your hotel. I'll go a step of the way with you."

"Is that safe?"

"Well, you're clean enough if we meet an army patrol, and who's going to worry about a poor old priest like me?"

He wore a hat and a raincoat over his cassock and sheltered us with his umbrella as we walked through the mean streets, passing here and there the devastation of a bombing.

"Would you look at this place?" he demanded. "Rat's alley where the dead men left their bones."

"Why do you keep on?" I asked him. "The bombings, the killings?"

"When it started, back in August sixty-nine, it seemed like a good idea. Orange mobs trying to burn Catholics out, the B Special Police giving them a hand."

"And now?"

"To be honest with you, son, I'm getting tired, and I never did like soft target hits, the indiscriminate bomb that kills passersby, women, children. That farmhouse above Killala Bay. My old aunt Eileen left it to me, and there's a job waiting as professor of English at Trinity College in Dublin whenever I want." He stopped on the corner and sniffed the smoky air. "Time to get the hell out of this and let those who want to get on with it."

"You mean you've finally got tired of the game playing you instead of you playing the game?"

He nodded. "That's what Steiner always says."

"Interesting," I commented. "You said, 'Steiner *says.*'"

He smiled. "Is that a fact?" The rain increased suddenly. We were on the corner of the Falls Road. In the distance was a foot patrol of the Parachute Regiment and a Saracen armored car. "I think I'll leave you here, son."

"A wise decision." I took his hand.

"You can look me up in Killala any time." He turned away and paused. "One thing."

"What's that?" I asked.

"The Cohen girl, the hit-and-run accident. You were right. Convenient for someone, that. I'd watch my back if I were you."

I lit a cigarette in cupped hands and watched him go, the cassock like skirts around his ankles, the umbrella against the rain. I glanced down the Falls Road. The patrol was nearer now, but when I turned to take a last look at Liam Devlin, he'd gone, disappeared into the shadows as if he had never been.

DATE			
JY22 '93			